# HIGHLAND BEAST

Alice knew she would have to let him feed from her. There was no choice. Even if he was not as close to dying as she feared he was, he needed her blood to heal. Between the weakness caused by the sun and the injuries he had suffered, it would take him a very long time to heal enough to travel.

Slipping one arm beneath Gybbon's head and lifting him up enough so that he would not choke as he fed, she placed her bleeding wrist against his mouth. For a moment his lips remained cold and still against her skin and her blood seeped down over his chin. Alice feared she was too late, that he was already beyond the ability to take what could save him. Then he grabbed hold of her arm and pressed her wrist hard against his mouth.

A heartbeat later, he sank his fangs into her skin and began to feed. . . .

**Books by Hannah Howell**

ONLY FOR YOU * MY VALIANT KNIGHT
UNCONQUERED * WILD ROSES
A TASTE OF FIRE * HIGHLAND DESTINY
HIGHLAND HONOR * HIGHLAND PROMISE
A STOCKINGFUL OF JOY * HIGHLAND VOW
HIGHLAND KNIGHT * HIGHLAND HEARTS
HIGHLAND BRIDE * HIGHLAND ANGEL
HIGHLAND GROOM * HIGHLAND WARRIOR
RECKLESS * HIGHLAND CONQUEROR
HIGHLAND CHAMPION * HIGHLAND LOVER
HIGHLAND VAMPIRE * THE ETERNAL HIGHLANDER
MY IMMORTAL HIGHLANDER * CONQUEROR'S KISS
HIGHLAND BARBARIAN * BEAUTY AND THE BEAST
HIGHLAND SAVAGE * HIGHLAND THIRST
HIGHLAND WEDDING * HIGHLAND WOLF
SILVER FLAME * HIGHLAND FIRE
NATURE OF THE BEAST * HIGHLAND CAPTIVE
HIGHLAND SINNER * MY LADY CAPTOR
IF HE'S WICKED * WILD CONQUEST
IF HE'S SINFUL * KENTUCKY BRIDE
IF HE'S WILD

**Books by Heather Grothaus**

THE WARRIOR * THE CHAMPION
THE HIGHLANDER * TAMING THE BEAST

**Books by Victoria Dahl**

TO TEMPT A SCOTSMAN
A RAKE'S GUIDE TO PLEASURE
ONE WEEK AS LOVERS * A LITTLE BIT WILD

Published by Kensington Publishing Corporation

# HIGHLAND BEAST

## HANNAH HOWELL

### HEATHER GROTHAUS

### VICTORIA DAHL

ZEBRA BOOKS
KENSINGTON PUBLISHING CORP.
http://www.kensingtonbooks.com

ZEBRA BOOKS are published by

Kensington Publishing Corp.
119 West 40th Street
New York, NY 10018

All Kensington titles, imprints, and distributed lines are available
at special quantity discounts for bulk purchases for sales pro-
motion, premiums, fund-raising, educational, or institutional
use.

Special book excerpts or customized printings can also be created to fit specific needs. For details, write or phone the office
of the Kensington Special Sales Manager: Attn. Special Sales
Department. Kensington Publishing Corp., 119 West 40th Street,
New York, NY 10018. Phone: 1-800-221-2647.

Zebra and the Z logo Reg. U.S. Pat. & TM Off.

ISBN-13: 978-1-4201-0672-5
ISBN-10: 1-4201-0672-4

First Kensington Books Trade Paperback Printing: September
2009
First Zebra Books Mass-Market Paperback Printing: September 2010

10  9  8  7  6  5  4  3  2  1

Printed in the United States of America

# CONTENTS

# THE BEAST WITHIN

## Hannah Howell

# Chapter One

*Scotland—spring, 1513*

Silence descended upon the forest like a shroud. It was as if all of nature had just drawn its breath in, holding it in fearful anticipation. But of what? thought Gybbon MacNachton. He looked at his two cousins and saw that Lachann and Martyn had gone as tense as he had. They gripped the hilts of their swords just as he did.

"Hunters?" he asked as they dismounted, in a whisper so soft only a MacNachton could hear him.

Lachann opened his mouth but had no chance to reply. A cry as chilling and feral as any MacNachton could make tore through the woods. The heavy silence was shattered. Some animals echoed the fury in that cry while others revealed little caution as they scrambled to flee from whatever made the sound, filling the air with their cries of alarm.

"I believe that was one of the Hunted," Lachann drawled. "Which way?"

Gybbon knew his cousins had a good idea of where the cry had come from; they only sought confirmation. One of the gifts he had gained from the blending of Callan and MacNachton blood was superior hear-

ing, one even few MacNachtons could equal. A gift
that could all too often be a curse, he thought idly as
he concentrated. It was a struggle to push aside all the
other noises crowding his ears, but he finally caught
the sounds he sought. The soft but heavy breathing
of hard-run horses, the sharp sound of armor, and even
the clear, sleek sound of swords being unsheathed.

"Straight ahead. A short run and we will reach a
clearing at the foot of the hills ye can see rising above
the trees," he replied. "There are at least six armed
men. The noise the horses are making makes it difficult to be certain. And one other," he added softly as
he heard a soft, low growl. "I believe we have just
found one of the Lost Ones."

"Then we had best hurry," said Martyn even as he
secured their horses deep in the shadows of several
old beeches. "I have no wish to have come so close to
the prize we have sought only to bury it."

"Agreed," said Gybbon. "I go straight. Martyn, ye go
to the right, and Lachann, ye go to the left. We halt
when we sight our prey and then ye wait for my signal."

They moved swiftly, and silently, through the trees.
Gybbon was not surprised to hear the sounds of animals moving out of their way. Animals recognized
predators. The beasts kept at Cambrun had to be
carefully raised from birth to accept a MacNachton
or a Callan. The MacNachtons' human allies cared
for the animals that were bred for the table.

The scent of blood stained the air as they drew
closer to their target. Gybbon had to swiftly cage the
beast that stirred within him, its dark hunger awak-
ened by the smell. Every instinct he had told him they
had found one of the Lost Ones their clan searched
for. If he was wrong, however, the last thing he and
his cousins needed was to approach a group of Out-

siders with their MacNachton blood running hot and hungry. The whispers about their clan were already too loud. Attacking a few Outsiders who were doing no more than fighting each other with fangs bared and the bloodlust running high would only add to the rumors that got them hunted down and decried as demons.

Gybbon felt anger grow within his heart, an anger aimed at the carelessness of his ancestors. Not only had the MacNachtons of the past done little to hide their dark nature, becoming the Nightriders of people's worst nightmares, but they had also bred outside the clan. They left behind living proof of their existence but, far worse and unforgivable, they had deserted their offspring, leaving children behind to grow up with gifts they did not understand and that, all too often, got them killed.

The moment the MacNachton laird Cathal had become aware of the problem, he had sent out as many of his men as he could. Dozens of MacNachtons were on a hunt for the ones they now all called the Lost Ones. Not only did their clan need the new blood the Lost Ones would bring to Cambrun, but the Mac-Nachtons' greatest enemy now hunted the Lost Ones as well. An ever-growing number of Hunters were on the trail of anyone with MacNachton blood and it had become a hard-run race to see who would find all the Lost Ones first.

As soon as the trees began to thin out, Gybbon signaled his cousins to go down on their bellies. The three of them crept along, barely rustling a single leaf, until they reached the edge of a clearing. Gybbon was idly thinking of how good they were at sneaking up on Outsiders when the clouds suddenly slid away from the full moon and he got a good look at the person facing down eight well-armed men.

They had definitely found a Lost One, was the only clear thought he had for a moment. She was small and looked as if she badly needed sustenance. She was also dressed in rags and needed a bath. Crouched as if prepared to spring at her enemy, she had her small, long-fingered hands held up, long nails that Gybbon knew could easily rip out a throat readied for attack. A snarl twisted her full mouth and exposed her fangs. One man already lay sprawled on the ground between her and the other men. Her ragged gown and pale face were spattered with the wounded man's blood.

A man of fastidious tastes and habits, Gybbon was shocked by the abrupt, fierce attraction he felt. She was a feral creature, as unlike the women he favored as a thistle was to a rose. Even the Pureblood women of his clan had never looked this feral, this dangerous. The fact that he could not even see her eyes or face very clearly due to the tangled mess of her long, thick hair did nothing to dim the attraction suddenly knotting his innards. He felt his fangs fill his mouth and he knew it was not just because of the strong scent of blood. He wanted to sink them into the woman standing there covered in blood and mud.

Forcing aside his confusion, he signaled to his cousins. They needed to slip into the clearing at her side and her back. They also needed to show the Hunters that they faced not one, but four Mac-Nachtons. Gybbon hoped that would be enough to cause the men to flee. Although he ached to rid the world of this pack of Hunters, a battle now could lose him the girl, and returning a Lost One to the nest was of greater importance. Women with Outsider blood were fertile and his clan was in desperate need of those. When the thought of her bearing a child for some other MacNachton nearly made him growl, he pushed all thought of the woman from his mind. He had an enemy to rout.

"Ye killed Donald!" cried a short, stocky man.

"Nay, but I will if ye take even one step closer," said the woman, her voice clear and sweet despite her battle-ready stance.

Gybbon nearly shook his head as he used the shadows to get as close to her as possible before he was seen. He did not understand why she did not just run. Why would she face so many armed men when she could outrun them or disappear into the shadows? They had not cornered her. She still had routes of escape opened to her.

"Ye will die here, demon bitch, and we will sniff out your stinking spawn and kill him, too."

It was hard not to curse aloud at the words "stinking spawn." Now Gybbon knew why she did not run. Somewhere, close at hand, was a child. A child that might also have MacNachton blood. He signaled his cousins and, one by one, each of them stepped out of the shadows. Martyn moved to the woman's right, Lachann to her left, and Gybbon stepped up behind her. He wanted to stand in front of her but he had to make sure she did not try to flee from them once the Hunters were gone. When she spun around, Gybbon smiled, revealing his fangs. It was the quickest way he knew of letting her know they were allies.

Alice Boyd stared at the man who had crept up behind her. The fact that he had been able to get so close to her without her hearing a sound stunned her. It had been a mistake to turn around, however, exposing her back to the men who had been hunting her for far too long, but she had responded to a presence at her back with blind instinct. The fact that the men now flanking her and the one behind her all had fangs did little to comfort her. Just because they appeared to be as cursed as she was did not mean they were allies.

The man behind her grabbed her by the wrist and yanked her to his side. Still reeling from seeing that there were others like her, Alice did not fight his hold. She told herself that if these men sent her enemies running, at the end of the battle she would have only three men to deal with. It gave her a slightly better chance of coming out of this confrontation alive. She forced herself not to think of the fact that if they were like her, they would be a lot harder to beat or flee from than the Hunters. She could not let fear weaken her now.

For a moment all the men did was stare at each other. Alice was tempted to tell them to all cease posturing and get on with the fight. Then the man she had injured moaned, rolled onto his belly, and started to crawl toward his companions. She pushed aside the pinch of guilt and horror over the fact that she had so badly injured him. He had been trying to kill her, she reminded herself sternly.

She waited for the three men with her to do something but they only closed ranks around her. They were protecting her but she had no idea why. She did not know them. She was sure they did not know her. Even though they appeared to be like her, she had no knowledge of any kinsmen, either.

"There are only four of them," protested the short, stocky man as two of the Hunters grabbed the wounded man and hefted him onto the back of a horse. "We should stand and fight."

"Nay, not this time," said a tall, muscular man as he mounted, never once taking his gaze off the woman and the men standing at her side. "Mount, Geordie. Now."

"They will return," said Alice the moment the last of her tormentors had disappeared into the night.

"Aye," agreed the man still holding her wrist. "They will try to creep up on us and take us down one by one."

"Then, mayhap, ye best hie right back to where ye came from."

"Not without ye."

Fear was a sharp pain in her heart but Alice fought to hide it from the men watching her so closely. "Why should I go with ye? I dinnae ken who ye are."

"I am Gybbon MacNachton," said the man holding her. He nodded toward the man on her left. "My cousin Lachann." He nodded toward the other man. "My cousin Martyn. We have been searching for ye."

MacNachton was but one of the names her tormentors had called her. It meant nothing to her. It did, however, add weight to what her instincts told her. These men were like her. Either the curse that plagued her was more widespread than she thought or they all shared a kinship. Yet, if there was a kinship, why had her mother or father never mentioned it?

Alice studied all three men before fixing her gaze on the one who still held her wrist. She beat down a surge of embarrassment, of humiliation, over being found in such a ragged state by three such handsome men. That was of no consequence. All that mattered was if she could trust them. It was not only her life that was at risk.

Her captor was achingly handsome, more so than his dark cousins, which made her feel even more ragged and filthy. She did not need her keen nose to know that he was clean. His skin and his clothes proclaimed it. He was tall, lean, and obviously strong.

His face was all elegant lines and fair, unmarked skin. As close as she was to him, aided by both the bright moonlight and her own keen eyesight, she could even see the color of his eyes. They were a brilliant green and the look in them was one of wariness. Set beneath straight, dark brows and rimmed with thick, dark lashes, they were beautiful eyes, too beautiful for such a strong warrior. His long hair was so black the moonlight caused it to gleam with a slight blue sheen. Monsters should not be so handsome.

"Why have ye searched for me?" She tried to pull free of his grasp when she caught herself thinking his slightly full lips looked soft, and tempting, but he held fast to her.

"Weel, nay for ye exactly. We were sent out by our laird to find people we call the Lost Ones."

"The Lost Ones?"

"Aye," said the man called Lachann. "Kin born outside our lands, ones lost to us."

Martyn nodded. "Our ancestors were nay verra good men. They raided villages and towns for miles about. They were called Nightriders. It wasnae until recently that we became aware of the fact that they left behind children, ones born of rape or seduction. First there was a man called Simon, then a lass and her wee brother running from the Hunters just as ye are, came to us."

"Hunters," she hissed, her fury at her tormentors rising up to choke her. " 'Tis too fine a name for them."

"Aye," agreed Gybbon, "yet 'tis what they do. They hunt down MacNachtons."

"I am a Boyd. Alice Boyd."

"Ye hold MacNachton blood, lass. That makes ye one of us. As ye now ken, we have an enemy, one that wishes to see every MacNachton dead."

"Because we are demons, cursed and damned."

"Nay, we are but different." He ignored the soft, derisive noise she made. "We can talk of this later. Tell me why ye faced these men, why ye didnae use the gifts I ken ye have to just run and hide."

Gifts? Alice nearly laughed but knew her bitterness would make it a harsh, unpleasant noise. Her family had not been slaughtered because she had gifts. She had not been beaten and raped because she had some God-blessed gift. It was fear of the darkness in her that caused such tragedy. If she had gifts she would not be filthy, ragged, hungry, and huddling in caves.

Quickly looking over the three men again, she frowned. They were clean, well dressed, and did not look hungry at all. Yet they knew what she was and, after seeing their fangs, she could not dispute their claim that they were like her. Did they have some safe haven or had they escaped true suffering because they were strong, well-armed men who had banded together?

She thought over their talk of Lost Ones, of children bred by their ancestors and deserted, or ignored because the men never considered the possibility that their widely cast seed had taken root somewhere. Her mother had once told her that, years ago, Grandmere had taken a lover, a dark man who had visited her only at night. Her mother had been the result of that union and had said that she was certain that was where the darkness inside of them had come from. Once her grandmother had spoken of that lover, calling him her dark knight, her sinful Nightrider. Everything these men told her matched what little she knew or could remember. Alice was not sure that meant she should trust them, however. She had too much to protect to trust too easily.

And yet, these men obviously knew how to stay safe, warm, and well fed. She desperately wanted to stop running, stop crouching in caves like a cornered animal. Neither could she ignore the fact that she was changing, was becoming more animal than woman. Alice also knew that all she had done, all she could do, was not enough to gain what these men had.

She was facing defeat and death and she knew it. She was not the only one, either. Once she was gone, the ones she fought so hard to save would be lost as well. Alice had to admit that she was also tired, so very tired, of carrying all that weight alone.

"Lass, we mean ye nay harm," Gybbon said quietly, knowing that she was trying to decide if she could trust them or not. "Ye are nay alone, are ye. There is a child, aye? Let us help ye. Let us take ye to your people, to Cambrun. Ye will be safe there, far safer than ye are now. Ye and the child."

"Ah, aye, my stinking spawn." Alice felt his hand briefly clench and saw anger tighten his handsome face. Oddly, that sign of the anger he felt over the insult to her child helped decide her course. "I have to trust in what ye say. There is no other choice for me. If these bastards hunting me dinnae succeed, hunger, cold, and exhaustion will. So, I believe ye had best follow me."

Gybbon released her and then found that he and his cousins had to move quickly to keep pace with her. She scrambled over rocks with ease despite her unshod feet and climbed the rocky hill with a speed and agility he and his cousins were hard-pressed to match. Either she had a natural skill or she had lived like this for a long time.

When she slipped into a crevice between two huge

boulders, he followed. The soft curses from his cousins told Gybbon they were finding it as tight a squeeze as he was. He stopped inside a small cave and was about to complain a little when he looked toward the small fire in the center of the cave. The sight that met his eyes trapped his petty grumblings in his throat.

# Chapter Two

Four pairs of eyes stared back at Gybbon. Even as his stunned mind struggled to accept the fact that Alice Boyd was protecting not just one child, but four, the largest of the children shifted just enough to place his too-thin body between the smaller children and the adults. Gybbon studied the boy who studied him, and judged the child to be nine or ten years of age. The MacNachton mark was strong on the boy.

Two small dark-haired girls huddled behind the boy. Gybbon did not even try to guess their ages but he doubted they were long out of infancy. One small boy kept trying to get next to the oldest child only to keep being gently shoved back. All four children looked as ragged, dirty, and feral as Alice. Gybbon doubted they were all her children, however, as she did not look to be more than twenty years old and only one had the look of her.

"Be at ease, Alyn," Alice said as she moved to crouch at the oldest boy's side.

"Ye brought the Hunters to us," Alyn said, his tone of voice wavering between question and accusation.

"Nay, I would ne'er do so. E'en if ye cannae believe I would die to keep ye safe, can ye doubt that I would do so for Donn, my own son? Or for wee Jayne or Norma?"

Alyn bit his lip and shook his head. "Nay. But if they arenae our enemies, who are they?"

"MacNachtons," replied Gybbon as he and his cousins cautiously moved closer. "We are like you, and the men hunting ye hunt us as weel. 'Tis our belief that ye all have some MacNachton blood."

"I dinnae ken what blood runs in my veins, but 'tis a curse nay matter where it comes from," said Alyn, a very adult bitterness tainting his words.

Gybbon sat and stared at the boy from across the small fire, his gaze never wavering even when his cousins sat down flanking him. "Aye, at times it does feel like a curse, holding us firm in the shadows and causing our innards to gnaw with a dark hunger. 'Tisnae the devil's work, however, and we are nay demons. We are but a different people. Our ancestors reveled in those differences, acting with both arrogance and cruelty. My laird's father put a final end to that long ago. What we ne'er kenned was that while our ancestors took whate'er they wanted or needed, they also left their seed behind. I would like to say they would have cared if they had kenned they had bred children, but I am nay sure they would have. I do believe, however, that it ne'er occurred to them that their seed would take root."

"Any mon with wit kens that if ye scatter your seed about some of it will root and grow."

There was such anger and pain behind Alyn's words it made Gybbon's heart ache. "Aye, so they should. Howbeit, MacNachton seed doesnae often take root. We have clung to our home, away from others—the ones we call the Outsiders—for a verra long time. We also bred within the clan far too often. One day the laird looked about and realized that in forty years, only one full MacNachton, what we call a Pureblood, had born a child and that the only other child born at Cambrun had come from a MacNachton and an Outsider. So, ye can see why it ne'er occurred to us that ones of MacNachton blood had been born outside of our lands." He shrugged. "If ye cannae breed at home, why should ye be able to breed away from it, aye?"

"Your clan has no bairns?" asked Alice, suddenly understanding why the men had stared at the children as if they truly were gifts from God.

"There are more now, for our laird and my father both wed Outsiders. It was my laird's plan. He himself is born of a MacNachton and an Outsider." Gybbon briefly flashed his fangs. "Few Outsiders can tolerate what we are. Our laird hopes to slowly breed out what makes us so feared. Although we begin to think the best we can do is lessen the differences between ourselves and the Outsiders enough to more easily move among them."

"Why would ye want to?" grumbled Alyn.

"To survive, Alyn," Alice whispered, easily seeing the path the MacNachton laird was walking.

"Aye," agreed Gybbon. "We may be stronger, fiercer, and all of that, but there are far more Outsiders than there are MacNachtons and there always will be."

"Even if ye gather all the Lost Ones."

The fact that she had seen that reason for their search told him she had a keen wit. "Ye could rightfully cry me a liar if I said that wasnae in our minds when we started searching for any with some MacNachton blood in their veins. It wasnae what truly started the search, however. There are many reasons."

"We have time," she said as she sat down beside Alyn and the small boy named Donn crawled up onto her lap.

"Nay, I dinnae think we do. Those men didnae flee home and I think ye ken it."

Alice sighed. "Aye, I ken it, but they will halt and plot for a wee while. 'Tis their way. They have a wounded mon they need to tend to." Or bury, she thought, and felt the pinch of horror and shame. She quickly shook that away. She was fighting for her life.

"Time that we should use to flee this place." Gybbon looked at Martyn. "Can ye fetch the horses?"

"Aye." Martyn stood and signaled Lachann to join him. "We will bring them closer, hide them, and fetch some supplies. I think it best if we eat ere we set out for Cambrun."

Gybbon briefly glanced at the children and nodded. "Watch your backs." As soon as his cousins slipped away, he said, "We will travel to Cambrun as soon as we have eaten. That is all the time I dare linger here. Ye can eat food, aye?"

"Aye," replied Alice, wondering just which Mac-Nachtons might not be able to and hoping it was not an added curse that would come to her later in her life, "though that cursed hunger isnae silenced by it."

"I ken it. It can be leashed, however. Can ye abide the sun?"

"A wee bit. Morning and dusk. Longer if the clouds are heavy. High noon, the heart of the day, is dangerous for all of us. And, ere ye ask, we all have those cursed fangs, all our senses are keener than most people's, we move faster, heal faster, are stronger than most, and, if my grandmere wasnae lying about when my maman was born, dinnae age too quickly. My maman was two score and ten when she was butchered but she didnae look much older than I am now." She smiled faintly when he just cocked one dark brow in question. "I am but two and twenty."

"And this is your son?" he asked, nodding toward the boy seated in her lap.

"Aye, Donn is my son. He is four now and has kenned naught in his short life but running and hiding. It isnae the life I would choose for any child, but at least they all still live."

"Your husband?"

Alice held his gaze with her own, hoping he could read in her face what she did not want to say in front of the children. "I have ne'er had one. Nay, nor a lover or a love."

Gybbon could see the fury and grief in her eyes, eyes that appeared golden in the firelight, and knew what she did not say. Donn was a child conceived in violence and humiliation. He felt a fierce urge to find the man who had abused her and make him suffer. Gybbon told himself that was because he had always abhorred men who abused women, but a small voice in his head scoffed at his excuse. This dirty, ragged woman was having a very unsettling effect on him and he was not sure what that meant or might portend.

With their callous arrogance and willful indifference, this was the hell his ancestors had condemned their children to. Alice had said that her mother had been butchered. Gybbon did not have to ask to know why the woman had been killed. The MacNachton blood had come from the mother, had left her different in a world that treated any differences with a dangerous superstition. He did not want to think on just how many MacNachton kin had met similar fates, but it was a fact that was hard to ignore, especially when he was facing a woman and four children who had all suffered losses. It fed the urgency his clan felt, fed the strong need to collect up all the Lost Ones they could find as quickly as they could.

"The boy will be cherished at Cambrun, as will all

these children," he said when he was certain his anger would not seep into his words. "Having accepted that we have become a dying people, any child with e'en the smallest drop of MacNachton blood is considered a gift, a sign that we arenae destined to fade into the mists."

"Mayhap we should just fade away."

"Nay. I told ye, we arenae demons and we arenae cursed. We are but a different breed of man. Kenning what Outsiders say about us, what they do to all who are so different, is why we are searching so hard for ones such as ye are. And we arenae the only different breed of man." He told them a little about the Callans, his mother's clan who claimed to be descended from a Celtic shape-shifter. "Who kens what others may be out there? Ones who can hide amongst the Outsiders better than we can. We have begun a search for others as weel, for our laird feels it would make us stronger if all who are different became allies."

"The Callans bred out what made them different? They dinnae act like cats any longer?" Alice actually considered the possibility that she was not some hell-born aberration.

"Ah, weel, nay. Not all of their differences have disappeared. We begin to think it is impossible to breed it all out, but Cathal, our laird, says we can soften the hard edges of our differences. 'Tis good enough. And, if ye and the others like ye had been made known to us, we could have helped ye hide what ye are, could have taught ye how to keep yourselves hidden amongst the crowd. By leaving ye to grow up untrained, without knowledge of who ye are, my ancestors condemned ye. It took a while, and a great deal of arguing, but even the Purebloods in the clan now see the truth of that."

"The Purebloods didnae want to change?"

"Nay, they were reluctant to change the way we have lived for so verra long, but they have come to see that Cathal is right. The recent discovery of Lost Ones has helped change their minds." He smiled faintly. "The fact that my mother and her sister, who married our laird, have bred easily and frequently hasnae hurt, either."

"So now ye do have children?" asked Alyn.

"Some, but nay enough. 'Tis difficult to find wives and husbands outside of the clan," explained Gybbon. "Especially since many would have to come and live amongst us for the safety of their mate and whatever children they might have."

"How can ye be so certain we will be welcomed by your clan?"

"I told ye, we are a dying breed. Ye need more than two women bearing children to keep a clan alive and strong. We need new blood. And my clan cherishes children if only because we have had so few, have suffered a long time with no bairns born and ken the sorrow of barren nurseries. Our younger men, ones who have a skill for blending with Outsiders, leave us to try and find a mate and some have succeeded. That only tempts others to do the same. Not all of them return, making their lives where their mates live."

"Another loss that weakens your clan," said Alice.

"Aye." Gybbon tensed when he heard the faint sound of a horse, then relaxed when he recognized the soft tread of his cousins. "My cousins return," he said quickly when he saw that Alice and the children had all tensed with fear.

When his cousins sat down by the fire and began to pull food from a saddle-pack, Gybbon quickly took charge of it. He had once suffered hunger and knew he should not give in to the urge to feed the starving children all they wanted. He suspected it had been a

very long time since any of them had known the
comfort of a full belly. Too much food now would
only make them ill. He gave them each a modest portion of the bread, cheese, and cold venison, plus one
honey-sweetened oatcake each. Then he served the
adults the same and signaled Martyn to pack the food
away. At first the children tried to stuff their mouths
full, but one sharp look from Alice halted that mind-
less greed. Gybbon began to think that Alice had once
been a well-taught lady from a family of means as,
once the urge to gorge had been ended, she and the
children ate their food with surprising delicacy.

"How long have ye been running and hiding?" he
asked Alice as she helped the smaller children drink
some cider from his wineskin. Later, he thought, he
would offer them some of the blood-enriched wine
MacNachtons always carried with them, for they could
all use the strength it would give them.

"Six years," she replied. "I was away from home,
collecting berries, when the men attacked my family.
If they had not fired the stable I might weel have
stumbled into their grasp. Instead, the smell of smoke
caused me to approach slowly. What I saw—" She
took a deep breath and let it out slowly in an effort to
maintain her calm, to push back the grief that could
still choke her at times. "It was clear to see that I was
too late to help my family, could only die as they had,
so I hid myself away. Once I was certain the men were
gone, I slipped back, collected what little was left and
might be of use, and then placed the bodies of my
family in our ruined home. I made it their tomb."

"How many did you lose?"

"Mother, father, grandmother, and sister."

"Thrice curse the bastards," muttered Lachann,
then blushed faintly as he recalled that he was in the

presence of a woman and children. "Forgive my harsh language."

"Mine has often been far harsher," Alice said, "and the ills I wish upon those murderers far bloodier."

"Ye were caught once, though, aye?" Gybbon glanced at Donn, who was savoring his sweetened oatcake bite by little bite.

"Aye. Once. The fools may think me a demon but they also still see me as a woman, weak and easily cowed as they think all women are. I escaped. I willnae be caught alive again," she added softly, hoping she could keep that vow despite her strong will to survive at all costs. "As I ran and hid I found first Alyn, then Jayne, and then Norma. All orphaned."

"I wasnae orphaned," said Alyn. "I was thrown out."

"And thus orphaned through ignorant fear instead of the death of loved ones." Alice reached out to pat his cheek. "We make our own family now," she said as she handed Gybbon back his wineskin.

"Ye will soon have a verra large family," said Gybbon and smiled. "So large ye will soon wish to get away from it now and then."

"Will adding five more nay crowd ye all even more?"

"Nay, for Cambrun has a massive keep, above and below the ground. There is also a large village in the valley. The MacNachtons' Outsider allies, the Mac-Martins, live there. The MacMartins have been our allies for hundreds of years," he added when he saw her frown. "Their loyalty to us is steadfast."

Alice was not sure she believed that, but she would still follow these men to Cambrun. The meal they had just eaten had swept aside the last vestiges of hesitation. Even carefully meted out as the food had been, it had still been far more than she and the children had enjoyed in a very long time.

Gybbon studied Alice and the children. He knew the Hunters they had driven away had not given up. They had dealt with this enemy enough to know the men never gave up. Taking a woman, three children of nursery age, and one underfed boy along with them was going to make the journey to Cambrun long and hazardous. If the Hunters caught up with them, the ensuing battle could easily hurt the children. There had to be a way to keep the Hunters off the trail of the children.

The Hunters were after the woman, he suddenly realized. She was the one they looked for. It was her trail they followed. They had also only referred to one child, her child. There was a good chance they did not know about the others. If they did not see the child, they would just assume that she had hidden the boy away, as she had done this time. If he wanted to ensure that the children reached Cambrun safely, he had to lead the Hunters away from them. Alice Boyd was the bait their enemies would follow. He was just not sure if she would entrust the children to anyone else.

"The children will ride to Cambrun with my cousins," Gybbon said and was not surprised when Alice tensed and opened her mouth to argue his abrupt command. She had already done a lot to protect the children, only one of whom was her blood child. "Ye and I, Alice Boyd, will lead the Hunters away from them." He repeated all his thoughts on the matter and was pleased when she only frowned in thought. After six years of being hunted like an animal, she obviously had the cunning needed to recognize the worthiness of his plan.

"Ye think they will follow our trail and nay try to hunt down the others?" she asked.

"I do. They hunt ye, nay the bairns. The bairns

would be killed once found, nay doubt, but 'tis ye they hunt." Gybbon heard his cousins mutter their agreement, but he kept his gaze fixed on Alice.

Alice looked at the children. They were as weary and hungry as she was. It astonished her that they had all survived as long as they had. The very differences that condemned them were obviously what gave them the strength to survive. These men offered the children the chance of a better, safer life, one where the differences that had endangered them for so long would be fully accepted. It would be nearly a sin to deny them that. All she had to do was trust the men long enough to let her children go, to hand their safety over to someone else for the first time in years.

# Chapter Three

Alice watched her children ride away with Lachann and Martyn until they could no longer be seen. Everything within her, heart, soul, and mind, cried to pull them back, but she fought the urge. Each time the Hunters found her, the lives of her children were put in danger. They were all so young. If something happened to her she knew they would suffer, could even die. Alyn was a clever boy but he was only nine. He would do his best to protect the younger children if she was captured or killed, but Alice knew he would fail. And each time the men found her, her chances of escape grew ever smaller.

They were being taken to safety, she reminded herself. It was something she had done far too often to count since the moment Gybbon had announced that they had to separate. Her mind knew his plan was sound, that it gave the children the best chance to escape. Doubts came from her heart and she had to ignore them. The men were like her, like the children, and that had to be enough to warrant her trust. That, and the look of delight and wonder on the men's faces when they had first seen the children. Holding that memory in her mind helped her still her doubts and fears.

"My cousins will guard the children with their lives," said Gybbon as he took her by the arm and led her to their horses.

Gybbon had watched her leave-taking of the children and was astonished she had allowed them to ride away with men she did not really know. The bond between her and the children, not just her blood son, was a powerful one, forged in fear and danger. What troubled him was why she had let them go. Gybbon did not need to ask. He knew. Alice had sent the children away with his cousins because she believed she was losing her battle against the Hunters, that she was soon to die. It was an admirable thing to do but he could not allow her to hold fast to that air of martyrdom. If they were to survive the next few days, she had to believe in him, believe that she could win this fight and finally reach a safe haven with her children at her side.

"Is that nay what we are doing as weel?" she asked as she mounted the sleek, black mare he led her to.

"In many ways, aye." Gybbon mounted his gelding Resolute, yet again pleased that they had had the foresight to bring two extra horses, for with both of them riding, it would be easier to lead the Hunters astray and stay out of their grasp. "We are the bait for the Hunters to follow, and when there are no more Hunters to plague us, we will ride to Cambrun."

"Ye sound so confident. The odds are heavy against us." Nudging her horse to keep pace with Gybbon's, Alice was pleased with the mare's obedience. It had been a long time since she had ridden a horse and it was good to know she had been given an easily controlled one.

" 'Tis best to ride into battle with confidence, with a surety that ye will be victorious."

"No one can be certain they will win when they go

into battle. E'en the best plans can go awry and e'en the most skilled of warriors can err or stumble."

"True, but thinking that, and only that, only increases the chance that such misfortunes will occur."

Alice suspected there was some truth to his words. If one expected the worst, one often got it. It was as if fate decided the worst was what you wanted and so gave it to you. She had begun to expect only the worst and had known it was a weakness, but each day it had gotten harder and harder to fight. Hope was what she needed to remain strong. Unfortunately, after running and hiding for so long her very bones ached with weariness, she had too little hope left within her.

"Exactly what is your plan?" she asked.

"To lead the Hunters far away from my cousins and the bairns and to lessen their numbers one by one until none are left or the survivors race home to their wee cottages to cower beneath their wee beds."

"Ye mean to kill them all."

"At least the ones who willnae give up. That troubles ye?"

"A wee bit."

"Why? They mean to kill ye and your child."

"Aye," Alice admitted, knowing that death was all that would shake most of the Hunters off her trail, for they thought they were doing God's work. "Ye dinnae need to fear that I will forget that."

"And one of the ones hunting ye now is Donn's father, aye?"

"Callum, the tall one who ordered Geordie to leave. The fact that I escaped him and bred a son from his cruelty appalls him. He wants me and Donn dead, wants what he calls his shame buried and gone." It hurt to even speak the words, to admit that her son's father thought of him as an abomination. Some day Donn would understand that, would figure out the whole ugly truth even if she did not tell him, and she dreaded the pain it would cause her child.

"Yet ye love the bairn, love a child born of rape."

"Rape only planted the seed. I grew and nurtured the child. He is mine. The fact that Callum can look at that small, sweet lad and see only evil that needs to be destroyed is nay something I will ever understand."

"The fact that he can look at his own bairn, his own son, and see that is but another good reason to kill him."

Although the chill in Gybbon's voice made Alice shiver, she had to agree with him. One thing she had hated about being hunted was that it had forced her to kill. In the six years she had been running she had seen the life fade from the eyes of four men. It was a sight that haunted her dreams. She suspected a few of the men she had injured had died later but she had been able to shrug most thoughts of that aside. Watching death claim a man while his blood warmed her hands was not so easily ignored. Not even the reminder that those men had been trying to kill her, would have killed the children, eased the horror of what she had been forced to do to survive.

The touch of a warm hand smoothing down her arm drew her from her dark thoughts and she looked at Gybbon. The understanding in his beautiful eyes eased the grip of her tortured memories. He probably did not suffer as she did over the men he had to kill, but she suddenly knew that he did not choose to kill, did not enjoy the necessity of it.

"They hunt ye," he said. "They hunt the children. The stain is upon their souls."

She just nodded, not sure she believed him. Despite the occasional nightmare, she had accepted what she had done as necessary. She had killed to keep from being killed. What Gybbon planned, however, was not face-to-face fighting. He intended to strike in silence, to slip out of the shadows, kill their enemy, and move on. It was a brilliant strategy when they were so outnumbered. However, Alice was not sure she would be able to do that.

The sun had been up for over an hour before Gybbon signaled a halt. The only other stop they had made had been so that she could wash in a small, rocky burn and change her clothes. Alice had been so desperate to get clean and change her clothes, even though her clean clothes were almost as ragged as her dirty ones, that she had been able to push aside the fear of being naked anywhere within a mile of a man. Gybbon had used the time to scout for any sight of their enemy and then take a quick bath in the cold burn himself. It still astonished Alice that she had accepted his word that he would give her privacy, but, even more, that she had actually been tempted to peek at him while he bathed.

Gybbon dismounted, shaking her free of her puzzlement over why she should want to peer at a man bathing when all she had wanted to do for the last six years was stay as far away from men as possible. She quickly dismounted, caught up her mare's reins, and followed him up a dangerously narrow rocky path. It startled her when he and his horse appeared to melt into the hillside, but as she drew nearer to where he had last stood, she saw the crevice he had slipped into. Wind-contorted trees and large stones plus a bend in the very shape of the hill had hidden the opening very well. It took a little coaxing to get her horse to pass through such a narrow opening, one that had a blind corner so that it looked as if she was trying to push the horse into a wall of stone.

Once through the passage into a wider space, Alice stood very still until her eyes accepted the loss of daylight. It happened quickly and she knew she could see in the dark far better than any person without her cursed blood. When she realized she was suddenly seeing that skill as the gift Gybbon called it, she shook her head and studied their shelter.

She stood in a somewhat spacious cave, the wood for a fire already arranged in a smooth hollow in the stone floor, and more wood neatly stacked against a wall to her right. This was obviously a MacNachton retreat, one of those places Gybbon had said his clan had found so that they could shelter from the sun when they traveled. In a strange way, the preparations this clan of his made to survive eased her fears about entrusting the children to them.

"Your clan is truly weel prepared for all things, isnae it," she said as she led the mare to the back of the cave where Gybbon already tended to his horse.

"Aye. Unfortunately it does mean that we cannae always take the most direct route when we do travel." Gybbon grimaced. "An inn or the hospitality of some laird's keep isnae for us. Caves, weel-hidden shielings, e'en holes in the ground. There is even a crypt or two."

"Better to rest among the dead than to join them."

Gybbon laughed softly. "True enough. Tend to a fire for us, lass, and I will tend to Nightwind."

"Nightwind. A fine name," she murmured, giving the mare a pat before turning her attention to the building of a fire.

Alice made sure the fire would not go out the moment she turned her back on it before she collected the clothes she and Gybbon had rinsed clean in the burn. Placing the saddles close to the fire, she draped their clothes over them and hoped they would dry before the sun set. She fought down a surge of embarrassment over how poor, thin, and worn her clothes looked next to his. Six years of running and fighting for her life and the lives of four children did not give a woman time to fuss over the vanities of her appearance, she sternly reminded herself. She was alive and so were the children. That was all that mattered.

When Gybbon sat by the fire and began to carefully portion out some food, Alice quickly sat down across from him. Her stomach ached for what he put in a wooden bowl but she fought to hide her desperate need. A part of her feared becoming accustomed to such bounty only to have it disappear, just as her fine comfortable life had been brutally torn away from her six years ago.

As she ate, struggling to cling to the good manners her mother had taught her, Alice covertly studied Gybbon. The way she felt around him was a constant source of surprise. Since the night Callum had beaten and raped her, cursing her as a demon all the while, she had stayed as far away from men as she could. The repeated confrontations with Callum and his men had only hardened her resolve, driving her deeper into the wilder places. In the last two years, the only time she had approached even the most humble home was in the darkest hours of the night and then only to steal what she could so that the children could eat or stay warm. Yet she felt none of that constant, gnawing fear around Gybbon.

She felt safe. She felt accepted for all that had previously condemned her. That frightened her. For too long she had trusted no one, depended upon no one, and felt no safety no matter where she was. Alice was not sure it was wise to feel safe now.

Even worse, however, she liked looking at him. She had barely begun to feel an interest in young men when her life had been torn apart. Callum's vicious attack had ensured that she never again felt such an interest in any man. Or so she had thought. Alice knew what stirred inside her now was definitely an interest in Gybbon, the sort a woman felt for a man she might want for her own. Everything about the man pulled hard at something deep within her, and she knew that ought to have her running away from him as fast as she could. Instead she sat there staring at him like some foolish moonstruck maiden. She prayed he did not notice. It was both a surprise and an embarrassment to her and she certainly did not want to be caught at it.

Gybbon looked at Alice and caught her scowling at him. She had cleaned up well, he thought. Yet again the firelight made her eyes appear golden. In the early morning light he had caught one good look into her eyes and found them to be a rich, warm light brown. After she had washed her hair it had appeared more golden than brown and now the firelight touched upon hints of red in its thick length. Her small oval face, now cleaned of dirt, revealed clear, pale skin. Its delicate lines had been sharpened by hunger and tragedy but even those dark shadows did not mar its beauty.

She was, he realized with an inner start, really quite lovely. He suspected a few good meals would return some womanly softness to her thin body, but he could not convince himself that she was unattractive as she was. His body certainly stirred with interest as he glanced over her body, its slight curves revealed all too clearly by her ragged gown. Gybbon tried to tell himself that it was just a result of feeling protective of her, even sympathetic, but he knew that was a lie. She was nothing like the sort of women he usually felt a lusting for, but something about her definitely drew him. Even when she looked as if she wished to hit him over the head with her bowl, he thought, suddenly amused at himself.

"Are ye now regretting sending the children away with my cousins?" he asked.

Even his deep, smooth voice stirred her long-dead interest, she thought a little crossly, but she fought to keep that irritation out of her voice. "Nay. They had to go. Ye are like us. If I cannae trust the ones who are like us, then who can I trust?"

"No one. I wish I could say otherwise, but I cannae. As the Hunters gain strength 'tis even less safe for any MacNachton to let anyone outside of the clan ken what he is. There is a risk with each new Outsider who discovers how different we are. We have been fortunate so far, but the danger is there and cannae be ignored. Unfortunately, for ones like ye and your family, the need for such caution, for such solitude, only adds to the danger ye are in."

"Aye, true enough. It stirs questions when one keeps oneself apart from others."

"In the end, 'tis less dangerous than mixing too freely with Outsiders or letting too many ken our secrets." He smiled his thanks as she took his bowl to clean it out. "We need to rest now. I can abide the late-day sun so we can leave here when the sun is low in the sky."

"And then we just ride about hoping the Hunters sniff us out?"

Gybbon shrugged as he collected their blankets and handed her one. "That and, when they creep close enough, I intend to cull their numbers whenever I can."

Alice wrapped herself in the blanket and settled down on the stone floor. She stared through the low flames of the fire at Gybbon as he did the same. It took only a moment for her to begin to miss the children, especially the way they had all curled up against her when they had slept. Alice forced that longing aside and fixed her thoughts on Gybbon's plan. It could work to free them of any pursuit so that they could follow the others to Cambrun and she would see her children again. It would not, however, put an end to the threat men like Callum and his little army presented to all who were like her and Gybbon.

"I can almost believe we will win this fight," she said quietly, "but 'tis just one battle."

"Ah, ye dinnae think that beating these men will end the hunts."

"Nay, it willnae. And I suspicion there will be men quick to step into the hole left by any Hunter killed."

"And why are ye so certain of that?" Gybbon felt the same but was curious as to why she thought so.

"Because whoever gathers these men makes them believe they do the will of God, that they are fighting demons and will be blessed by God for their sacrifice."

Gybbon softly cursed. She was right and he had no argument to give her. The MacNachtons had become a crusade for the righteous. His clan had long debated the reasons they now had men hunting them and come up with many, including some quest to gain the MacNachton longevity, but Alice had spoken the truth of it all, concisely. He had no argument that would refute her. Someone was leading a crusade against the MacNachtons. This war would be long and bloody.

# Chapter Four

Gybbon used his sleeve to wipe the blood from his mouth. He stared down at the man sprawled at his feet. In deference to Alice's unease about a stealthy culling of their enemies, he had given the man a choice. Fight and die or give up his quest, run home, and live. The man had chosen to die. Alice was right. These men believed they fought evil, that they fought for good and God. Others who had taken up the cause might have a few other plans of their own, but not men like these. It almost felt wrong to kill the fools.

He cursed as he crouched down by the body to search it for anything of value. Gybbon always felt a twinge of revulsion when doing so, but he could not leave anything of worth to rot with the man or to be stolen by someone else. He and Alice needed whatever supplies they could scavenge. He regretted the fact that the man's horse had fled, for it was clear that it had been the man's only worthy asset.

The marks on the man's neck revealed the way he had died, so Gybbon put the body in a shallow grave and covered the newly turned earth with leaves. It had not been his intention to feed, but the man had struck a few telling blows with his sword before he had died and Gybbon could not afford to nurse wounds for any length of time. He could not regret the strength the blood had given him either.

Two days, two men. Gybbon thought that was a good accounting. Since he doubted the man Alice had nearly gutted was part of this hunt any longer, whether dead or because he had been sent away to heal, the number of their enemies was now six. If the Hunters had not gathered any new martyrs, he thought as he mounted Resolute and started back to where he had left Alice. His count depended on the possibility that all the Hunters after Alice had been in the clearing when he had first seen her. His instincts told him they had been.

What he hoped was that once the Hunters realized how their number had dwindled, they would flee. The glint of religious fervor he had seen in the eyes of the two men he had killed weakened that hope, however. Such men were often quite prepared to die, even expected some great reward since they would die in service to their God. Gybbon was coming to understand that most of the Hunters truly believed they were on a crusade against evil, were fighting the minions of Satan. That did not bode well for the future of the MacNachtons.

Gybbon found Alice sitting in front of the shieling he had left her in. The look of relief that briefly crossed her face told him she had worried about him. He did not want to be moved by that, but he was. Even telling himself that she was just afraid she would be left alone if anything happened to him did not completely dim the warmth that look of concern brought him.

Each hour he spent in her company made his attraction to her grow stronger. She was not as feral as he had first assumed when he had seen her standing over the body of a man she had savaged. She had just been hardened by six years of fighting for her life and the lives of the children she had to care for. Beneath the rags was a woman who had both education and good manners. She also had intelligence, strength, and courage. Gybbon supposed he should not be surprised that he wanted her as badly as he did.

"We now have but six men trailing us," he announced as he dismounted in front of her, deciding he would not hide what he had done. It had been necessary and she had to learn to accept that.

"That willnae be enough to make them cease hunting us down, will it." She sighed, for the hard look on his handsome face was answer enough.

"Nay, and ye ken weel why. Aye, and better than we did."

"Because they believe they do God's work."

He nodded. "I have seen the proof of their fervor in their eyes."

"And these men arenae the only ones, are they."

"Nay." He began to unsaddle Resolute. "There is an army of them. We nibble away at it from time to time but it just gains new men to take the place of those who were lost. When we first learned of them they were few, but word spreads and the numbers grow and become better funded and better organized. We need to find the head of the beast and lop it off."

"Ye believe there is a leader who is keeping this war alive?"

"I do, as does my laird." He grinned briefly. "He is my uncle, too. 'Tisnae often easy for him to be both." He sat down next to her and glanced up at the slowly lightening sky. "There is a leader, and mayhap a few close to him, who stirs the fervor in the men. Someone discovered the truth about us, or some of it, and began to gather an army. That requires coin so 'tis nay some poor crofter."

Alice grimaced. "Nay, poor crofters are always the arrow fodder. The fact that these men dinnae hesitate to cut down women and children only proves how deeply they believe we are demons. They only wish to send all of us to hell."

"Weel, there are a few who want something else from us. 'Tis why we didnae really think hard on the reasons so many men were joining the fight, on the religious side of it."

"What else could they want?"

"What makes us so strong and live for so long. That is one of the things the men who lead this fight are after. It nearly cost two of my cousins their lives. Two men came close to discovering that secret, that 'tis in our blood. We only recently realized ourselves what our blood can do for Outsiders. We can only hope the men didnae tell anyone else. As far as we ken, no other MacNachton has been caught and held as my cousins were."

"I wager that is something they dinnae tell their arrow fodder."

Gybbon offered her his wineskin, the one filled with wine fortified with blood. Her hesitation in taking it grew less each time he offered it. It was making her stronger, however, and she knew it. Even the few small drinks she had taken over the last few days had softened the hard edges of hunger on her face and body. He knew it would have also sharpened her senses and she would need that keenness in the days ahead. There might be only six Hunters left, but they were determined men.

"Do ye think your cousins have reached Cambrun by now?" she asked as she handed back his wineskin. Alice hated the fact that she needed blood to survive and remain strong, even as she appreciated how it helped her in this fight.

"They should be there on the morrow if they have suffered no trouble," he replied.

"The children willnae slow them down. They are weel accustomed to travel, to long hard journeys in the dead of night, and to the value of being verra quiet."

"Aye, and isnae that just a wee bit sad. My cousins will appreciate that, however, for they will be eager to get the bairns to the safety of Cambrun. The children will be weel cared for there, Alice," he added gently, trying to ease the worry he knew she felt.

"I think a lot of the concern I feel is borne of how much I miss them. There were times when I wondered if I was a complete lack-wit for dragging four children about with me. It shames me to admit it, but, sometimes, I even wished them gone. Aye, I would think, did I nay have enough trouble just keeping myself alive? Why carry the added weight of them on my back?"

"Ye shouldnae feel shamed. 'Twas only a passing thought, a wee one borne of a hard day or a long night of running, of hunger and exhaustion. It isnae what ye thought when your spirits were low, but what ye did, and ye kept them with ye, fed them, hid them, kept them alive." He frowned. "Did they ne'er need any blood?"

"Aye, but we all need only a wee bit now and then. Enough so that the gnawing in our bellies doesnae grow too strong, for that brings the beast too close to the skin, doesnae it. Alyn suffers it the most."

Gybbon frowned. "He has the strong mark of a MacNachton. I wouldnae be surprised to find out his father was a Pureblood, or near to. I dinnae like thinking any MacNachton still beds women with nay thought to the breeding of a child. Ten years past we all kenned it could happen and that being so careless was wrong. Then, too, 'tis verra possible the one who sired Alyn ne'er returned because he was killed. I will find out, but now, we had best get inside. Ye go and I will join ye as soon as I secure the horses in amongst the trees."

Alice grabbed his saddle and moved inside the shieling. It was tiny and the roof was so low she knew Gybbon would not be able to stand fully upright. What troubled her most was that she and Gybbon would be side by side as they slept through the day. She sternly told herself not to be such a coward as she hurriedly washed up. Gybbon was not like Callum. They had been together for two days and nights and the man had barely touched her.

Yet, the few times he had, she had felt no fear, she thought as she spread a blanket on the dirt floor. What she had felt made her think that Callum had not destroyed all chance that she would ever be with a man again. Gybbon's touches, though light and all that was gentlemanly, stirred a warmth inside her. She had even found herself wishing for a touch that was not so gentlemanly. Such thoughts did make her a little afraid, but they also intrigued and excited her.

Gybbon joined her and they sat on the blanket to share the last of their bread and cheese. Alice tried to ignore the warmth of his body when they had to sit so close together their sides touched. For the first time in years she felt a woman's interest in a handsome man. It made her nervous, but she also savored the feeling. She could actually see a chance at the future she had dreamed of years ago, one of a man who cared for her, one who would give her children and a home.

It was a dream she had thought Callum had stolen from her. Even thinking of that elusive future made her look at Gybbon and she knew that was beyond foolish. Not only was the man well-born and rich, he had shown no interest in her beyond that of a man helping to save a kinswoman. And that was a good thing, she told herself firmly, and did not believe a word of it.

The crack of Gybbon's head hitting the low ceiling of their shelter startled her. She had been so caught up in her own thoughts she had not even seen him move. Alice reached out as he staggered a little and fell to his knees. She grasped him by the arms to keep him from falling over completely. He was muttering some very creative curses, but Alice pretended she did not hear him. Seeing the way he kept one hand on the top of his head, Alice rose up on her knees to push his hand aside and inspect the wound he had received.

It served him right, Gybbon thought, and winced as Alice's slender fingers moved over the part of his head that had made such hard contact with the ceiling. He had only thought of putting some distance between himself and Alice, of running from the desire he felt for her. It grew stronger with every moment he spent in her company, making it more difficult to fight and control. Now his head hurt as much as his groin, only easing the pain of the latter would at least be pleasurable.

He opened his eyes and nearly groaned aloud. The way Alice was kneeling in front of him put her plump, firm breasts far too close to his mouth. He stared at them, watching them rise and fall gently with every breath she took, and his mouth watered. Exhausted though he was after a night of hunting, sleep was suddenly the last thing he wanted. He told himself not to touch her even as he placed his hands around her small waist.

Alice slowly lowered herself until she was face-to-face with Gybbon, one hand still lightly tangled in his thick hair. He was just steadying her, she told herself, and felt strangely disappointed. The look in his eyes disputed that conclusion but she did not know enough of men to be confident of that. For all she knew, it could be anger putting that heated look in his eyes.

"There was a wee gash," she said, "but it healed e'en as I looked at it."

"That is because I fed tonight," he explained and saw her quickly hide a flinch. "I gave the man a choice, lass. Flee or die. He chose to die. Since he wanted to toss his life away, I saw nay reason to waste what he could give me."

"Strength."

"Aye. And two blankets, a wee bit of food, and a few coins."

"I have robbed the dead, too," she confessed softly, trying not to stare at his tempting mouth so close to hers and failing miserably. "A wee part of me cringed but my mind kept saying that he didnae need it now and I did, the children did."

"And that it would only be taken by someone else."

"Aye."

"I am going to give ye a choice now, lass. Ye can stay right where ye are and let me kiss ye, or ye can move away. Best decide quickly, as I have waited a long time."

"Ye have only kenned me for two days." She knew she ought to move but curiosity and temptation held her in place.

"As I said, a verra long time."

He pressed his lips to hers. The soft warmth of them surprised Alice. She slid her hand down the back of his head until it rested upon the back of his neck. The heat of his kiss seeped through her body and she blindly pressed closer to him. When he teased her lips with the tip of his tongue it caused her lips to tingle and she gasped softly. Alice was startled when he put his tongue in her mouth. Her astonishment disappeared in a haze of heat as he stroked the inside of her mouth.

The slow caresses of his hands up and down her back and sides made Alice tremble with the strength of the desire he was stirring to life inside her. The feeling was both exhilarating and terrifying. She offered no resistance as he pushed her down onto the blanket, wrapping her arms around him to hold him close as he sprawled on top of her. The soft growl he made as the full length of their bodies pressed together aroused her more than the sweetest of flatteries.

Then she became aware of the long, hard length of his manhood rubbing against her. Alice fought to push aside the insidious advance of fear. She told herself it was not a thing to fear, that this man would never wield that part of him as a weapon, but the fear grew stronger. It chilled the heat of desire she had been enjoying and then forced her mind into the dark quagmire of terrifying memory.

Gybbon suddenly found his arms full of a terrified woman intent on doing him harm. He silently cursed himself for a fool for forgetting what Alice had suffered in the past. As quickly as he could, he moved to kneel beside her, his hands out to the side as he called her name.

" 'Tis Gybbon, Alice," he said in as soothing a voice as he could manage while his body was knotted up with unsatisfied need. "Ye are safe. I am nay Callum. I willnae hurt ye."

"I ken it," Alice said, taking several deep breaths as she continued to push aside the icy fear that had conquered her heart and mind. "I am sorry." Too embarrassed to look at him, she wrapped herself in her blanket and curled on her side, facing away from him. "I had thought the scars had healed," she whispered, her disappointment nearly choking her.

"They will heal," he said as he wrapped himself in a blanket as well and settled down at her back. " 'Tis just the first time ye have tested the strength of them."

"Aye."

He put his arm around her and pulled her close, pleased when she only tensed a little. "I was too quick. Next time I will go slowly."

Alice knew she ought to firmly tell him that there would be no next time, but she just closed her eyes.

# Chapter Five

"He is late," Alice complained to Nightwind.

She paced in front of the mare that placidly nuzzled the ground looking for tasty things to chew. It was foolish to be so concerned, she told herself. Gybbon was a big, strong man, one skilled in battle. He was also far better at hunting and killing than the men he now hunted. Even though the Hunters had grown more cautious, in the last three days Gybbon had lessened their numbers to four. He was a deadly shadow at their heels.

Yet, the cursed Hunters did not give up. Alice did not understand that. When a man could lessen your numbers by half without even being seen, when the female you hunted could bring down a grown man with only her hands and teeth, why continue? Why not at least return home to plan and gather more men and weapons?

She could understand why Callum continued, for she knew he needed to remove what he saw as a grave sin and a stain upon his honor, his very soul. He had made that increasingly clear in every confrontation they had had since he had raped her. That did not, however, explain why the others continued to follow him as they watched one after another of their companions disappear into the night never to return. It was madness. Alice knew the men believed they were trying to rid the world of what they saw as a great evil, but did that mean they could not even rest now and then?

"Whate'er this fervor is that has grasped these Hunters, it robs the men of all good sense, of even their soul-deep need to survive," she muttered, earning only a brief glance from her mare. "And I begin to think Gybbon has tumbled into the same madness." She crossed her arms over her chest and scowled in the direction Gybbon had ridden. "The two of us together could face down and defeat our foe now. Why does Gybbon continue to do it alone? I shall tell ye why. He doesnae think I can fight despite surviving for so long without his blessed help. He probably thinks I have just been lucky or that the ones hunting us are unskilled lack-wits. I may nay be one of those mighty Purebloods but I have strength and fighting skills, ones I have learned weel over the last six years."

Alice glanced up at the sky and cursed. Gybbon had said he would return in time for them to reach shelter before the sun peeked over the horizon. Unless he rode up in the next few minutes he would not be keeping that promise. They certainly would not reach the next place of shelter before the sun was up and shining on both of them. Even if they started right now and the shelter they needed was close by, Gybbon would still be out in the sun long enough for it to begin to leech his strength away.

"Gybbon is never late," she said and felt a chill wiggle through her that had nothing to do with the cold mists of dawn. " 'Tis true that I havenae even kenned the mon for a sennight yet, but he is always where he has said he would be exactly when he said he would be there. Especially when it concerns getting to a shelter ere the sun has risen too high in the sky. Instead I stand here alone talking to a horse. Nay, something isnae right, Nightwind."

She clenched her fists at her side and struggled against the urge to start bellowing his name. Despite not being a Pureblood, Gybbon could not abide much sun, far less than she could. He was always intensely aware of when the sun would rise and set. He simply would not risk his life like this. Nor would he want to have her suffer from the sun in even the smallest way. Alice feared that this time Gybbon had not been as quick or as stealthy as before or, worse, he had stumbled into a trap.

That last word nearly stopped her heart beating. Just thinking the possibility that Gybbon had fallen into a trap made her tremble with fear for Gybbon. Alice could not claim that she had the sight, even if she did have the occasional dream that gave her a timely warning. What she did know was that she had very keen instincts, and every one of them was telling her that Gybbon was in grave danger. In the years she had been running and hiding she had learned to heed those instincts. They had saved her more times than she cared to count. Now she felt sure they were trying to save Gybbon with their alarums.

Grabbing Nightwind's reins, Alice began to follow Gybbon's trail. The man was careful not to leave enough sign of his passing for the Hunters to see, but her eyesight was far keener than their enemies' and the blood Gybbon had been making her drink in the wine had made them even keener. She knew he would be angry with her for following him but she did not care. Far better to be lectured by him than to discover much later that if she had just done something, she might have saved his life. Alice did not want those chains of guilt dragging her down for the rest of her life.

And when they reached shelter this time, she would conquer the last of her fear, she silently vowed. It had lessened with each one of Gybbon's kisses, with each stroke of his hand. It was past time to vanquish the last of it. The fear that something had happened to Gybbon had made one thing very clear to Alice. It was far more than lust that kept her returning to Gybbon's arms, kept her risking the chance of recalling the horror of Callum's attack every time she felt the hard proof of Gybbon's desire press against her. She had no intention of allowing Gybbon to get himself killed until she had discovered just what that more was. He had started the seduction and he could damn well stay around until he finished it, she thought crossly.

Gybbon echoed every move the Hunter made as he waited for the man to strike. This man was not going to be a quick kill. The Hunter had not only refused to flee, he had been cocky in that refusal. Considering how many of the man's companions had already died, that made no sense to Gybbon. He doubted the fool considered himself a far more skilled fighter than his dead companions, although such arrogance was a possibility. This man did not have the same look of religious fervor in his small dark eyes, either.

Bait.

The word whispered through Gybbon's mind and he cursed. He did not want to believe he had been foolish enough to step into a trap but every instinct he had was suddenly screaming that that was exactly what he had done. This man had not been caught;

he had done the catching. And if Gybbon did not break free of the trap soon, Alice would be left alone. The thought chilled him to the bone.

He had not even told her how to get to Cambrun, he suddenly thought. In his arrogance, he had assumed he would be the victor of this battle and would take her there when it was all over. Gybbon quickly pushed aside what tasted too much like fear, a fear for Alice's safety. He could not allow himself to be distracted by concern for her. He had to worry about himself. If luck was still on his side, he could escape this trap. The fact that he was already hoping for luck to save him did not make Gybbon feel much better.

A heartbeat later he knew there would be no escape for him, that he had allowed his thoughts to distract him enough to miss someone creeping up behind him. Pain crashed through his head. Gybbon tried to turn and face whoever had struck him from behind, but staggered and fell to his knees. A second blow fell and the cascade of agony laid him out on the ground, bringing him down so swiftly that he had no chance to even put out his hands to ease his fall. His last clear thought before he was dragged into blackness was of Alice and how he had failed her.

Gybbon instinctively smothered a groan as he woke up, slowly dragging himself out of the dark he had been plunged into. The pounding in his head was so fierce his eyes hurt, felt as if they were trying to escape his skull. For a moment he wondered what was wrong with him and then the memory of two hard blows to his head seeped into his mind. The fact that his head still throbbed told him the injury done to it had been a serious one. He started to lift his hand to his aching head and froze.

He was tied down. All reluctance to open his eyes fled. Gybbon ignored the increased ache in his head as the soft light of dawn struck his eyes like a blow, and looked around. He was staked out on the ground just inside the woods surrounding a small clearing, his arms and legs tethered to four thick tree trunks. A brief tug was enough to let him know those ropes were thick and strong, the knots tight. His strength had been too badly leeched away by the injury to his head, and the others he was beginning to feel, to allow him to snap the ropes quickly. The way the four men moving toward him were watching him, he would have to break his ties very quickly to have even the smallest chance of escape. At his full strength he could have done it, and leapt into the fight before the fools even knew he had freed himself. At the moment, just the thought of leaping anywhere was more than he could bear.

The man Gybbon now knew was Callum stopped barely a foot away. A snarl rose up inside Gybbon and rumbled in his throat as he met the cold gray gaze of the one who had so badly hurt Alice. The way the three men with Callum took a slight step back would have pleased him if his attention had not been so fixed upon Callum. The beast that lived inside every MacNachton wanted this man's blood and was enraged by the weakness that prevented him from tearing out the man's throat.

He would not feed from him, Gybbon decided coldly, only taking enough to let the man know he had been right about some of what he had believed about the MacNachtons. Enough to make the man fear for his soul just before he died. As far as Gybbon was concerned the man's soul was already damned for what he had done to Alice and what he yet planned to do to her and his own child. Unfortunately, he knew a man like Callum would not see what he had done or wanted to do as a crime.

"They say the sun kills demons like ye," Callum said.

The man's voice was rough and unusually hoarse. Gybbon wondered why he had not noticed that when the man had spoken that night Gybbon had found Alice. Fighting to see clearly despite the faint haze of pain clouding his eyes, Gybbon studied the man closely. After a good long look, he finally saw why the man's voice was so unusual. A ragged scar marred his throat, a mark he recognized as having been made by an animal or, he almost smiled, a MacNachton. Alice had nearly killed the man. With either her teeth or the lethal claws her fingernails could become, she had tried to tear out the man's throat. His Alice was a strong fighter, he thought with pride.

His Alice? Gybbon silently cursed. She was that and more. He wondered what twist of fate made him realize that now. It was a poor time for such a revelation. He had no time to sort through his feelings or question just why he had marked her. If nothing else it would probably only add to the pain he felt, for there was a very good chance he would never see her again. Telling himself that if she found her way to Cambrun his clan would care for her only brought him small comfort.

"They say a lot of foolish things," he replied, not surprised when his calm, faintly derisive words caused Callum to narrow his eyes in anger. "One has to question the wit of any who would listen to such mad talk." Gybbon hid his pain when the man kicked him in the side. "Ah, time for the gentle persuasion, is it?"

"Ye willnae be so cocky soon. Despite the shade the trees offer, the sun will soon be shining down on ye."

"Aye. A rare sight in this land and one to enjoy the few times we are blessed to see it."

"Mayhap that talk of the sun killing them wasnae right, Callum," muttered a short, thick-set man. "And werenae we supposed to try to catch us one of these demons?"

"We have caught one, Duncan," said Callum.

"I was meaning catch one to be taking back to the laird so that he can be made to talk and all. The laird badly wants one of these demons so he can look them over. Has him some questions for the beastie, aye?"

"This beastie has killed four of our men. And we will be answering a few questions by watching what does happen to demons like him once they are forced to meet the light of day, aye?"

Duncan scratched his weak chin. "I be thinking the laird has more than one question he is wanting answered."

"Then he can hunt down and capture one of these thrice-cursed beasts himself. This one is ours. There is also one more of his ilk creeping about, isnae there. Mayhap we should take the lass to the laird. Aye, there is a thought. I suspicion the laird would like to see what a female demon is like."

A chill rippled through Gybbon. He could not halt the memories of what had happened to his cousins Heming and Tearlach when they had been captured by Hunters from swamping his mind. Their tales of captivity had enraged every MacNachton alive and sent the icy chill of dread he felt now down many a spine. The thought of Alice enduring such tortures made his heart clench with fear for her, but he kept that fear hidden from Callum and his men. It would only please them and could even add to the danger Alice would face without him at her side. Reminding himself of how long Alice had escaped these men, even with the added burden of four children, made swallowing that fear a little easier.

"Ye have been trying to catch and hold fast to Alice for six years," Gybbon said, "and ye have failed. Why do ye think ye can do so now?" When those words earned him another kick in his side, Gybbon had to fight even harder to hide how much pain it caused him, for he was certain he had felt his rib crack under the blow.

"Because ye are going to tell us where the bitch is."

"Och, nay, I dinnae think so. She wasnae too pleased with your hospitality the last time ye had her as your guest."

"She and that loathsome whelp she bred need to die, but how long it takes them to do so isnae my concern. They will be caught and I will take them to the laird."

"Which laird do ye mean to give your son to?"

"That beast she bore isnae my son! And I am nay fool enough to give ye the laird's name just so that ye can lay some curse upon his righteous head. Just think on this as ye die, demon. Soon your woman and her wee bastard will be in the hands of your enemy, and I think ye can guess how much she will be enjoying that mon's hospitality."

Gybbon watched the man walk back to the fire burning in the center of the clearing, his men shuffling along behind him. There was a confidence behind the man's words that deeply unsettled Gybbon. Why, after six long years of chasing Alice all over Scotland, did the men believe she would soon be caught? It made no sense.

Then he almost cursed aloud, barely stopping himself from wildly fighting against his bonds as an icy panic seized his heart. He was bait. Just as they had used a lone man to draw him in and capture him, they planned to use him to draw Alice into a trap. It had been hard enough to think on how Alice would be alone, unprotected because he had foolishly stumbled into a snare. Now he added the fear that she would be taken captive. Gybbon had not thought there could be anything worse than thinking Alice could die because of his carelessness, but Callum had just shown him that there was.

He fought to smother the ugly memories of all his cousins had endured when they had been taken prisoner, but they refused to leave his mind. Only it was not Tearlach or Heming he saw in chains. It was Alice. It was Alice's soft skin marred with bloody lash marks and bruises from repeated beatings.

Even more horrifying was the thought that, if the men who had caged his cousins had told anyone of their assumptions about the value of MacNachton blood, Alice would spend her long years in chains while her blood was used to give those monsters the strength and longevity of a MacNachton. Even if the men who held her did not have that knowledge, they would still make her life a hell on earth as they used her to try to discover every strength and weakness the MacNachtons had. And such prodding, such long study, could easily reveal that secret the MacNachtons themselves had only just fully understood and wanted no Outsider to ever know—that drinking MacNachton blood could heal, could strengthen, and could lengthen an Outsider's life by many, many years. The secret they had hoped had died with Heming's captors. That realization brought Gybbon's thoughts right back to the chance that Alice could be held as a source for that blood for a very long time and he nearly bellowed out his pain and rage at the thought.

For the first time in a long time, Gybbon found

himself praying. He prayed that some miracle would occur and that he would regain enough strength and luck to escape so that he could slaughter these men who thought themselves so much more blessed than he despite their plans to hand a woman and child over to ones who would torture them for years. But mostly, he prayed that Alice had the good sense to stay very far away.

# Chapter Six

Sweat trickled down Alice's spine as she inched her way closer to Gybbon. When she had first seen him tied down she had nearly charged the Hunters' camp, blindly eager to free him and slaughter his captors. She had needed several moments to quell that urge. The good sense to know that it would be an utterly foolish thing to do had been slow to come and cool her blood,

Still shaking from the need to kill the men who had hunted her for so long, who now left Gybbon staked out to suffer a slow bleeding away of his strength and his life beneath the slowly rising sun, she had taken her bow and arrows from her saddle. The weapon was one of the few things she had rescued from her home before running for her life. Her father had made the bow to suit her small hands and taught her to hunt with it. Unable to buy, make, or steal any new arrows, she had treated each one she had like gold but she was willing to lose a few now if they finally rid her of these men and saved Gybbon.

As she continued to creep closer to Gybbon, Alice tried to plan exactly how she would free him. She knew she could take down at least one man with an arrow, possibly two, before the Hunters even knew she was there, but then they would be on her. Freeing Gybbon as much as possible had to come first. Then all she could do was hope that the threat of being taken down by an arrow would be enough to hold the Hunters back. As she held them at bay, Gybbon could finish freeing himself.

If he still had the strength to do so, she thought, glancing up at the sun. Its light was already eking through the trees to touch him, each shaft of its light slowly sucking the strength from his body. If the amount of blood she could see on his now dirty, tattered clothing was anything to judge by, he had wounds that would also steal his strength. She could tolerate a lot more sun than he could, but it was still vital to get him to some shelter as swiftly as possible. For that to happen he had to be able to ride, and that took strength. She certainly did not have the strength to drag him about for miles if he lost consciousness.

Her stomach cramped with fear as she moved the last few inches to where one of the ropes holding him down was wrapped around a tree. She kept her gaze fixed upon the Hunters as she sawed at the thick rope with her dagger. Each faint rasp of the blade against the rope made her heart skip with alarm but she did not hesitate. Even if she got only one of Gybbon's arms free before she was discovered, that would still give them some chance to flee. She could put the dagger in his hand and hold their enemies back as he finished cutting himself loose.

"There be sun on him now, Callum, but he doesnae act like he feels any pain," said one of the Hunters, a tall, too-thin youth with pockmarked skin. "I thought ye said they were supposed to burn."

"That is what we will soon discover for certain," said Callum.

Alice fought the fear that rough voice stirred inside her, a fear so deep her muscles tensed with the need to run. Instead she concentrated on the fact that his once fine, deep voice was ruined because of her. The memory of how she had escaped him gave her strength. Even so, she felt a dizzying surge of relief when the blade of her dagger finally cut through the rope, for it meant she was now a little closer to getting far away from Callum. Still keeping her gaze on the men by the fire, she began the slow, exhausting crawl toward the tree that Gybbon's other arm was lashed to.

Gybbon looked toward the Hunters when the youngest of them spoke. The youth's words proved that the rumor that MacNachtons caught fire in the sun's light had not died. Although the result was wrong, the men obviously knew, or had been told, that the light of day was dangerous to the people they hunted. Gybbon had to wonder what idiocy made the men continue to track MacNachtons at night if they believed that. It could be as simple as the Hunters not knowing where their prey would hide, but Gybbon could not help but think that some of it was a simple following of the rules of war. Striking at night often gave the attacker an advantage. Since striking at MacNachtons in the full light of a sunny day could cost his clan dearly, he prayed these men and the ones sending them out to hunt remained so blindly foolish.

A faint tug on his wrist startled him but he hid his surprise. He also swallowed a sudden wave of hope. It might not be a rescue. It could just be some woodland creature testing the rope for food or nesting material. Gybbon took a slow, deep breath to restore his calm and his nose filled with a light scent he knew all too well. Alice was near. He had the wild thought that he should have left the need of bloody retribution out of his prayers.

The urge to shout at her to run was hard to beat down. At full strength he and Alice could take down all four men, but neither of them was. He suffered because of his wounds, that weakness only added to by the sun's effect on him, and she had not yet regained the strength six years of running for her life had stolen from her. Her reluctance to feed only made her recovery take longer. If she was seen, she could be captured, and the thought of that was nearly more than he could bear.

When the pull of the rope on his wrist went abruptly lax, Gybbon struggled to remain still. He did not give in to the temptation to see where Alice was moving to next. Instead, he concentrated on how she moved without making a sound, silently slipping from shadow to shadow, and how none of their enemies appeared to be aware of her presence. To ensure that they remained ignorant, he attempted to keep their attention fixed firmly on him.

"Did ye expect me to blaze like some Hogmanay bonfire?" he asked, mockery thick behind every word.

"It fair disappoints me that ye havenae, but the sun will soon kill ye, be it slow or swift," said Callum. "Of course, ye could save your life by telling us what we need to ken. Where are Alice and the bairn?"

*Alice is probably near enough to spit on ye,* he thought with grim satisfaction. "Och, nay, I willnae help ye catch her. I ken all too weel the tortures your laird and his ilk would put her through. Her and your son."

"That whelp isnae my son!" Callum cursed and glared at Gybbon. "She tries to blame me for her bearing that demon's spawn, but he didnae grow from my seed."

Gybbon felt the rope around his other wrist fall limp. A heartbeat later the hilt of a dagger filled his palm. It was the hardest thing he had ever done but he resisted the urge to hurl it at Callum. He also resisted the need to move. Since he now had Alice's dagger, he knew she was not planning to cut his legs free of their tethers. That meant she had something else planned, something he hoped would hold the Hunters back as he finished freeing himself. And something, he thought as his insides clenched with anticipation, that did not require any sacrifice from Alice. He would not allow her to trade her freedom for his.

"It was your seed, ye raping bastard," Alice said as she leapt to her feet, her bow drawn and an arrow aimed right at Callum's heart. It took all of her willpower not to let it fly.

Despite his weakness, Gybbon moved swiftly to cut the ropes at his ankles. Every bone and sinew inside him ached with weariness but he leapt to Alice's side the moment he was free. One man drew his sword and stepped toward them but the man had barely completed the move when an arrow through his leg took him down. Gybbon glanced at Alice to see that she already had another arrow notched in her bow.

"Ye are admirably quick with that, lass," he murmured.

"Thank ye," she said. "Now what?"

"Ye mean this is where all your clever plotting ended?"

"More or less. I fear I thought it all up a wee bit quickly."

He moved to grab his weapons that had been set down not far from where he had been staked out. One quick look toward his horse revealed that the animal was still saddled and only lightly tethered to a tangled bush. Gybbon whistled softly and Resolute easily tugged himself free. In the brief moment the horse crossed in front of Alice, another man tried to rush forward. Gybbon watched as, the moment Resolute moved past Alice, she took the man down with an arrow to the shoulder. She was good, he mused, but she was going to have to overcome her aversion to killing when dealing with men like these. They might not be holding a blade against her throat, but they were still a threat to her life.

"Keep your bow drawn, lass, and come here to me," he said quietly as he drew his sword. "Your horse?"

"A few yards behind us," she replied as she did as he had ordered.

"Mount Resolute. We will catch the mare as we pass it."

It was not easy, and she had to release her guard on the men for a moment, but Alice mounted the horse. She then resumed her armed watch on the Hunters as Gybbon mounted behind her. She frowned when he caught up the reins and the animal began to back up, but not straight back. It was not until Gybbon cut free the men's horses, slapping one on its flank with the flat of his sword and sending all the horses trotting away, that she realized what he had planned. Even as the Hunters cried out their fury, Gybbon turned Resolute in the direction she had come, and kicked him into a fast trot. Alice hastily shoved her arrow back into its quiver and slung her bow over her shoulder so that she could hang on.

When they reached Nightwind, Alice halted Gybbon's attempt to grab the reins of her horse and keep on riding. She moved nimbly from Resolute's back to the mare's. They would travel faster this way, and getting to a shelter was as important as eluding their enemies. The sun would soon be high enough to cause her trouble. She did not want to even think of what it was doing to Gybbon.

He gave her no chance to ask him how he felt, however. Alice quickly nudged her horse to a pace to keep up with Gybbon as he rode through the forest at a speed that was just short of dangerous. She kept her attention fixed upon the path he led them along for over an hour, ducking low limbs and praying her horse did not stumble. The time had passed in utter silence before Alice thought to ask Gybbon if the Hunters were still on their trail. If he did not think so, they could, perhaps, slow their pace a little to one that did not offer so many chances for disaster.

When she looked at Gybbon, however, she could not fully smother a gasp of shock. There was no color left in his face and, even as she watched, he swayed in the saddle. He shook himself and sat upright again but Alice doubted he would be able to do that for much longer.

"Stop," she ordered. "Stop right now, Gybbon MacNachton."

Gybbon reined to a halt and looked at her, all the while fighting to remain conscious enough to get her moving again. "Why?"

"Because ye are about to fall out of your saddle. The sun has leeched away all your strength," she said as she dismounted and stepped up beside him.

"Nay. 'Tis near. The shelter is near. We can reach it if we keep moving."

The ease with which she pulled the reins out of his hands alarmed Alice. "Ye willnae make it any farther than the next tree if ye keep on as ye are."

"Near enough."

He reached for the reins only to sprawl facedown on his horse. Gybbon told himself that he just needed to rest for a moment but he knew that was a lie. He felt as if his bones had turned to water. Ordering himself to rise up, to take the reins back and get Alice to safety did not stir up even the smallest spark of strength.

"What are ye doing?" he asked as he felt something cover him.

"I am securing ye to the saddle and covering ye with blankets," she replied, knotting the ends of a blanket beneath Resolute's belly. "And dinnae argue with me. Ye are near to falling out of your saddle and I could ne'er get ye back in it if that happened. And I wouldnae have time to try, for I will soon be suffering as ye are if we dinnae get out of this sun. And why, when it so rarely does so, is that cursed sun so bright today?"

Gybbon did not even have the strength to sigh with relief when she finished covering him up, shielding him from the sun with their blankets. He used that respite to gather what few shreds of strength he could and told her where to go. He did not want to admit that he was no longer sure of how much farther they had to go and was pleased that she did not ask. As Resolute began to move, Gybbon prayed he had not waited too long, pushed himself too hard, or the sleep he was tumbling into could be an eternal one.

Alice was beginning to feel the dangerous effects of the sun by the time she found the shelter Gybbon had been traveling to. It was an old stone hovel, one of the ones people believed the ancients had left behind, so well shielded from view by trees and vines she had nearly missed it. She was able to rouse Gybbon just enough so that she did not have to drag him inside, but left him where he fell facedown on the dirt floor. Muttering apologies to the horses for her rushed care of them, she tossed the saddles and their packs into the shelter and then secured the animals beneath the heavy shade of the trees.

Once inside the shelter she spread a blanket over the floor and then dragged and rolled Gybbon's body onto it. She undressed him and washed his wounds, cursing the Hunters for every bruise and cut Gybbon had suffered. Just as she was about to make certain he still breathed, and ease her growing fear for him, he opened his eyes. Alice frowned when his lips moved but she could hear little more than his breath passing through them. She leaned closer, turning her ear toward his mouth.

"Blood. Need blood."

She sat back on her heels and stared at him, pleased that his eyes were shut again. He would not see her fear. Alice did not understand why she felt that chill at his request. Fear and dislike it though she did, she had long ago accepted the dark hunger that afflicted her, one that had come from his clan. She had let the children feed from her, seen it only as a necessity to keep them strong and healthy. Then she cursed softly as she realized what held her back. This was a man; this was Gybbon. Alice knew that letting him feed from her would be far more than an act of healing. Every instinct she had told her it would also be an intimate act.

Cautiously, and silently ridiculing herself for that caution, Alice touched his face. He was cold, so cold that grief clutched at her heart. It felt as if she touched a corpse. She placed her hand over his heart. It beat, but slowly, wearily. It would not be long before it stopped.

Alice knew she would have to let him feed from her. There was no choice. Even if he was not as close to dying as she feared he was, he needed her blood to heal. Between the weakness caused by the sun and the injuries he had suffered, it would take him a very long time to heal enough to travel. They did not have that

time. One of the reasons she and Gybbon had been
so successful thus far was that they had never stayed
in one place for very long. She also had the strong
feeling that she would grieve hard if he died. If it
happened because she was too great a coward to let
him take her blood, that grief would be tenfold.

Abruptly, she cursed and bit her wrist. Slipping
one arm beneath Gybbon's head and lifting him up
enough so that he would not choke as he fed, she
placed her bleeding wrist against his mouth. For a
moment his lips remained cold and still against her
skin and her blood seeped down over his chin. Alice
feared she was too late, that he was already beyond
the ability to take what could save him. Then he
grabbed hold of her arm and pressed her wrist hard
against his mouth. A heartbeat later, he sank his
fangs into her skin and began to feed.

The surge of what Alice could only assume was lust
flooded her body. Her breasts quickly grew heavy and
the tips hardened, even began to ache in an itchy sort
of way. What began to alarm Alice a little was the growing heated fullness between her thighs. With each
pull of his mouth upon her wrist, she felt a faint,
cramping need low in her belly. And she was getting
wet down there, she thought, nearly yanking her wrist
away from Gybbon. As if sensing her plan to retreat,
he growled softly and held tight. Only her deep need
to help him grow strong again held her in place. By
the time he stopped feeding, stroked the wound on her
wrist with his tongue, and promptly fell unconscious
again, Alice was fighting the urge to shove her hand
between her legs and stroke herself. That shocked
her so much that she pulled away from Gybbon so
fast she nearly fell over.

Was this lust? she wondered, staring at the closed
wound on her wrist with utter fascination. Since the

only time she had known a man intimately was when Callum had brutally assaulted her, Alice could not be sure. She had not even kissed a man before that horrible night. In truth, she had never kissed a man before Gybbon. Callum had not bothered with kisses. Whatever it was that she had felt, she knew it was no threat to her despite the alarm that rippled through her. Behind all the strange feelings that had just afflicted her was one she had recognized. Need.

She looked down at Gybbon and sighed. Instinct told her that need could only be fed by Gybbon Mac-Nachton, and not with the blood that dark hunger in her sometimes demanded. If that was true, and what she had just felt was lust, she might be wise to rethink her decision to cast aside the fear Callum had scarred her with and take Gybbon as her lover. Alice was absolutely sure that Gybbon would never hurt her in body, but she could not be sure that he would never shred her heart.

# Chapter Seven

A sweet-scented warmth was the first thing Gybbon was aware of as he woke up. He glanced down to discover Alice curled up beside him, one slender arm draped over his belly. Then his memories rushed into his mind and he tensed. It took him a moment to calm himself, for his sleep-dulled mind to fully grasp that memories were not a threat. Not an immediate one, at least, he thought as he stroked one hand down Alice's long, thick hair.

Peering around, he realized she had gotten him to the shelter, although he recalled nothing of the journey after she had covered him with the blanket. Gybbon was embarrassed by the weakness that had taken him down, by his inability to save himself, but he was also proud of Alice's courage and strength. She was his; she just did not know it yet. It would require some hard wooing but he was more than willing to work for his prize.

In the midst of an idle, pleasant dream of the future with Alice as his mate, Gybbon finally became aware of how good he felt. Too good for a man who had suffered the wounds he had and then spent too long in the sun. He should still have a few aches to deal with, yet he felt as if he could easily chase a buck to ground for their next meal.

He carefully lifted Alice's small hand from his chest and stared at her wrist. The marks were faint, nearly fully healed, but he recognized them easily. Alice had fed him. Gybbon suddenly feared he had fed too long, left her weak, but a quick, thorough look at her eased his fear. There was color in her cheeks, her breathing was deep and even, and beneath his fingers, the pulse in her wrist was steady and strong. The food and the blood she had taken in over the last few days had done their work. Alice was not only stronger, she was strong enough to give him what he needed to heal and suffer no weakness for it.

Shifting just a little to free the arm Alice was sleeping on, Gybbon trailed his fingers up and down her spine. He touched his nose to her hair and breathed deeply of her clean scent. Then he frowned and, lifting his head slightly, took another deep breath. He grinned, experienced enough to easily recognize that faint scent in the air. It was arousal. He knew exactly what had stirred Alice's lust as well. Allowing him to feed from her had obviously stirred her desires.

Gybbon idly ran his tongue over his lips. He could still taste her sweetness there, feel the bright glory of her blood inside him. The taste of her still lingering in his mouth was a heady one, and one he was eager to taste again.

He lightly stroked her soft cheek with his fingers. Thus far frustration was his only reward for the desire he felt for Alice, but he hoped the fact that she had let him feed from her indicated that she was finally breaking the chains of fear. When there was an attraction between a man and a woman, a sharing of blood became an extremely intimate act. The arousal that had stirred in Alice, one that still lightly perfumed the air with its tantalizing promise, should have terrified Alice. Yet here she was, curled up against him.

Gently tilting her face up to his, Gybbon brushed his lips over hers. He felt a twinge of conscience over his plan to seduce her, to use what lusty feelings the feeding had stirred within her to his advantage, but he ignored it. For Alice to completely conquer her fear about all that could happen between a man and a woman, she needed to be shown that it could be pleasurable. She needed to see that lovemaking was not painful, that violence had nothing to do with it. She needed to be shown tenderness and passion so that she could finally begin to heal from the scars of the violence she had suffered at Callum's cruel hands. Gybbon was certain that once he and Alice had made love, she would lose the fear that ate at her. He was not arrogant or fool enough to think that all her ghosts would disappear, but he felt certain that most of them would.

Pulling her on top of him, he kissed her awake. The way she quickly roused from her sleep to return his kiss made his body rapidly harden with need. She wore only her thin linen shift, but he ached to tear it from her body. He wanted to be skin to skin with her so badly he could feel a growl of demand gathering in his throat. Weaving his fingers into her thick hair, he plunged his tongue into her mouth, craving the taste of her.

Alice gasped when Gybbon ceased kissing her and gently scraped his teeth along the side of her throat where her pulse throbbed. She was sprawled on top of his large, naked body in a wanton manner but felt no inclination to move. Her blood ran hot and all the aching need she had thought sleep had conquered now rushed back so swiftly she felt dazed by it. His manhood rose big and hard between her thighs but it stirred no fear inside her.

"I see ye are healed and strong again," she said, shivering with delight as his lightly calloused hands stroked the back of her thighs.

"Aye." Gybbon was not surprised when his answer sounded more like a groan than a word, for Alice was rubbing herself against his aching manhood. "I can still taste ye on my tongue. Your blood now races alongside mine."

It surprised Alice that she could be so aroused by those words. She had done what she needed to survive over the years, but the dark hunger for blood she had been cursed with had always appalled her. Instead of disgust and shame, she found herself wanting to feel what he did, wanting to taste his blood and make it part of hers. The mere thought of that brought her fangs out. When she lightly nipped his shoulder, letting him feel the sharpness of them, his growl held such hungry pleasure she felt her womb clench with demand.

"Take your shift off, lass," he ordered. "I need to feel your flesh against mine."

Without hesitation, Alice sat up straddling him and yanked off her shift. He ran his hands up her rib cage and covered her breasts. When he teased her hardened nipples with his thumbs, she closed her eyes and placed her hands over his. He suddenly wrapped one strong arm around her, pulled her down closer to him, and then took the aching tip of her breast deep into his mouth. Alice cried out from the strength of the pleasure that seared through her body.

Through the haze of desire that was clouding her mind a demand made itself known. Alice realized she was wet and rubbing herself against his warm, hard length. There was an aching hollowness inside her that cried to be filled. It shocked her to admit it but she knew exactly what her body wanted. Her own body's needs were strangling her blind fear of that part of Gybbon, and she knew she had to take that final step now.

"Inside," she gasped. "Get inside." She started to move off him to lie on her back but he held her in place.

"This way, love," Gybbon said. "Ye ride me."

"I dinnae understand."

"Put me inside ye, lass."

Gybbon struggled for some control over the fierce desire gripping him. He was so desperate to be inside her that even the way she fumbled as she tried to unite their bodies excited him beyond words simply because her hand was wrapped around his shaft. After only a moment, however, he moved to show her what she needed to do, placing his hand over hers to help her aim him in the right direction. The moment he began to ease inside her, he yanked her hand away and pushed deep inside. He knew he should go slowly but the way her tight heat wrapped around him seared away the last of his control. A small part of him was aware of how she began to move on him, revealing the same greed infecting him, and he gave himself over to the passion ruling them both.

Alice's release came quickly. Gybbon felt her body clench around him as she cried out his name in an alluring mixture of delight and surprise. Then she fell against him and he growled with pleasure as she sank her teeth into his chest.

Gybbon looked down at her feeding from him and shuddered from the force of the ecstasy pouring through his body. His dark hunger grew and his fangs ached for the taste of her. Since he could not reach her neck and did not want to stop her, he grabbed her arm and brought her wrist to his mouth, sinking his fangs into her soft flesh. As the taste of her entered his mouth, she shook with another release, her heat constricting around him. He held her writhing hips steady and thrust deep inside her, once, before joining her in rapture's fall.

Alice blinked as she realized she was still sprawled on top of Gybbon, her cheek pressed against his broad chest. As her mind cleared a little more and she recalled all that had just happened, she did not know whether to be embarrassed or to spring up and do a dance of joy. She started to lift her head and her gaze fell on his chest, upon the mark she recognized all too well even though it was already faint and growing fainter. All her joy over conquering her fear, over finding out what pleasure could be found in a man's arms, faded away so quickly she felt chilled.

"I bit ye," she whispered in shock as she slowly sat up. "I fed from ye."

"Aye, that ye did." Gybbon idly wondered when she would recall that she was as naked as he was as he savored the sight of her soft skin and full breasts. He hoped it would not be too soon. "I bit ye, too."

Alice frowned at him. "Why do ye sound so pleased by that?"

"Because I am." He lightly trailed his fingers over her taut stomach, enjoying the way her skin flushed beneath his touch, and thinking that even her belly hole was beautiful. He almost laughed at how besotted he was. "Lass, we may nay be Purebloods, but we are MacNachtons."

"But I didnae need to feed. I am nay wounded. I—" She ceased talking when he pressed a finger to her lips.

"E'en people who arenae of our ilk give each other wee love bites whilst in the throes of passion. Alice, for a MacNachton who still feels the dark hunger of what we just did, the sharing of our blood only adds to the pleasure to be found in lovemaking. It can make it richer, wilder, fiercer. Aye?"

She blushed. "Aye. I think it will take me a wee while to shake free of fearing all that has made me different."

When she felt his hand enclose her breast, she sighed with pleasure until she realized that they were both still naked. With a squeak of embarrassment, she tried to scramble off him and get her clothes, only to find herself on her back with a grinning Gybbon crouched over her. She could not stop herself from looking at him, at his big strong body. He was all lean muscles and smooth skin. Her hands itched to touch him.

"We have at least another hour ere the sun sets, Alice Boyd," he said and kissed the tip of her nose.

"Ye want to do that again?" Even as she asked that question she felt him grow hard against her.

"Shall we try it this way? Do ye think ye are ready for that?"

"Do ye think I grew afraid because of ye being on top of me? It cannae be that simple, can it?"

"Nay, but once passion clouded your wits, I think it became that way." Gybbon brushed his lips over hers. "The moment ye feel that old fear nudging at ye, give me a wee push and I will turn us around."

The sun had fully set by the time Alice opened her eyes again. She blinked a few times before she could see clearly and then studied the man snoring softly with his head pillowed on her breasts. He was so handsome it made her heart ache. So, too, did the knowledge that he was not for her. Gybbon MacNachton was too fine for a shepherd's daughter. Her mother had been from a better-bred, more prosperous family, but that mattered little to people. All the finer things her mother had brought to the family were gone, anyway. There was no land or coin or even linen Alice could bring to a marriage, even if Gybbon had any inclination to offer her such a thing. All she had to offer was her heart, and a man like Gybbon MacNachton looked for more than that when he sought out a wife.

She pushed away those thoughts, for they made her eyes sting with tears she knew she could not shed. Instead she thought on the passion she and Gybbon had shared, and would share again if only for a little while. No matter what else happened between her and Gybbon, Alice knew she would always be grateful for the healing he had brought her. She knew he had not slain all her dragons, but he had cut the chains fear had wrapped around her.

When the man she had thought was asleep suddenly pushed himself up onto his forearms and gave her a quick hard kiss, she heard herself squeak in surprise. "I thought ye were asleep."

"I was," he said as he forced himself to leave her arms and reached for his clothes. "But I fear we cannae rest and enjoy each other any longer. I think 'tis also time we make straight for Cambrun."

Alice hurriedly dressed, regretting the abrupt end to her time in his arms but knowing it was necessary. "There are only two Hunters left. I didnae kill those other two men but I cannae see them continuing on with the wounds I gave them. Dinnae ye think Callum will give up now?" As she laced up her gown she turned to look at him and could tell by the expression on his face that she was not going to like his answer.

"The wounded men may weel give up but I am nay sure Callum will e'er stop." He pulled her into his arms and lightly kissed her frowning mouth. "I think 'tis more than some crusade to rid the land of perceived demons that keeps that mon on your trail, sweet Alice."

"He wants me and Donn dead, aye? We are living proof of what he sees as his sin and his shame."

Gybbon nodded as he rolled up the blankets. "In his mind, 'tis all your fault that he fell from grace and ye must pay. What troubles me most is that he spoke of capturing ye and taking ye back to the mon who sent these Hunters out. I wish I had had the chance to kill him for that thought alone."

"I would still be alive, though."

"Ye would soon wish that ye were dead." He put his arm around her shoulder when she paled a little at the hard fury in his voice. "Trust me in that, loving. My cousins Heming and Tearlach suffered mightily when they were held captive. Naked, caged, and chained, they were beaten, cut, and bled. Our enemies search for our weaknesses. The ones who held my cousins had a plan that, if they shared it with others, could cause the MacNachtons far more trouble than they have now."

"What could be worse than being treated as if we are evil demons, like we are naught but beasts?"

"They decided that the secret to the MacNachtons' strength and long lives is in their blood." He nodded when she paled again. "Aye. Just before Heming was freed, his rescuers heard his captors talk of making a potion from his blood and, if it made them stronger, to keep him alive so that they could keep dosing themselves."

"And they think we are evil?"

Gybbon almost grinned at her use of the word "we." She was already thinking of herself as a Mac-Nachton. It would make settling her at Cambrun a lot easier. He glanced at the mark on her neck, one she had not noticed yet, and felt his chest swell with pride and possession. She was his and that mark would let every MacNachton male know it. When they had the time, were no longer eluding an enemy, he would let her know it, too.

# Chapter Eight

"Cowards!"

Callum stood staring at the empty campsite, his hands clenched into fists at his side. His men had deserted him. That would not make him turn back, he swore. He could not. He had to clean away the sin on his soul. As long as Alice Boyd and her bastard lived, his weakness and his shame were there for anyone to see. He could never redeem himself as long as she and her son drew breath.

He looked at the place where the MacNachton beast had been tethered, at the remains of the ropes that had held the man in place. He should have killed the demon the moment he had brought him down. Callum cursed and kicked at the dirt. Now he was one against two, but he would not run with his tail tucked between his legs like the others had.

There was no going home for him until Alice Boyd and her bastard child were dead. He could not allow that proof of his weakness, of his succumbing to temptation and breeding evil, to walk around. The stain on his honor, on his soul, had to be cleansed with the blood of the ones who had put it there.

"I will see her dead," he vowed. "And then I will

search for that bastard she bred and see it in the
ground. On this I swear."

Alice cautiously eased away from a sleeping Gybbon's warm body and ignored the immediate chill of
loss that swept over her. She was getting far too accustomed to the feel of him at her side, of sleeping
wrapped in his arms. Worse, she was becoming too
bewitched by the pleasure she could find there. Alice
hated to think of how much it was going to hurt
when he left her, when their love affair ended as such
things too often did. She just hoped she had the
strength and dignity not to make a fool of herself
when his ardor began to cool and he looked else-
where for his pleasure.

She sat up and looked around her, then grimaced.
They slept surrounded by the dead. She was not one
given to fears about ghosts but she reluctantly admitted to herself that bedding down in a crypt caused
her a shiver or two. It had actually taken Gybbon a
moment or two to kiss and caress away her unease
and turn her full attention to the passion that burned
so hot between them. Now looking at the stone coffins
and effigies carved on the lids made her feel embarrassed. It seemed disrespectful to make love in such a
place. She also prayed that there really were no such
things as ghosts or they would have gotten an eyeful
during the hours she and Gybbon had sheltered
here.

She stood up and dressed. Alice suspected the sun
was still up, still too much of a danger to Gybbon, but
that it was probably safe enough for her to go outside. They needed food. Their supplies were almost
gone and she doubted there would be much chance
to stop anywhere and gain more before they got to

Cambrun. A meal of rabbit or fowl would give them some strength for the rest of their journey.

As she collected her bow and arrow, she pushed aside the small voice that told her to stay where she was. They had seen no sign of the Hunters for three days. It was obvious that the men she had wounded had needed care and she was sure they would have needed at least one of the last two hale men to help them get it. Alice did not think even Callum would hunt her and Gybbon all on his own. She ignored the little whisper of caution in her mind, the one trying to remind her that Callum was not completely sane when it came to her.

Slipping out of the little church the crypt lay beneath, she looked around to be sure no one was near before hurrying into the shelter of the wood. It was yet another sunny day and she was beginning to think some mean spirit was keeping the weather so fine just to make matters more difficult for her and Gybbon. Smiling at such a foolish thought, she set her mind to getting her and Gybbon some meat.

The sun was nearly finished setting by the time Alice had caught a rabbit and prepared it for the spit. Her hunt had been quickly successful but not as quick as she had thought. She cursed herself for becoming too intent upon the hunt and not paying attention to how much time had passed. Gybbon would awaken soon, if he had not already, and he would wonder where she was. She might not be certain of the depth of what he felt for her, but she knew he would worry about her if he found her gone. Wrapping the carcass of the rabbit in a scrap of cloth, she shoved it into her quiver and hurried back toward the church, a little surprised at how far she had gone.

A faint rustle of leaves was her only warning and it came too late for her to save herself. She was just drawing her dagger from its sheath when a body slammed into her back. Alice hit the ground hard, the fall and the heavy weight on her back robbing her of the ability to breathe. She could only flail weakly as her weapons were torn from her and tossed out of her reach.

"Finally, ye demon bitch," rasped a voice that sent chills down her spine. "Finally, I have ye. Where are your wee bastard and that devil ye have taken as your lover?"

Still struggling to regain her breath, Alice replied, "I dinnae ken who ye are talking about."

Callum turned her onto her back, straddling her and pinning her wrists to the ground with his knees. He had obviously learned a thing or two from the last time he had captured her, she thought a little wildly. Alice felt the old fear he had bred in her start to stir, but fought it. She needed to keep her wits about her if she had any chance of surviving this confrontation. A quick glance around revealed that Callum was alone and she cursed herself for not heeding the instinct that had tried to make her stay inside the crypt with Gybbon, the one that had tried to argue her assumption that Callum would not continue the hunt on his own.

He slapped her. "Lying bitch. Ye will tell me where they are."

"So ye can kill them? Nay, Callum. Ye will nay beat or frighten me into giving ye more innocents to slaughter as ye slaughtered my family. Even if I was fool enough to believe ye would let me live, I willnae buy my life with the blood of others."

"Your family were demons! A foul affront to God's eyes."

"They were just trying to live, to raise a family. They ne'er hurt anyone." Alice knew that trying to reason with this man was a waste of words, but it might buy her enough time to think of a way to escape. It might even buy enough time for Gybbon to come looking for her.

"Ye cannae say that about your braw lover, can ye? He has killed four of my men and he drank their blood. We found one of the bodies and ye could see the marks in the neck where he sank those fangs in and sucked out the mon's soul along with his blood. And ye tried to kill the rest of my men."

"Did ye expect me to stand still and let ye kill me? I fight because ye willnae leave me alone. Ye mean to kill me and my bairn. Aye, I fight as would anyone. Wanting to live hardly makes me a demon. Or Gybbon evil. And there is no soul sucking, ye great fool. Someone is telling ye a lot of lies and ye are getting your hands bloodied for naught."

He pressed the blade of his knife against her throat. "Ye are the creations of the devil and he always makes his minions take souls. Ye have to hide in the shadows and ye feed on people like wild beasts do. There is naught ye can say to change that or what it makes ye. Now tell me where he is."

"Nay."

She bit back a cry of pain when he coldly thrust his knife into her shoulder. Breathing deeply to try and push aside the agony as he pulled the knife free, she looked up into his cold eyes. Too many wounds like that and she would never regain enough strength to fight him.

"I ken ye and your ilk have a lot of strength," he said as he tore the shoulder of her gown aside to stare at the wound he had delivered. "And ye heal fast, dinnae ye. But ye still bleed and, with enough wounds, with enough of your blood spilled into the dirt, ye will die. Then what will happen to your wee bastard?"

"He will live, for he is where ye will never reach him."

"Nay, he is close. Ye would ne'er let him leave ye, nay after dragging him about with ye for years. And e'en if ye have tucked him somewhere ye wouldnae leave your braw lover, would ye. Nay, a whore cannae last long without a mon between her thighs. Weel, I willnae weaken this time. I willnae let ye take my seed and corrupt it into the devil's weapon."

"Oh, 'tis all my fault ye are a raping, brutish swine, is it? Is that how ye free yourself of any guilt for what ye did?"

"Ye were bred by the devil to tempt a mon but I am wiser now."

"Ye are certainly madder now," she muttered and she tried to buck him off her, furious at her failure to move him even a little.

"Where is your lover?"

"Here, ye mad bastard."

Callum was yanked off her and seemed to fly through the air. Alice stared up at Gybbon, but he gave her just one furious glare before turning his attention to Callum. The fury in Gybbon was so strong and fierce, Alice was surprised it was not lighting up the woods with its heat. She scrambled up on her knees and, afraid that she would faint if she stood up, crawled backward until she was out of the way of the fight she knew was to come.

It surprised her when Callum got to his feet with no sign that being tossed through the air had injured him. She had to wonder if madness gave him strength. The man drew his sword and faced Gybbon looking as if he actually thought he had a chance to win this fight. Gybbon had also drawn his sword and just stood there, obviously wanting for Callum to make the first move.

"Ye willnae take my soul, demon," Callum said.

"I wouldnae want the foul thing," replied Gybbon.

"Ye and your ilk are doomed, ye ken. We will hunt ye down and slaughter ye until there isnae a one of ye left, mon, woman, or bairn."

"I ken it. 'Tis why I will feel no sorrow over killing ye, e'en if ye are a pitiful fool. Of course, after what ye did to Alice, I do feel a wee bit inclined to make your death as slow and painful as I can."

"She is a whore, a tool of the devil sent to tempt a righteous mon into sin," Callum yelled.

"It isnae wise to anger me, Callum. Ye make that wee inclination I just mentioned become stronger. Now, do ye fight or do ye mean to keep trying to talk me to death? Ah, but wait, mayhap I should offer ye the same chance to survive as ye offered me. Tell me the name of the laird who sent ye after Alice and I will give ye a chance to flee."

Alice noticed that Gybbon did not actually say he would allow Callum to live. The battle began so abruptly that the first clash of the swords startled her. Callum proved he was strong and skilled with a sword, but she could see that Gybbon was even more so. It only took her a moment to see that Gybbon was teasing the man, allowing Callum to think he actually had some chance to win. She supposed she ought to be appalled by that cruelty but Callum had tormented her for too long, had too much blood on his hands, for her to care.

"When ye are dead, I will take your whore to my laird," Callum said. "He will show her how the righteous deal with evil."

The way Gybbon suddenly moved, knocking Callum's sword from his hand and grabbing the man by the throat, told Alice that Callum's taunt had broken the last shred of control Gybbon had. Remembering what Gybbon had told her of all that had been done to his cousins, she was not really surprised. As she rubbed her hand over her healing wound, she watched Gybbon slam Callum up against a tree. The Callum who had raped her and viciously beaten her was gone now. In his place was a white-faced, trembling man who could see his death in Gybbon's eyes.

"Ye are a fool, Callum," Gybbon said softly. "If ye hadnae raped Alice, hadnae sought her death and denied your own child, I might feel some sympathy for ye. Pity, even. Ye have been led to your death by the lies of others, ones too cowardly to come and face us themselves. Ere ye die, I will tell ye one thing about the men ye so blindly follow, tell ye why they keep trying to capture one of us. They think we have the secret to immortality. They dinnae care about demons or sin or God, they just want to live longer."

Gybbon could tell by the look in Callum's eyes that he believed that, suddenly knew at the moment of his death that he had been used. Not wanting the taste of the man in his mouth, Gybbon simply cut his throat and let his body fall to the ground. He knew he would not be haunted by this man's face.

He turned to see Alice getting to her feet and hurriedly cleaned his dagger on Callum's shirt. Sheathing it, he went to stand in front of her. Part of him wanted to pull her close and reassure himself that she was alive while another part wanted to shake her until her teeth rattled for scaring him half to death. His heart had not ceased pounding with fear from the moment he had woken up alone until he had taken Callum off her and seen that she was still alive. The wound Callum had given her was already healed and he felt a little more of the tight fear for her ease.

"Ye never should have come out alone," he said.

"I ken it, but all I could think of was that we needed some food." She grimaced. "I had the brief thought that Callum might come hunting me on his own, but shrugged it aside. Odd thing is, I didnae even hear him until he was already leaping toward my back. Lost in my own thoughts of needing to get back to ye, I suspicion. It certainly wasnae worth the rabbit I caught."

"Nay, but, if it hasnae been ruined during your fight, we might as weel cook and eat it."

It was hard to lecture someone when they so openly admitted to making a mistake, Gybbon thought with a sigh. He put his arm around her and led her back to the church. They would have a meal and then start on their way to Cambrun. The last of the Hunters now lay in the dirt and would not be found until morning. There was a chance they might actually be able to enjoy some of the journey ahead of them.

He had learned one thing from the fright she had given him. He could call what he felt for her lust, possession, need, and whatever other word he could think of, but it did not change the facts. He loved her. Somehow, in the days they had been running from the Hunters, he had given her his heart. The fear he had felt when he had found her gone had been all-consuming. In his mind's eyes, he had seen his future without her and it had been cold and bleak.

It explained why he had marked her as his mate so quickly. Instinct had ruled. Something within him, something beyond his ken, had recognized her as his mate. His heart had tried to tell him that she was more but he, in his manly ignorance, had consistently misnamed that more. Gybbon wanted to tell her what he felt, what she meant to him, but decided he would wait until they reached Cambrun. They might not have Hunters trailing them anymore, but the journey would still not be so easy that he could include wooing the heart of his mate along the way.

Gybbon also, reluctantly, admitted that he was not sure about how she felt. She had not noticed the mating mark on her neck and probably would not know what it was if she did. Her passion was sweet and hot, and considering the abuse she had suffered and the scars she had carried, the fact that she felt such passion for him was no small thing. He just could not accept that as a sign that she loved him. He needed something more before he bared his heart to her; he was just not sure what that more was.

As they cooked and ate the rabbit, he told her about Cambrun and its people. Gybbon wanted her to feel as if she knew the place and the people before they rode through Cambrun's gates. When they reached his home, he would have to speak to her about the future, however. His clan would see the mating mark on her neck and he could not be sure that no one would mention it. Before someone else told Alice that she was mated to him, marked as his for life, he knew he had to say something. He just prayed he could cough up the right words before they reached his home.

# Chapter Nine

Cambrun rose up out of the mists so suddenly that Alice almost gasped. One look was all it took for her to see the strength of the keep. It was huge, dark, and would certainly look threatening to an enemy. Alice suspected it could make grown men shiver with awe and fear when they saw it. She saw it as a haven and nearly wept with the realization that she and the children could finally just live without constantly worrying about where their enemies would appear next or even where their next meal might come from.

" 'Tis so verra big," she whispered.

"Aye," Gybbon agreed and, seeing no fear in her eyes, only a sort of dazed wonder, he smiled. "And nay easy to get to, either."

"Nay. I began to think ye were just leading me to another cave and then suddenly the mists parted, and there it was. Your ancestors chose weel."

"Aye, and the need of this place has ne'er been stronger."

As they neared the gates, he tried to think of how to say she wore his mark on her neck, but the words still would not come. He had wooed her as best he could during the last five days but he found he had no confidence when it came to guessing how she felt about him. Not knowing if he was about to throw his heart at the feet of a woman who only desired him had shown him that he could succumb to cowardice. He would pay for that soon, he thought, as they rode through the gates and his kinsmen rushed to greet him.

The large number of very handsome men at Cambrun astonished Alice. She dismounted and huddled close to Gybbon, a little intimidated by them all, as well as the beautiful women who slowly began to join the welcoming crowd. They smiled and greeted her with warmth but all she could think of was that she could never hold a man like Gybbon when he was accustomed to such beauty.

"Maman!"

That clear, high child's voice was sweet music to Alice's ears. She looked around and saw Donn rushing toward her. When he leapt into her open arms, she nearly cried from the strength of the joy that swept through her. A heartbeat later the other children were by her side, hugging her skirts and all talking at once.

All Alice could see through her tear-clouded eyes was how healthy and clean they looked. They wore warm clothing and looked as if they had never known the lack of a meal. But what touched her heart the most was that they were all smiling, all happy and eager to tell her all they had been doing, even solemn little Alyn.

After that everything moved so swiftly, she was dazed by it all. It was not until she was bathed, dressed in a warm blue gown, and having her hair brushed dry by the laird's wife Bridget that Alice felt she could at least speak sensibly. She looked at the woman who did not look any older than Gybbon even though

Alice knew she had to be as old as her own mother had been, perhaps even older.

"M'lady, I ken from all Gybbon told me that ye dinnae have MacNachton blood. Yet ye dinnae look any older than I." Alice hoped she was not saying the wrong thing but curiosity forced her to press on. "So, 'tis true that MacNachton blood is what makes us strong and gives us a long life? And that can be given to others through our blood?"

"Aye, and 'tis a secret we pray daily no Outsider will discover," said Bridget.

Alice shivered with horror at the thought. "I think I shall join in those prayers. If one could be certain it would be fairly shared and our lives nay put in danger, then 'twould be a gift we could share, but that would ne'er happen, I fear."

"I ne'er looked at it in that way, but aye, it would be wondrous if it could be used to do good, but aye, that would never happen and we would all be in danger if the secret got out. Howbeit, now that ye are here and ye and Gybbon are mated, ye need nay fear for your safety. Weel, nay as much as ye have had to."

"Um, Gybbon and I arenae married, m'lady."

"Weel, mayhap not by the laws of the land or church, but we can sort that out in time. Ye are mated, though. Ye bear his mark and a MacNachton doesnae mark anyone but his mate."

"His mark?"

"Aye. Havenae ye seen it?" Bridget held Alice's hair to the side and touched the mark on her neck. "Look in the looking glass. Right there. See it?"

"Aye, 'tis a bite." She could not completely subdue a blush as she thought of what she and Gybbon had been doing when he had bitten her. Several times. " 'Tis odd that it hasnae healed and faded away as the others did."

"Ah, he hasnae told ye."

"Told me what?"

"Nay, I willnae be the one. Ye had best speak to the great fool and sort this out yourselves." Bridget put the brush down. "In truth, I believe I shall fetch my nephew and send him here to take care of this right now." She paused at the door. "And, Alice, we all thank ye for sending the children to us, for trusting us to care for them."

Before Alice could say anything, the laird's wife was gone. Shrugging her shoulders, she pulled her hair back and stared at the mark on her neck. It should have disappeared. Gybbon had fed off her more than once yet there was only the one mark. It was faint but it was clear to see what it was. Neither was it sore, so she knew it had healed all it was going to.

Mates, Bridget had said. A mating mark. The thought of that sent a heated shiver through her body as she wanted it to be true, wanted to be marked and claimed by Gybbon. Yet, if he had done that, why had he not told her?

The answers that cropped up in Alice's mind robbed her of all pleasure she felt. It had been a mistake. Gybbon had not meant to do it. Or he had done it but did not want it to be true.

Gybbon rushed into the room and then came to a quick halt. Alice was staring at the mark on her neck. The look she turned on him was not one of joyous welcome and he sighed. Shutting the door behind him, he cautiously approached her. His aunt had seared his ears with her scolding and he deserved it. He should have swallowed his foolish cowardice and just told Alice, offered her all he had to offer and hoped he did not get his heart stomped on.

"She called this a mating mark," Alice said, not encouraged by the guilty look on his face. "She thinks we are mated."

"We are. That marks ye as mine."

"If ye marked me, why didnae ye tell me? Or ask me if I e'en wanted to be yours?"

Alice wanted to be his more than she had ever wanted anything in her life. She would not let that lead her into a marriage, or mating, that did not have any more to hold it together than lust and possession. She wanted what her parents had. They had loved each other. She loved Gybbon and wanted him to love her back. Until she was sure he did, she was not going to be claimed no matter how many marks he put on her.

"I was surprised when I realized I had done it, done it the verra first time we made love." He knelt before her and took her hands in his. "I then thought, weel, there it is, 'tis fate and we will sort it all out when we arenae busy fighting for our lives."

"Yet ye still didnae tell me and ye have had days where we werenae fighting for our lives."

"I ken it but I found that I can be a coward."

"If ye dinnae want to tell me the truth, then dinnae, but dinnae say such nonsense."

He could not help it, he grinned. "I thank ye for being so certain of my courage that ye think I could never cower from anything. Ah, but I can, my sweet Alice. I called what we shared everything but what it should have been called. Passion." He brushed his lips across hers, taking strength in the fact that she did not pull away. "Possession." He kissed the mark on her neck.

Alice did not know whether to be disgusted with herself or afraid when those two little kisses and the warm look in his beautiful green eyes was enough to make her desire him naked and in her arms. "What should it be called, then?"

"Love."

Gybbon was not sure what he should think when she gaped at him. Just as he began to feel uneasy and was going to demand she say something, a tear rolled down her cheek. His stomach clenched with alarm.

"Alice?" He brushed the tear away with his thumb only to have another follow it. "Why do ye cry? Is it so appalling to ken that I love ye?" He grunted when she hurled herself into his arms so forcefully he fell backward onto the floor, still clutching her in his arms.

"I so hoped ye might come to love me," she said, her words muffled because she had her face pressed into his chest. "I love ye so much that I was willing to accept less if I could just stay with ye, but to ken ye love me, too, is nearly too much."

"Ye never said ye loved me."

Gybbon was shaking with the relief he felt. She returned his love; she was his mate in every way. He knew of only one way to celebrate such a miracle and began to undo her gown.

"Of course I didnae. I didnae want to make ye stay with me out of pity, or even worse."

"What could be worse?" He tossed her gown aside and started to unlace her shift.

"That ye would be so burdened and embarrassed that ye would send me away."

He picked her up and carried her to the bed. As he started to shed his clothes he looked at her sprawled out on the heavy coverlet, her shift unlaced and falling open, and felt everything that was male in him roar its need for her. The moment the last of his clothes were tossed aside he hurriedly pulled the rest of hers off.

"Gybbon?"

"I think I have loved ye from the beginning. 'Tis why I marked ye." He sprawled in her arms and began to kiss a circle around her breasts. "I accepted it but didnae think much on it except to be pleased that fate chose a woman who could make my blood burn. Then"—he teased her nipples into hard points with his tongue—"when I was held captive I realized it was more, more than passion and possession." He began to kiss his way down her smooth midriff. "When ye were attacked by Callum, when I woke up to find ye gone, that was when I accepted that the more was love. And now that I have had the woman I love tell me that she loves me, too, there is only one thing I want to do almost more than breathing."

Alice was trembling with the need to have him inside her but she said, "Weel, your aunt said there will be a fine meal set out within the hour."

Her words ended on a gasp of shock as he kissed her. Right there between her legs. She was so stunned by the intimacy that she could not move. By the time her mind cleared of shock enough for her to speak, passion had roared in to clear every coherent thought from her mind. Alice threaded her hands through his hair and gave herself over to the pleasure he gave her until she could not bear it any longer.

"Gybbon," she cried out, tugging on his hair until he began to kiss his way back up to her breasts. "I need ye to be one with me."

"Aye, lass, always."

She cried out again when he thrust himself deep inside her. Ecstasy swept over her as his fangs sank into her neck. When he placed his wrist against her mouth, she did not hesitate, but cupped his hand in hers and stroked it as she gently fed from him. The moment the spicy taste of him hit her tongue, all clear thought fled her mind and she sank into the fierce passion only he could make her feel.

Feeling as limp as if he had been in the sun too long, Gybbon rolled off Alice and pulled her into his arms. She was as limp as he felt and he found the strength to grin with male pride. She was his, mind, heart, and soul. He had no words for how complete, how blessed that made him feel, but somehow he would do his best, for the rest of their long lives, to make her know just how necessary she was to him.

"We will be married as soon as my mother and aunt can arrange it," he said when he finally had the strength to speak.

"Can ye get a priest up here?" she asked, idly wondering if she would have the strength to get dressed in time to go have something to eat.

"Aye, one of our kinsmen. He can abide a fair lot of time in the sun and took a place within the church." He kissed the top of her head. "I hope we have just made a bairn."

"Weel, even though we already have four, so do I."

"Ah, my mother found Alyn's kinsmen. I fear his father was killed even as he was traveling back to Alyn's mother. The boy does have several aunts and uncles, however, as weel as a grandmother. My mother says they are all madly in love with the lad even now. She is working to see if she can find who ye and the others may be related to."

Alice raised herself up on her forearms and kissed him. "I dinnae ken how I can be so blessed. I also dinnae ken how I can be thinking of food right now, but I am."

Gybbon laughed and helped her sit up. They dressed, each fighting the urge to toss aside the clothes and return to bed. Their stomachs won that battle and Gybbon was soon leading her into the great hall.

\* \* \*

Her belly full, Alice sipped her wine and looked around at all the MacNachtons. Alyn sat with his newfound family and she could see how their delight in him was easing all that anger and bitterness he had held for most of his young life. Even though Jayne and Norma did not yet know who amongst the crowd of dark, handsome people they might be related to, they were being so showered with love and attention she doubted it would matter if they ever found out. The fact that they were females who would grow up to be the mates of some MacNachton male undoubtedly added to their worth, but Alice could see that the joy the clan felt in all the children had no ties to it. Even Donn, already seen as Gybbon's son since he was mated to the child's mother, was being cosseted and feted. Alice knew she was going to have to do her best to make sure the children were not spoiled.

She knew she was basking a little in the acceptance of the clan. The shyness and uneasiness she had felt as Gybbon had presented her to his clan had fled quickly. It was hard to keep tears of joy at bay as she realized that she and the children had come home. Grief pinched her for a moment as she wished her family could have known this joy, but she shook it aside. She knew they would be happy for her and the children and that had to be enough.

The laird stood up and everyone went silent. Gybbon took her hand in his and flashed a smile at her. Alice stared at Gybbon's uncle, thought of how he would also remain so handsome for years and years and almost grinned back at him, but the laird began to speak.

"We are blessed tonight," he said, and paused to smile at Alice and each of the children. "We have brought five of the Lost Ones home. The number of fledglings returned to the nest will surely grow. And, since my nephew has had the good sense to mate himself with this fine brave lass who kept these children safe until they could come home, we will soon be celebrating a wedding as weel."

Everyone cheered as Alice blushed so hotly she was amazed her cheeks did not catch on fire. Gybbon laughed and kissed her cheek but it did little to ease the heat there. It was several minutes after everyone had returned to their talk and their food, or tankards of enriched wine, before Alice calmed down.

"All right now, love?" Gybbon asked, a teasing note in his voice.

"I was just a wee bit unsettled by how everyone was cheering," she murmured.

"Ye are a heroine to them, love. Aye," he said when she shook her head. "As my uncle says, ye kept those children alive. That is no small thing. And everyone is overjoyed to have so many Lost Ones brought home."

"And I am home now, arenae I."

"Aye, love, ye are. That is what is being celebrated and 'tis a worthy thing to celebrate. Of course," he murmured close to her ear, "I am eager to return to our bed so that I may celebrate in a manner more to my liking."

"Ah." She felt the desire he could so effortlessly stir in her begin to rise. "I thought ye had celebrated it quite thoroughly already."

"Och, nay. Having ye as mine can ne'er be celebrated enough."

He sounded so cocky, and looked it, that Alice had to smile. She also felt a strong inclination to wipe that arrogant smirk off his handsome face. "Gybbon," she whispered in his ear, "ye do recall that, er, kiss ye gave me a wee while ago, aye?"

"Oh, aye, and I recall how sweet ye tasted as weel."

"Tell me, oh great lover of mine, do ye think I would find ye as sweet to taste?"

He choked on his wine. Alice was still laughing about that when he grabbed her by the hand and dragged her out of the hall. She doubted the joy that filled her would fade anytime soon. She had spent six years in hell, running, hiding, and fighting to stay alive, but now she was home, home with a man who loved her and a people who accepted her because she was truly one of them. Alice realized that she had been lost and she thanked God that the man who was dragging her to their bedchamber as fast as he could was the one to find her.

# THE
# VAMPIRE
# HUNTER

Heather Grothaus

*For my family*

# Chapter One

*October 1, 1104*
*The Leamhan Forest of the Scottish Highlands*

"Like that, do you?" Beatrix whispered into the stranger's ear as he moaned and bucked against her body. She had pinned him against the rear wall behind the White Wolf Inn—foolishly close to the patrons reveling just steps inside the kitchen door, perhaps—but the added danger was exhilarating. And although his stealthy appearance had interrupted her countless nightly chores as the inn's sole proprietor, she could not pass up the opportunity he offered.

She thrust against him again and her blood rushed in her veins like liquid moonlight when he gave a choked cry.

"That's right—take it," Beatrix gasped. "Take it, you bastard."

She felt sudden wetness soaking through her long apron and into the front of her gown and knew a moment's rue at the telltale stain that would be left behind. But concerns for the condition of her gown whirled away as she felt the cold heat of the stranger's lips skitter desperately along the side of her neck.

"Doona . . . *dare*," Beatrix growled and, throwing herself upon him with all her strength, finished him.

He fell against her fully and Beatrix stepped away from the wall, letting the man's body tumble into the muddy dooryard behind the inn, near the now-splintered slop bucket she had come outside to empty. She stood over him, gasping.

A bright bar of moonlight divided by the roof peak above fell across his unnaturally pale and frozen face, setting free a single starburst from a pointed fang only just glimpsed through slack, gray lips as his head came to its final rest in the wet filth. The startling strip of light showed a slice of his torn and dirtied clothes, his ashen and decimated skin, his cratered chest ornamented with—

"Ah, dammit," Beatrix muttered, realizing her loss. She stepped to the corpse and, placing one foot on his rapidly sinking chest, grasped the springy fan of her short wooden fork with both hands and yanked it free. A hissing sound chased the fork's release. She staggered backward and looked at her ruined utensil— the black blood was already soaked into the wood.

"Third one this week," she lamented and then pitched the fork in the direction of the refuse heap.

Her eyes found the body once more, now sizzling away into shimmery dust, the high-pitched squeal of a soulless void being squicked away from the earth causing Beatrix to wince. Before the corpse could vanish completely, she spat on him.

Beatrix Levenach took her time scanning the black wall of trees just beyond the inn's back door. She could detect no movement in the thick dark—at least, not of any creature not properly alive—nor was there a return of the ominous prickle that warned her of impending attack. Save for the highland wind on its whistling journey through the elms, carrying a cumbersome winter on its back, the wood was still.

For now.

The night seemed colder after her kill, but perspiration trickled between her shoulder blades and breasts as she fumbled with the strings of her apron and whisked it over her head. Beatrix wadded it into a ball and tossed it to the same fate as her muck fork, and then turned into the moonlight so as to appraise the damage to her gown while walking to the rain barrel at the corner of the inn.

*Nae so bad*, she thought. A streak of black here, a splotch there. She could disguise the freshness of the stains tonight with a good dollop of her rich, dark stew—Eternal Mother knew she ended each night wearing enough of the stuff, any matter—but her skirt would forever bear the marks of tonight's kill. She reached the barrel and plunged her arms into her turned-up sleeves, scrubbing doggedly at the cold, sticky black blood.

"Frocking vampires," she muttered as her skin burned from both the icy water and the thought of the muck that contaminated her. She sniffed. It happened every time—this delayed release of . . . not fear, exactly. When faced with the undead she never flinched, never hesitated—she let her hatred for the unnatural beings and her sense of honor lead her into battle with a fearless vengeance. Only when the kill was made and the threat no more did the uncharacteristic tears creep in, the trembling seize her.

Beatrix gripped the rim of the barrel with both dripping hands, her reddened arms stiff, her head hanging down for a moment. Then she turned up her eyes to the ripe, white moon and took a deep breath.

*You are Levenach,* she heard her father say once more, only now that he was dead, the words came from her memory instead of his smiling mouth. *Protector. Guardian of the Leamhnaigh, of the forest . . . of all the highlands.*

A splintering crash sounded through the open rear door of the inn, but Beatrix did not flinch. Yet another one of her clay pitchers meeting its empty end against the hearth stones. Likely a retaliatory act by one of the innocent Leamhnaigh—her shoulders hitched in a soundless chuckle—she was sworn to protect, in a pique at not receiving more ale straightaway.

Beatrix straightened from the barrel and swiped at her eyes so that she could look upon the moon clearly one last time before returning to the common room and the score or so of forest folk impatient to be tended to. The people who whispered about her, who drank her ale and ate her stew while watching her with suspicious eyes. Who grudgingly paid their dues to her in meager rations of supplies—adhering to the centuries-old tradition of supporting the Levenach even as they muttered about her black and wicked ways.

*Beatrix the witch.*

*Bring us all to ruin and damnation.*

Nae, she didn't want to go back into the White Wolf Inn, but she would.

Because she *was* Levenach. And she was the last.

After dropping the bar on the door following the departure of the last, straggling patrons, Beatrix felt as though she could slide to the floor and fall asleep that instant. But she only allowed herself to rest her forehead against the splintery wood and sigh. Her muscles ached miserably with fatigue and her eyelids felt lined with sand. Tomorrow was the Christian Sabbath, and then she could rest all the day.

But she could not escape into sleep just yet. Although she boarded no travelers, and she had already destroyed one vampire this evening—ensuring that the rest of the demonic pack would likely keep their distance from the inn and townsfolk for mayhap a day or two—her mundane duties were not complete. After another deep breath, she pushed away from the door and turned to face the common room, surveying the damage.

The tables were shoved out of rank, sticky-wet with the leavings of drink and food; mugs and wooden bowls lay strewn over tables and floor like giant, mis-shapen acorns shaken loose from a tree in a gale. Overturned stools tangled legs obscenely with each other. She'd not bothered to sweep up the shards of broken pitcher earlier—not wishing to expose her upturned backside to a roomful of drunken folk— and so the pieces still waited patiently for her on the hearth stones in the weary glow of the fading coals. The air was already stale with fermented grain and smoke, and for the thousandth time, Beatrix wished she could do the washing up with the door and windows thrown wide to the cold night air. But then, she might as well hang a shingle over her lintel: LONE WITCH IN RESIDENCE—VAMPIRES ENTER HERE.

She lit several fat candles and then set about her chores with grim purpose, wishing them done, wishing she had someone to talk with and pass the dirty hour, wishing she was her great-grandmother, who, Beatrix had been told, could charm the furniture to dance and the old shake broom to herd the dirt with only a glance of her sharp green eyes.

The room set to rights at last, Beatrix straightened

from her bucket with a groan and tossed her rag into the scummy gray water. The broom, which had not so much as twitched on its own during her efforts even though she had glared heavily at it several times, leaned against a table and ignored her. A sweaty string of red hair fell into her eyes and she blew it upward. Her feet dragged as she crossed to the hearth to bank the coals and then circuited the room, blowing out each candle in turn, save the last, which she took in hand and carried with her through the door to the inn's kitchen.

There was little to do in this back room—Beatrix set the iron pot containing the congealed remains of stew on the floor with a heavy clunk and scrape and then tipped it onto its side. A white and then a black shape swirled out of the shadows draping the wall shelves and leapt silently to the floor at the telltale sounds of the meal being served, and the two cats attended their supper with their usual aloofness.

The work bench wiped clean and the mugs and bowls left soaking, Beatrix picked up the fat yellow candle once more and walked to the small, woven mat covering a far corner of the kitchen floor. She bent and pulled the stiff rug aside with a huff and then grasped the metal pull ring set in the heavy wooden trapdoor and pulled it wide.

A cool, minerally smelling breeze sighed through the quiet black square, and Beatrix took a deep breath. She thought of her stained and dirtied gown for a moment, but then let the worry go. It was nearing dawn already, and she could take no time to make herself more presentable. She smoothed her hair back behind her ears, wiped her cheeks and forehead high on her sleeve.

The steps were old, steep and narrow, but did not spring or creak under her feet as she made her careful way into the cellar, the candle glow acting like a queer, reverse sunrise on the stone walls, dropping flickering light like a curtain. The very roots of her hair tingled as she landed on the cellar floor.

*"Teine,"* she called into the cold, quiet room.

Tall, standing iron candelabras immediately emerged from the darkness of each of the four corners of the cellar as their seven candles sparked to life.

Beatrix set her own, crude light on the bottom riser and walked to the center of the room, where a massive, polished black slab comprised the largest portion of the floor, resting like a gem on a setting of dull gray. The points of light from the candelabras glinted off the hard surface like a mirror, and in an instant, so did Beatrix's own image. She let her mind clear, becoming lost in the glossy black for a moment, before raising her arms away from her sides.

*"Fosgail."*

As the command left her lips, a hairline crack appeared in the heretofore solid rock at her feet, and the slab began to slide apart in two halves with barely a whisper. In the widening seam was a black unlike any polished jet stone, darker than the depths of the deepest loch, colder than winter's thick ice at midnight.

Beatrix reveled in the moment, as she had ever since she'd first been allowed to visit the hidden, magical Levenach well as a young child. Here she could at last believe she was what legend reported: a witch of the mighty and ancient Levenach clan. A woman with powerful blood in her veins, strong magic in her heart. A warrior against evil, a protector of the highlands and of the innocent peoples who dwelt in the sheltering arms of the wood. Here, she could ofttimes see the people who had shared her blood, her home, and who had now been called on to the Beyond.

Here were her only friends, her only strengths, her only comfort—that of the dead, and their cryptic promises.

Beatrix's gaze was soft, and now in the wavering black water colors began to swirl into brightness. A man with white hair and short, neat beard.

"Hello, Honey Bea."

"Hello, Da," Beatrix whispered. "I'm missing you."

"And I am for certain missing you, lass," her father assured her.

" 'Twas a wearisome night, this one," Beatrix offered.

Her father only nodded. "But still he comes."

Beatrix shook her head. She didn't want to talk about that tonight—she wanted only a conversation with her father. Someone to comfort her. "I canna do this any longer, Da. I'm so tired."

"You *can* do this. You *must*. He comes, and he will save the Leamhnaigh."

"I doona want him to come, and I doona care about the Leamhnaigh," Beatrix insisted in a shaky voice. "I'm lonesome for company that doesna think me the devil."

The smile was gone from her father's face now, and his tone was grave. "It was sworn, Beatrix."

Even though her voice was still quiet, little more than a whisper, her tone matched the desperate tears now rolling down her cheeks. " 'Tis nae fair, Da! I'm all alone and the folk have turned from me since you've gone on. They grow more convinced each day that 'tis *I* committing the slaughter."

"But still he comes, and you will wait," her father insisted. "You are—"

"Levenach. I ken," Beatrix sniffed. "But what good Levenach am I? I command naught beyond some simple candles and a goodly sized rock! I canna so much as charm water to boil!"

"You are a strong witch, Beatrix, but aye, 'tis true that your powers grow less obvious—"

*"Less obvious?"*

"But 'tis only for your protection. With no other Levenach to stand with you, your power would make you a target. It is how it has been for one hundred years. As our family has diminished in numbers, some of our powers became hidden. They will return when the most evil hour is at hand, and when you are matched with a strength equal to your own."

"Of what use is a witch with nae power?" Beatrix said, her voice growing petulant now. " 'Tis like a man with nae pecker."

"Beatrix!" Her father roared with laughter.

"Well?" Beatrix challenged. " 'Tis what I am— Beatrix Levenach, the eunuch witch."

"You have all the powers you need for now," her father said, still chuckling. "You can come to the well to scry, and the most important thing—you can hunt and kill vampires better than any Levenach that has ever been told in our history. You will be the resurrection of our clan."

"The folk will likely see me hanged for a witch. Ironic, as 'tis what I am and yet I canna *do* anything!"

"Are you still holding to your tale of betrothal?"

"Aye, but 'tis wearing thin. They keep asking of my intended, and I keep forgetting what it is I've already told them."

"It will be over and done with soon enough," her father promised. "He comes—*look*. Godspeed, Honey Bea."

"Da, nay," Bea pleaded as her father's image began to ripple apart in the water. She didn't want him to go, to have his comfort replaced by the tired old image of the white beast roaming through field and forest. She'd seen it countless times and still it meant naught to her.

But even as she lamented it, a blur of white began to coalesce on the rippling black, and Beatrix knew it would be the four-legged creature for which the Levenach inn had been named—the white wolf. Perhaps drinking at a stream, perhaps lounging in some woodland glade or loping down a narrow path, but the same cryptic symbol that had long ago lost any significance or interest for Beatrix the Downtrodden, Beatrix the Alone, Beatrix the Eunuch Witch.

She stared down into the fluttering image as it cleared and stilled. Beatrix's frown deepened.

It was indeed the white wolf.

But this time, the animal was sitting on a chair at a table, in a common room not unlike the one above her head, and he was holding a mug of ale in one paw.

# Chapter Two

*October 1, 1104*
*Edinburgh*

"So you've come to learn of the bloodsuckers, have you?"

Alder picked up his mug of ale carefully, deliberately, as he regarded the fat, dirtied man sitting across from him. He nodded slightly in answer and then took a sip, his eyes never leaving the sleazy excuse for a mortal.

The man chuckled, his rounded belly shuddering under his frayed and filthy tunic. The shirt had likely been quite fine at one time, and Alder wondered briefly what had happened to the nobleman from whom it had been stolen. The whoremonger leaned over his ponderous abdomen toward Alder, as if readying to impart a great secret, and the rush of movement caused a stirring of the man's foul odor—strong spirits and cologne and weeks-old perspiration mixed with other bodily secretions.

"Well, you've come to the right man." The whoremonger winked and then settled back in his groaning chair to finger one of the long gold chains around his neck. "What are you called, my fellow Englishman?"

Alder hesitated only briefly. It mattered not that the louse knew his given name—no one alive today would recognize it.

"Alder the White," he said, realizing a faint stab of melancholy. That moniker had once held such power. Did that man still exist?

"Alder de White, eh? A fittin' name, I'd reckon!" The man roared laughter at his own attempt at wit and his eyes flicked over Alder's features, obviously scrutinizing his white-blond hair and pale skin.

Alder let his lips curl slightly, to keep the man at ease and talking.

"Well, Alder de White, I will be most glad to share the secrets of the bloodthirsty killers, right after I quench me own thirst." His head swiveled and he bellowed at a passing woman. "Whore! Drink!"

A young woman, clothed only in an underdress that was much too small for her, bore a tray to the table Alder shared with her disgusting master. Alder could clearly see that she was naked under the worn linen. Her nipples, flattened against the straining material, and the dark V of pubic hair advertised her occupation more than the shortened hem that revealed most of her calves above short leather boots. Her black hair piled in knots atop her crown nearly matched the color of the shadows under her hard eyes and the fading bruises on her arms and one cheek.

She leaned low over the table as she filled the whoremonger's mug, giving Alder a deliberate view of her breasts. Alder's keen sight easily caught the ghostly impressions of fingertip-sized bruises on the white globes of skin.

"You fancy her?" the whoremonger simpered. "She's

me own bit at the moment, but for the right count of coin I'd share her with a good friend for the eve." The man winked again. "She'll suck, too."

As if on cue, the woman turned fully toward Alder and, with no change in her expression, pulled down the bodice of her underdress, popping her breasts free as if for Alder's approval.

"Perhaps," Alder said, looking only into the woman's eyes. She met his gaze for a moment before frowning slightly, as if being stirred from a deep sleep.

*Put away your tray. Clothe yourself. Gather your belongings and leave this place, woman, else you die here tonight.*

She hurriedly hid her breasts in her gown, her eyes widening and turning fearful with confusion. Alder faced the whoremonger. "After our talk."

"Of course," the man chuckled and waved the woman away with a bored hand, not knowing he would never see his pet again. "I think *she* fancies *you*."

"They all fancy me," Alder said without a trace of pride—that quality had been killed in him long ago, strangled by the deep scar around his neck, hidden by his tunic. It was simply true that most found Alder irresistibly attractive. Whether whore or noblewoman, peasant or soldier, both men and women, meek and depraved, were drawn to Alder the White. They all shared in common a hunger, a deep, aching want— be it for wealth or beauty or love, or even the solace of eternal darkness. Perhaps they did not sense any one particular prize in Alder, but only his great power, sinister and primitive. And they yearned for that unknown power. Yearned to be closer to him, to touch him, and have that touch returned.

They did not know until it was too late that Alder's touch meant their destruction.

"And why not fancy you, I ask!" the whoremonger

chuckled. "A comely bloke such as yourself, obviously in no want for coin." His smile turned even slimier. "I'd wager you've got a big cock, too, ain't ye?"

Alder shrugged. "The vampires?"

The whoremonger's eyes turned smug and knowing. "I've heard tales of men like yerself—wantin' a spot of adventure, rushin' into the forest to see 'em with yer very own eyes. 'Tis dangerous business, me friend. Most never return."

"I've no fear," Alder said, and that was also true. "Tell your tale." He was growing impatient, and the ripe, dripping moon beyond the inn's roof was moaning to him in throbbing whispers. His blood ached.

"The highlands once crawled with the beasts," the man said. "They roamed the thick forests, attacking the towns and travelers in packs. Held in check only by an ancient family of witches, who some say were as evil, if not more so, than the bloodsuckers themselves."

A shiver overtook Alder, and a roaring of memories like the sea in a tempest begged to be set free. "Witches, you say?" Alder was pleased that the tone of his voice conveyed only mild interest.

"Aye. Witches. The Levenachs. As red haired as the Devil hisself. They were the only ones who could slay the beasts, and they feasted on the rotting corpses to feed their power."

Alder knew that last bit to be untrue, but he did not bother to correct the man, as his hope was growing. "You said the land once crawled with the vampires—are they no more? Destroyed by the Levenachs?"

"Nearly so, nearly so . . . but not quite." The man gave another of his disgusting winks. "A hundred years ago, 'tis said the vampires and the Levenachs came to a great battle, led by a mortal man. Both sides were nearly wiped out when the Wild Hunt came down upon them and swept many of their numbers away to hell."

This too was a falsehood. The Hunt had indeed come to the battle, but Alder had been the band's archangel leader's only prisoner. 'Twould have been more merciful had he been swept away to hell, for even though he had escaped his captivity, still Alder smelled the sulphured smoke from the winged horse's hooves, felt the snap of the golden lead around his own neck. Even while he spent his nights running from the vengeful pack who would not rest until they had reclaimed their slave once more, Alder was chased also by the screams of the damned echoing in his ears, and craved still their evil, tainted blood. . . .

The whoremonger continued. "But the king of the bloodsuckers as well as a handful of witches managed to escape, leaving the corpses of their brethren about as a warning to all who would disobey the laws of Christendom." The whoremonger had the audacity to cross himself reverently. "The land lay in relative peace for a time. But now . . ."

"Now?" Alder urged.

"The vampires roam again, a new generation spawned by the solitary demon that thwarted hell's band one hundred years ago."

*Laszlo,* Alder thought, the name echoing in his mind as if in a cave, and Alder's blood bubbled, itched, threatened to burst from his cool veins and through his skin. *Laszlo has crowned himself king.*

"What of the Levenachs?" Alder insisted, for it was on this family his very soul depended.

The man blew obscenely through his lips and fluttered his fingers. "All but gone. 'Tis why I try to kindly warn you—one true Englishman to another—to stay away. There is no more safeguard to the bloodthirsty killers for mortal men who venture through the enchanted wood seeking adventure. The Levenach would just as soon kill you for sport. No one goes near the cursed wood lest they have a wish to die a horrible death."

Alder had to force the words from his throat. "You said the Levenachs were *all but gone*—there are still some?"

*"Levenach. One,"* the whoremonger said, lifting his mug as if in a toast. He drained the vessel and then set it back on the table with a loud thump and even louder belch. "A witch-woman. The most beautiful and deadly sorceress in all of the highlands."

"And she is the last?" Alder pressed.

"Aye. The last. And good riddance to her when she is gone, I say."

"Indeed," Alder agreed, pleased that his voice still emerged smooth and even from his constricted throat. "Where would a man wishing to die a horrible death find this last Levenach?"

The whoremonger raised his eyebrows, seemed to consider Alder for a long moment, and then leaned forward once more. The table shrugged and creaked.

"There is a road," he said in a conspiratorial tone. "West from Edinburgh toward the coast and Loch Lomond. Just past the loch, a forest seems to grow up from nowhere. A dark, narrow path joins the road in a clearing of black trees, their branches stripped from the trunks."

*They were burned,* Alder remembered to himself. The archangel Michael's fiery warning still remained.

*"That* path leads into the Leamhan forest, and to the White Wolf Inn, where the Levenach lies in wait for her victims."

Alder started and his ears rang with the ominous words. "The White Wolf Inn?"

"Aye. 'Tis a ruse concocted by the Levenach to lure in the innocent and lost traveler, though I hear trade is quite slow of late." The whoremonger roared with laughter.

Alder did not bother to feign amusement. "You're certain of where this inn lies? Quite certain?"

"My friend, I have me very hand on the pulse of Edinburgh—indeed, of all of Scotland! Many a tale is told in my rooms and on me own pillow, no less. If you're wishin' for a bloody adventure, take the dark path into the Leamhan. But I warn you, you'll not likely come out the other side the same condition as you went in."

"That is very much my plan," Alder murmured.

The whoremonger frowned. "What say ye?"

"Naught." Alder leaned back in his chair and smiled at the whoremonger, a bit more relaxed now even though his hunger gnawed at him more impatiently than when the obscene man had begun his tale. Alder sipped from his all but forgotten mug. It was so very pleasant to be able to drink mortal refreshments once more, even if they did not satisfy him completely. His senses were so keen he could taste the faint tang of the brewer's sweat in his fine, sweet drink.

Alder noticed that the inn where he and the detestable human had passed the evening was now all but deserted at the late hour, and the patrons had left for their own pallets or to the upper floors with their evening's entertainment of the flesh. Alder could smell the depraved beings in the rooms above his head like so many roasted chickens tied up in sacks—only waiting to be brought out and consumed by the famished.

And Alder was starving.

But before the feast proper, a well-deserved prelude . . .

The whoremonger seemed to notice he and Alder were alone at that moment, although foolishly, it seemed to please the man rather than frighten him. He looked casually over each shoulder, then pinned Alder with a greasy smile.

"It seems we are without company, my strange and inquisitive friend. Shall I call a whore for you to take or have your desires been satisfied by me own grand presence?"

"I do find myself rather loath to be alone this eve," Alder said, returning the man's smile.

"Ah, so I reckoned," the whoremonger chuckled and made to move his watery mass from his chair. "For you, and only you, I shall summon that fine knot of arse and send her to—"

Alder cut off the man's words by reaching out and grasping his forearm. The moon's own howl rang in his ears until he was nearly deaf with it.

"What would you answer should I request *your* company . . . friend?" Alder all but whispered.

The whoremonger paused and then a sick smile slid across his face as Alder stood and moved to stand just over him.

"Well, now, I would say that I don't usually turn that way, but for a wealthy and comely friend like yourself . . ." He let the sentence trail away and licked at his thick lips as his eyes crawled up Alder's body. "I am more than a mite curious at what lies beneath those fine, tight breeches."

Alder easily pulled the man's bulk from the chair and locked his arms tightly around the mortal's shoulders. The whoremonger gave an almost feminine sigh of desire, and Alder knew his base presence was affecting the lowlife. The more evil and depraved the mortal, the easier prey they made. Like all the others, the whoremonger had a hunger.

So did Alder. And he could not resist speaking once more to the man.

"Do you wish to know," he whispered into the greasy hair behind the man's ear, "why it is I seek the Levenach, whoremonger?"

"Aye," the man moaned, his need making him limp and dazed in Alder's embrace. "Tell me."

"The mortal man who sparked the battle between the vampires and the witches—'twas I."

The whoremonger stiffened slightly and struggled to shake his head, his warning instinct of impending doom coming much too late to save him. "Nay—that battle was one hundred years ago," he whispered.

"Indeed," Alder agreed, and let his lips peel back from his fangs, at last stretching his mouth luxuriously. "And I am no longer mortal."

# Chapter Three

Beatrix felt resigned two nights later as she prepared to open the White Wolf for trade. She had spent the Sabbath in rest and reflection—between batches of ale in varying stages of brewing—and had decided to trust her father's word.

She was Levenach. And she would wait.

The Leamhan around the inn had been peaceful and still since her last vampire kill, so although she would be forced to hunt tonight to preempt any attacks on the forest folk, she was heartened by the serenity she now felt. Especially since last eve, when the ancient Levenach well had once more reverted to showing her only images of the inn's namesake running on swift feet over some unknown land, and no longer behaving like a human.

Bea skipped down the stairs and into the common room with purpose, replacing dried warding herbs over the door and window frames with fresh, potent bunches, and shooing the cats into the kitchen.

"Go on—you know how they like to make targets of the pair of you when they get into their cups." But it was said with a wry smile.

The Leamhnaigh could not be blamed for their behavior. They *were* innocent, and must remain so for very good reasons. Should they learn the truth about the creatures stalking them, should they even think to take the old legends as truth, their realities would shift, change, and then Beatrix Levenach as well as witches throughout the highlands would have more to fear than the bloodsuckers.

It was up to Beatrix alone to end the vampires' reign, once and for all. She didn't know how that was to be accomplished, but she would do as her father—and the very blood in her veins—requested, and wait for the white wolf to arrive.

She let the smile linger over her face as she gave the stew a final stir and then reentered the common room to unbar the door. Dusk was falling through the fog, and the folk would be thirsty. Beatrix was thankful her inn and her presence would provide them a safe haven in which to pass the most dangerous hours of the night. It made her solitude feel a twitch more bearable.

She was only halfway across the floor when she heard the shouts from beyond the door.


Alder paced behind the fringe of trees along the woodland path, his long-sought destination directly before him, but the sunlight of late evening still too strong for him to take his human shape.

Yea, surely this was the place of the Levenach, for trouble was already afoot, and it was brought not only by his own—currently four—feet.

The faded timber and mud exterior of the humble-looking cottage was awash with the yellow glow of a score of torches, borne by a few more than that number of humans. Those which did not carry the sources of light wielded axes or thick staffs, and a pair of folk bore a long, cloth-wrapped bundle.

"Beatrix Levenach!" a man closest to the cottage shouted. "We summon thee, witch! Come and look upon what your wickedness has wrought and take your punishment, lest we set fire to your lair while you cower inside!"

The crowd roared in agreement and then seemed to wait for the door to open. When it did not, the appointed spokesman for the group continued his haranguing.

"*Levenach!* We have had enough! Your sorcery on our people has come to its end and we are here to finish your evil bloodline!"

Behind his thin fringe of trees, Alder paced, and flicked his black eyes to the pinnacle of the tree line and the orange glow of sunset that lingered there.

*Don't come out,* Alder said in his mind. If she came out, the people were certain to kill her. A dead Levenach was of no use to Alder. Indeed, the *last* Levenach, dead by mortals, would mean Alder's destruction.

*He* was the one who must spill her blood. He and no one else.

*Don't come out,* he repeated.

The door to the inn opened, and Alder froze in his pacing as his savior, his nemesis, his destiny, stepped into the dangerous crowd of folk.

"What is the meaning of this?" the witch demanded, and Alder felt his pupils dilate as they took in the whole of the last living Levenach, his senses screaming out from the very power of her, even at the distance he kept in the sheltering tree line. His breaths shortened to stuttering pants, the hair on his back bristled.

The damnable sunlight, weak and ruddy though it was, threw back sparks from her fiery hair and the whoremonger's words whispered in Alder's ear: *as red as the Devil hisself.* She was as tall as half the menfolk gathered around her, and her arms, cocked on her hips defiantly, appeared long and slim in their rough garments. With each swish of her plain skirt, Alder thought he could see silvery washes of tracing light.

And he knew a shiver of fear for his soul.

He was shaken from his stupor as the mob leader again took up his grievances.

"And yet another, Levenach!" the man shouted and gestured impatiently for the pair of folk bearing the long-wrapped burden to come forth. Several women lingered on the fringes of the crowd, and their wailings pierced the air around the man's accusations. "You canna explain this away inna longer! Your blood-thirst has drunk of its last victim!"

"Who?" Alder heard her shocked whisper clearly.

*"My boy!"* a woman screamed and fought her way toward the inn. She was seized by a pair of folk before she could reach the Levenach woman. "My Tom! Only ten and six—not yet a man and yet you had to have him, did ye nae? Ye monstrous whore! Evil! Evil!"

"Nae," the witch whispered, and Alder thought he could hear physical anguish in the word. "Nae Tom!"

"Aye!" the mob leader shouted, shaking a torch at the Levenach. "Ye've lied to us, fed off'n us long enough, Beatrix Levenach. And now we will put an end to it!"

"Dunstan, surely you doona think that I—"

"What else are we to think, I ask ye?" the thick man—Dunstan—charged. "And unmarried woman, carrying on as if she were a man of business, a chief even—"

"But my betrothed—"

"He doesna exist!" Dunstan sneered. "For years we swallowed yer lies and those of yer father. The old tales are just that—stories. You nae more protect the Leamhnaigh than does the Devil hisself."

Alder shuddered at the words, a sharp, frozen fingernail between his shoulder blades.

"And now you'll pay for the lives you've taken. I know how to put an end to a witch," Dunstan threatened, shaking his torch at her again. He looked over his shoulder at the group of forest men gathered behind him, their own torches growing progressively and ominously brighter as the sun sank slowly, too slowly. "Take her, and light the inn!"

The crowd shouted encouragement as the Levenach was taken roughly in hand. Alder saw her lips move, whispering words too low for even his sensitive ears to hear. A spell of some sort, perhaps, but if it was, it had no effect on her captors. Alder looked to the glowing treetops again.

Three more minutes. Two, mayhap . . .

"Light it!" Dunstan insisted again while the folk who held her dragged the Levenach to a gnarled old elm spread wide in the clearing before the inn. As they drew closer to his hiding place, Alder could feel the power of the Levenach throbbing in rhythm to his own shuddering heartbeat.

The folk charged with destroying the inn stood before it without action, as if hesitant to approach the humble building. But the inn's fate was of no concern to Alder—he knew the Levenach's moments on earth could be counted on one hand.

He looked to the glowing treetops again. A feral whine escaped his throat.

"Doona do this, I beg of you!" the Levenach screamed. "Dunstan, I am the Levenach! You are sworn to—"

"Doona threaten me with yer curses, witch!" the

mob's leader growled. He jerked her by her fiery hair. "The Leamhnaigh will be free from yer evil when we toss yer wicked corpse upon the burning coals of the White Wolf."

A pained yip escaped Alder's throat.

"Nay!" the Levenach shrieked and thrashed her willowy body side to side as a length of rough rope was produced and a crude noose was wrenched over her head. Alder felt his own throat constrict, his scar burn.

He could not wait a moment longer, sunlight or nay.

Alder crouched low, his white muzzle nearly touching the dirt. A squealing growl came from him as he shuddered, shuddered, then sprang from the tree line.

# Chapter Four

*I'm going to die,* Beatrix said to herself in disbelief as the noose fell over her collarbone and then scratched itself tight around her throat. Someone behind her—it wasn't Dunstan, as he still stood before her, glaring triumphantly—tied her wrists together.

Nothing had worked. The warding spell, the escape spell, the discernment spell—it was as if she sang a pretty lullaby to a group of savage sheep. Her father, the legends and prophesies—the well itself—had all been wrong.

She was going to be burned to death. And then the Leamhnaigh and all the highlands would fall to Laszlo and his vampires.

Tom's mother fought her way to the fore of the crowd, and even in her own mortal fear, Beatrix's heart wrenched for the poor woman, and for her sweet son, dead by the fang.

"Look, look!" The woman tore at the rough covering that shrouded her boy until Tom's face, gaunt and white and shriveled, was revealed. His brown eyes, forever holding their fear wide, gaped at Beatrix. A strangled cry wheezed from her throat at the sight of the two black puncture marks on the young man's neck. Whoever had fed upon the boy had drained him like a piece of winter fruit.

"His should be the last face your damned evil eyes look upon before you burn in hell, witch," the woman gasped, and then spat in Beatrix's face before collapsing in a half faint in the arms of one of her neighbors.

"I didna," Beatrix whispered the plea to the crowd. "I swear it!"

"Would you light the fucking place?" Dunstan shouted, and the rope began to tighten around Beatrix's neck. She rose onto her toes as her breath was cut off.

*Help me, Da,* Beatrix said in her mind as her eyes closed.

A low, wet snarl whispered in Beatrix's ear the instant before the commanding shout of "Release her!" seemed to echo from the very heart of the forest.

Beatrix's eyes opened, and a reedy stream of sparkling air slithered into her straining lungs. For a moment, Beatrix thought that she had already died, and that now she looked upon the angel that would bear her to her ancestors.

He . . . *glowed* as he emerged from the blackening forest, walking with a purposeful but rolling gait that emphasized his lanky grace, lean muscles crowded beneath his alabaster skin. His hair was so blond as to be nearly white, long and straight as it flowed back from his high forehead and disappeared down his back. He carried no pack, no obvious weapon—the stranger simply stepped into the forest clearing that was more than two days' travel from anywhere as if he'd just come from his own house.

His command had been for the Leamhnaigh, but his eyes, the irises as black as the Levenach well itself, were for Beatrix alone. He strode toward the crowd as if he would bowl them all over.

"I said, release . . . my betrothed." Around Beatrix, the Leamhnaigh gasped.

And then he was before her, his sinewy hands pulling the noose from her neck effortlessly as the crowd backed away. His scent enveloped her, like the perfume of a garden of night flowers, and the smell of a half-burnt piece of firewood, smoky and exotic. He spun Beatrix around to address the ties at her wrists and she could not help but gasp when his fingers found her own tender skin, like rogue sparks.

Beatrix heard Dunstan challenge the stranger. "Your betrothed, you say?" The suspicion in his voice was unmistakable.

"Aye, Beatrix Levenach is to be mine." She felt his cool breath at her ear. "My name is Alder," he hissed.

"Alder!" Beatrix stuttered as the ropes fell away from her hands and she turned to face him once more. "Why did you not send word?"

"I was . . ." the man paused, his eyes flicking over the crowd with a sneer. "Unexpectedly detained. Forgive me. Had I known that you were to be set upon by such savages I would have hastened to your side without concern for other business."

"Now just one bleedin' moment." Dunstan stepped toward the white man. "We doona know you from Jake, bloke, an' yer interference with the witch here is unwelcome. She's a killer, stalking good and innocent folk when they trusted her, murderin' 'em in their very homes!"

The man calling himself Alder whipped around and the queer sound of a hollow roar echoed in Beatrix's ear at the swift movement. It was little more than a blur.

"My name is neither bloke nor Jake, and if you should take one step closer to Beatrix Levenach, I will rip both your arms from your torso and beat you to death with them."

A shocked look of disgust came over Dunstan's ruddy face.

"My name," the man continued, now addressing the entire stunned crowd, "is Alder . . . de White. Beatrix Levenach was promised to me these many . . ."

"Six," Beatrix chirped.

"Six years past," Alder picked up. "By her father—"

"Aye, me da, Gerald."

The white man sent her a warning look. *Enough.* "Gerald Levenach promised his daughter to me six years ago. I have been delayed in claiming her due to . . . matters of my estate in England. A plague on you who would seek to do harm to the head of your clan family. What would Gerald say?"

Tom's mother staggered forward. "She's nae our clan head—she's a witch! She's killed my Tom!"

Alder looked to the corpse and then back to the woman, his voice growing low and thoughtful. "My dear woman, pray tell, do you think it reasonable that even a woman of the Levenach's stature could overtake a boy of Tom's size?" Beatrix had the strange feeling that she could fall right into Alder de White's voice and be lost forever. She found herself leaning toward him.

"Aye, he was strapping," Tom's mother admitted, standing a mite taller in her grief. "But she is a powerful evil, that one, and Tom trusted her. We all did!"

One eyebrow rose. "Yes, I could see her evil power evidenced by the easy way in which she escaped her own imminent death. Did anyone witness the attack?" Alder continued, looking around the crowd. Beatrix noticed that many of the folk were also leaning toward the white stranger, their gazes thoughtful, rather detached.

No one answered.

Alder swung around to face Dunstan, who was one of the few not mesmerized by Alder's presence. "Is this your quest to settle a personal vendetta, mayhap?"

"What?" Dunstan shouted, his eyes widening.

"Mayhap you propositioned my betrothed and she refused you. Is it your pride that wishes to see her destroyed? Shall I challenge you for the Levenach's honor?"

"I'm a married man!" Dunstan cried. "This is about murder, stranger! A concern of folk of which you are nae kin to, so—"

Before Dunstan could gather up the broken pieces of his speech, Alder addressed the crowd once more, taking Beatrix by her elbow.

"The inn will not trade this night, to give you good folk time to cool your tempers and see reason. My lady has had a trying evening at your very hands and I'm certain she wishes to rest."

Beatrix opened her mouth, to say what, she didn't know, but Alder frowned at her and she clearly heard the words "Say nothing," in her mind.

"Any matter," he continued, "I have a great desire to speak privately with my betrothed." He began pulling Beatrix toward the inn. "Perhaps we will meet on the morrow under happier circumstances. In the meantime . . ."

Their backs were at the inn's door now and he made a low bow to the crowd. "Will you not invite me in," he growled, the exasperated question meant for Beatrix alone.

She started, as if from sleep. "Won't you come in, Alder?" she said brightly, loudly.

"Thank you, my lady, I think I shall." Alder looked to the stunned and gaping crowd a final time. "We bid you good night."

Then he was bustling her inside the inn and barring the door behind them, leaving them both in the dark quiet of the common room.

Alder collapsed in a hard wooden chair as soon as the door was shut and locked, his mind's eye full of the near escape both he and the Levenach had had. All those sharpened staves . . .

The Levenach woman still stood perhaps five paces from him, where Alder had left her. Her mouth was slightly agape and there was a delicate frown laid across her rust-colored eyebrows.

"You're welcome," Alder prompted.

"You came," Beatrix Levenach said. "You actually came. The white wolf," she said in wonder.

Alder froze. Did she know of his true nature? If she was as powerful of a witch as had been rumored—and Alder suspected she was—who was sworn to rid the highlands of vampires, Alder could have very well just locked himself inside with his greatest enemy.

A gorgeous enemy, for certain, but one that would leave him just as destroyed.

"Aye," he said slowly. "Some do call me that."

"You are the only one who can help me."

"Didn't I just?"

"You're a killer of beasts," she continued, as if he'd not spoken. "Of . . . of"—she lowered her voice to a whisper—"vampires."

Alder nodded and then gestured to Beatrix with a wave of his hand. "As are you, so I hear tell."

The Levenach nodded. "My life, the lives of the

Leamhnaigh, are in grave danger. The vampires are multiplying."

"You know the one who stalks you?" Alder prompted, wanting yet dreading her to speak the name.

"He is called Laszlo," Beatrix whispered. "The king of the vampires. He is verra old. Ancient. Dangerous."

"As am I too all of those things," Alder said, wondering at the warning he was giving her. "Although perhaps not as ancient as he."

"Of course you're nae." A faint smile tilted her full lips for an instant and then was gone. "Why have you sought me?"

"It's Laszlo I seek. He stole something from me, many years ago. I've come to get it back, and destroy him. Though for both those tasks, *you*, Beatrix Levenach, are the only one who can help *me*." She gave him no comment, and so Alder continued. "You reside here alone?"

"Aye. My father died three months ago."

Alder let his own smile curve his lips. "Gerald?"

Her teeth flashed. "Aye. A fine ruse we've concocted, the two of us."

"There is no betrothed, then, is there? I'd not be set upon by an irate suitor as well as Laszlo and his fiends."

"Nay, nae suitor. 'Twas but a buy for time with the folk until you came. My father told me you would."

"Did he?"

"Aye."

Alder did not question her further on the matter. "You hunt at night?"

The Levenach nodded. "After the inn has closed, past midnight. I sleep during the day and then open the inn for trade at dusk."

Alder's heart pounded. It was almost too perfect. "Then we shall both hunt at night."

Beatrix's eyes raked him from head to toe, and Alder felt himself stiffen in his breeches. "Where are your stakes?"

"Ah . . . I don't carry any at the moment."

"You can borrow one of mine. They are old—well used, and very effective."

He gave her a seated bow, although he thought to himself that he would rather peel his own skin from his flesh than touch one of those ancient weapons.

After a long moment of each studying the other, Beatrix asked, "Are we to play at being betrothed, then?"

"I think it best under the circumstances, don't you agree?"

"I do. But what of after? When we've killed Laszlo and the rest? What shall I tell the folk?"

Alder found himself staring at the pale curve of her neck, just under her crimson hair, where he could see her pulse leaping. Her blood was calling to him already, and he wanted to grab her now, throw her onto her back on one of the inn's rough tables, drive himself into her while he drank his fill, mortal and undead passions united, slaked.

He shrugged. "Perhaps you will not have to tell them anything at all."

She nodded as if this was a perfectly acceptable answer. "Well, then. I'll show you to a room. The hunt should be an easy one tonight—the moon is waning now, and the beasts are not as heated." She started for the narrow staircase.

Alder followed her with his eyes for several moments, his nostrils flaring with her scent, before rising from the chair and stalking the Levenach into the dark upper level of the inn.

Waning moon or nay, Alder's own fire blazed.

# Chapter Five

In the bowels of the snaking, subterranean network of caves that was his palace, Laszlo le Morte slumped in his favorite chair. It was a throne of sorts, fashioned painstakingly from the bones of his most treasured victims, bleached and macabre and cold—like Laszlo himself. And while the chair perhaps didn't lend itself to a cushioned and pampered backside, it did give Laszlo a sense of lazy, privileged power, and he slouched regally in it whenever he could.

But this early evening, not even his regal throne could bring a cold smile to Laszlo's long and pointed face beneath his short beard. The king of the Leamhan Vampires was troubled.

Alder the White had returned. And he had set up house with the Levenach. Perhaps the white bloodsucker had only entered into the witch's abode to kill her in a spot of privacy, in which case, Laszlo would be pleased—after taking her blood, Alder would be mortal again and vulnerable to Laszlo's attack.

What gave Laszlo concern was the fact that Alder the White had returned at all. Laszlo had taken the ambitious human's blood—and his soul—personally. One hundred years ago, the Levenach witches had enchanted the forest, to prevent Laszlo and his unnatural and deadly children from capturing the magical well at its center. And so Laszlo had lured a mortal into the highlands with promises of vast tracts of land, choosing the young, power-hungry Alder de White for his fiery ambition, which had blinded him to the danger of Laszlo and his true vampire nature.

Laszlo's plan had worked, bringing his bloodsucking offspring to the very cusp of the enchanted water, which once claimed would guarantee Laszlo rule over that dark slice of Scotland and its people forever. Unfortunately for him, Alder de White had realized his folly too late—only when Laszlo had sunk his fangs into the proud English neck for that final indignity—his screaming promise of revenge seeming empty and futile.

When the archangel Michael and his Wild Hunt had descended upon the slaughter of witches, thwarting Laszlo's near victory, and seized Alder's body from the forest clearing, Laszlo had assumed that his unwilling co-conspirator was to spend a soulless eternity in hell.

But Alder had somehow escaped the Hunt after nearly a century, and returned to the highlands for what Laszlo could only surmise was revenge and retribution. The latter for the Levenach—to take her lifeblood in hopes of regaining his soul, and revenge on Laszlo, for sucking that soul from his mortal shell. Laszlo was not fearful of the White; more . . . *cautious*. As slave to the Hunt, Alder's power and knowledge of things, usually unseen to mortals, had undoubtedly grown. Engaging the rogue vampire directly could be very, very dangerous, but Laszlo would not be intimidated by a beast of his own making.

No, Alder the White must die a permanent death this time, while Laszlo himself kept a safe distance. Laszlo suspected the White would use the Levenach, as Laszlo had used the White a century ago. And so Laszlo must find a way to rid himself of Alder before Alder could rid himself of Laszlo.

Hmmm . . . puzzling.

He thought of the ways those of his kind could perish as he extended each long, bony, alabaster finger: sunlight, stake through the heart, several herbs were certainly potentially damaging, and being bled dry by another vampire. All of those possibilities were too dangerous for Laszlo to carry out personally. He could set his children to chase, but there were barely two score remaining now, thanks to that bitch, the Levenach. Laszlo could not risk lessening their numbers if he was to have a proper dynasty.

The only other choice was to build their ranks. The thought of tainting their exclusive tribe with the stupid forest folk caused Laszlo's lip to curl. But after Alder was dead, the undesirables could be pruned.

Laszlo thought of how close he had come to being rid of the Levenach—the oaf Dunstan had nearly done the job before Alder had arrived. Greedy, dense of brains, and ridiculously strong, the forest man would make the perfect grunt vampire. It was no secret that Dunstan disliked the female Levenach, and Laszlo thought it would be an easy matter to recruit the idiot. *That* task he would most definitely do himself, and with pleasure.

Laszlo's blood started to hum in his veins—the sun must have set. As if to confirm his suspicions, the screeching and mournful howls of his tribe itched at his eardrums as they roused themselves from the recesses of the caves. Laszlo pulled his lanky form from the chair and at last stretched with a lazy, satisfied smile, eager to slip behind the heavy curtain of darkness. Perhaps the folk had given in to their human weakness for drink only a pair of days after attempting to kill the inn's mistress, and in the next several hours would be staggering home to their pathetic woodland houses. It was very much like picking mushrooms—mortals were so unbelievably gullible when drunk. And quite tasty, as well. Laszlo would feed quickly and then retreat to the safety of his natural catacombs to plan.

He raised his face to the rocky and dank ceiling of the cave, stretched wide his thin gray lips, and let loose his own cry, the call that would gather his children to their bloody supper.

It was time to eat.


It was time to hunt.

Beatrix laid out the weapons on a table in the now empty and tidied common room while she waited for Alder to descend from the upper floor. She trailed a finger along the knotted embroidery of Gerald Levenach's quiver, which held the supply of freshly sharpened stakes. She'd never hunted with anyone save her father.

Was Alder de White truly a killer of beasts? Would his presence be an aid or a deadly hazard?

Beatrix suspected the latter, being unable to take her eyes off the man's muscular body and enigmatic smile for the past two days. He made her blood rush as if by magic—it sang and pumped through her veins and whispered to her in an old, old language things of heat and lust and naked moonlight. It was prophesied that the white wolf would come to save the Levenach, and he had already saved Beatrix's life in the clearing, true. But what was to become of her heart?

As the last living protector of the Leamhnaigh, Beatrix had always known there was little chance of her ever marrying. Who would she pair with? A man of the forest? None had ever shown the slightest interest in her as a woman, and it was clear now that the folk did not trust her. She could not leave the Leamhan forest while it still crawled with vampires, and even should she rid the land of the bloodsuckers, to where would she go? The wild highlands were her home and she had no friends or family left either here in the black thickness of forest or anywhere else. And what man was likely to wander into this cursed part of Scotland, seeking a witch for a bride?

She shook herself from her foolishness and turned her burning face once more to the tabletop as Alder de White's boots whispered against the stair treads. His approach was stealthy, but she could feel his energy press against her as he descended into the common room.

"I've brought out my father's things for you to use, if you wish," she said, not wanting to turn and look at him just yet, with her cheeks still heated from the mere thought of him. Instead, she waved her hand over or touched lightly the items she spoke of as he came to stand at her side. She felt as though the floor of the common room was tilting, swaying her body closer to his. She made a conscious effort to stand upright.

"His quiver and stakes." Her eyes only flicked at his shirt. "You'll likely have to tighten the strap—he was a bit thicker of chest than you. Here is a pouch of five finger grass, and a phial of blessed water. I also have his long staff, if you're the sort who prefers a bit of a fight before the kill."

Then she did turn her face to look at him directly, forcing herself not to retreat at the close scrutiny those black eyes placed on her as they skittered intently over her face, taking in her hair piled high atop her head and tied with thin twists of leather, then dropping deliberately to her shirt and breeches. His nostrils flared, as if picking up her scent through the thick, rough wool.

A smile quirked his lips suddenly and he blinked, as if just remembering she was there. "I see you've dressed for the occasion."

Beatrix's face heated once more. "I canna be stomping through the wood in a skirt now, can I? I'd be cut down in a blink."

"Take no offense, Levenach," Alder said smoothly. His cool smile widened and he leaned to the side slightly as if to peer behind her. " 'Tis a wise choice of attire. I particularly admire the backside. You will be leading me through the wood, won't you?"

Beatrix's mouth gaped open for a moment at his bold teasing and then she broke into a laugh, feeling at once at ease. "Is that how you speak to your woman in England?"

"I have no woman in England." Alder's smile relaxed into something only slightly less predatory. "Perhaps you are volunteering to be my woman in Scotland?"

"I am nae woman, Alder de White." Beatrix grinned and began to divide up the simple but deadly tools into their respective piles. "I am the Levenach. I am a hunter. 'Tis my only purpose, so you can roll your slick tongue back inside your mouth."

"I can think of somewhere else I'd rather put it."

At this, Beatrix did gasp, and she swung her face back to his.

"Too bold?" Alder challenged.

"Aye, too bold," Beatrix insisted, although her legs felt weak and her nipples tightened beneath the rough shirt she wore. "I may be Levenach and therefore nae meant for the mundane life of a husband and family, but I do demand respect."

"What I said was meant only with respect," Alder argued mildly, and picked up the quiver. He seemed fascinated by it, turning it this way and that in the dim candlelight. Then his black eyes pinned her again. "Neither of us are innocents, by the very role we play in this evil. I am not offering you marriage or children." Beatrix swallowed and Alder tilted his head, studying her now. "But I've wanted your body since the moment I saw you in yonder clearing. What say you to that?"

Beatrix wanted to swallow again but could not, her breath frozen in her throat.

And *aye* was dancing on the tip of her tongue. . . .

She cleared her throat, picked up her own quiver, and slung it over her head to seat the strap between her breasts. "Why do we nae see if we're compatible in the hunt first? Perhaps you'll be of nae use to me at all, and I'll be forced to banish you for your own safety."

He snatched her against his chest before the last word had cleared her lips, and the contact of his hard muscles against her loose breasts caused an involuntary mew.

She gave a nervous laugh. "Ah . . . or mayhap my own safety."

"You're not safe with me, Beatrix," Alder agreed quietly and the breath of his words stirred the tendrils of hair at her temple. "Indeed, at this very moment, you're in more danger than you have ever been the whole of your life."

Her eyes were fixed on his mouth and she couldn't help but let her tongue slide over her own lips. She wanted to taste that mouth. She felt a humming in her core. "I know."

" 'Tis well that you do."

He eased back from her and, after a quick adjustment to the knots, slipped the strap of Gerald Levenach's quiver over his head. Beatrix twisted, picked up the pouch containing the herbs and water, and held it out to him, but he did not take it.

"I've . . . no use for those," he said uneasily. "But I will take the staff you offered."

"Very well," Beatrix said, her heart still pounding. " 'Tis in the kitchen. We'll pick it up as we go."


Beatrix Levenach did in fact lead Alder through the wood for the first hour of their hunt, and he very much enjoyed the sight of her round ass in the men's breeches she wore. The night around them was pitch, but Alder's vampire eyes illuminated the shadows as if subjecting them to a white flame. Each time the Levenach high-stepped over a downed tree, the wool pulled tight over her curves, revealing her body in a way that was somehow more erotic than nudity. Seeing the freedom of her limbs, scissoring, stretching, lengthening—Alder could barely concentrate on his surroundings.

Until the first vampire launched himself from the blackness with a hiss and fell atop Beatrix.

Before Alder could reach her, the Levenach had spun out of the powerful claws of the bloodsucker, swinging her arms in a wide arc, and without even a cry of effort, drove a readied stake into the undead's chest with a wet *chunk*.

The entire confrontation was over within the count of ten, and it had been almost completely soundless. Beatrix Levenach stood over the now-sizzling corpse, her breathing barely labored. She looked up at Alder and the fire in her eyes caused him to squint.

Here then, was the true power of the Levenach witch. Perhaps Beatrix was not the only one in grave danger from the close company the two now shared. If she discovered Alder's nature, suspected his unnatural hunger, he could very well find himself beneath her sharpened stake.

"That's one for me, Alder de White." She smiled at him, and the magic of her caused Alder's cool blood to roil like floodwaters. "You'll need be a mite quicker than that if you're to keep pace with me."

He answered with a bow, not trusting himself to speak. He wanted to seize her, strip her, drink from her, there in the black forest with the danger all around them. He wanted to confess his own evil to her while he did base and very mortal things to her body. His hunger was nearly out of control.

He had to feed—to quench at least a portion of his black appetite lest he lose all control.

The dead vampire's corpse blinked into nothingness, and Beatrix nodded, satisfied with her work. "Well, then. Ready?" She turned and continued deeper into the forest.

Alder followed, his senses now tuned to the minutest signs of the wood around them. He could smell another vampire ahead and to the right and could barely suppress his howl. His eyes were all but blind with hunger, but before him, the Levenach glowed, taunting him. Should he not take this next kill, the witch—and perhaps Alder's immortal soul—was doomed.

Beatrix passed safely by the clump of bushes where Alder sensed the bloodsucker lurking, and continued into the wood. Alder slowed, stepped from the rough path they had been following just before the stand of scrub. He slid the long staff between his shoulder blades and the quiver strapped to his back—Alder had no desire to play with his food at the moment. He was nearly deaf with the bloodrush in his sensitive ears, his nostrils full of the rancid smell of the vampire crouched before him, who followed the Levenach's progress, readying to strike.

Alder let himself go. Moving so quickly, so quietly that even to himself his motions were a blur, he placed one hand on the vampire's greasy head and the other on the cusp of his shoulder and pushed his palms away, the cracking of bone perhaps audible to the Levenach, some lengths away. Before the vampire could scream, Alder fell upon the man's neck, crunching through the skin, his fangs sinking into cold flesh and setting loose the torrent of tainted but powerful blood. He drank and drank and drank. . . .

"Alder?"

The call seemed a whisper, but Alder raised his head, feeling his eyes dilated to their maximum capacity, and he knew that should the Levenach have a chance to look upon his eyes in the light, she would see no white at all. His guts, his veins burned as though he had swallowed glowing coals. For an instant, he half rose, intending with all his instinct to continue his gorging on the redheaded witch woman who now sought him in the black wood. But his heart was slowing, his head clearing, his will reshaping itself into heady control.

She was nearly upon him now. "Alder?" Her tone was filled with alarm.

Alder let the melting corpse slip onto the leaves and then he skittered soundlessly behind a sheltering tree, dropping his head back against the trunk and taking enormous gulps of air. He scrubbed at his mouth, chin, and neck with his forearm, hoping that when she saw the blood on his clothes, she would attribute it only to the kill and not his beastly, quenched thirst.

He knew the moment she came upon the vampire by her anxious tone. "Alder! Where are you?"

He rolled to his feet and stepped from behind the tree on the opposite side of her, causing the Levenach to swing around, her stake at the ready.

" 'Tis only I," he said, his palms out.

"Eternal Mother!" Beatrix gasped and lowered her stake. She took a brief moment to catch her breath and then gestured to the faint, silvery imprint in the leaves, like the intricate trails of a thousand slugs. "You nearly took his head off."

The vampire's fortifying blood having sated him, Alder no longer felt that he was in danger of feeding from Beatrix Levenach, although the heavier desire to take her body still ran through him like a hot iron bar.

He smiled. "I could not let you best me."

She laughed, seeming completely unconcerned that they were surrounded by a hostile wood littered with bloodsuckers. Her mirth and her ease caused Alder to stiffen completely in his breeches. What an odd combination of seasoned killer and soft woman the Levenach was revealing herself to be.

"The night is yet young," she taunted. "And I'm nae accustomed to losing."

Alder watched her forge ahead, leading the way once again through the darkness, and Alder's eyes went once more to the silvery slime where he had drained the vampire of its tainted blood. For the first time, Alder wondered how he would ever bring himself to do the same to Beatrix Levenach when the time came.

# Chapter Six

The Levenach, well-secreted away in the cellar, had spoken true—they were winning. Alder de White had been in residence for almost four weeks, and with his help, seventeen vampires had been sent to their ready hell. Although Laszlo still remained elusive, Beatrix felt that they were drawing closer to that devil as well. Soon, the king of the vampires would have no choice but to come out of his hiding and face them directly or flee the Leamhan forest forever.

In the meantime, the vampires' slaughter had been stanched and the forest folk were feeling more relaxed and hopeful, and most certainly possessed of a more charitable attitude toward the Levenach. The inn was crowded with village folk from wall to wall, and the atmosphere was easy, merry. Beatrix freely shared smiles with the patrons as she served her stew and poured pitchers of ale, marveling at the radical shift in her standing in the community.

Alder had helped with that as well, as the men were fascinated by this English stranger with the odd accent, and the women were sweetly enchanted. Although Alder boldly baited Beatrix nightly, never letting a hunt pass without some erotic comment or look—and lately, a glancing touch—he never encour-

aged the womenfolk's attention. They simply seemed
unable to help being drawn to the pale, intense man.
Beatrix told herself it was not jealousy she felt when a
woman engaged Alder in coquettish banter, simply
annoyance. Alder would not risk their mission by dal-
lying with a Leamhan woman when the folk were
under the assumption that Alder was Beatrix's intended.

Even though a lie, that thought always succeeded
in making Beatrix's stomach clench, and lately, she
had allowed herself the frequent folly of imagining
the lie as truth. She told herself it was but a harmless
way to pass the time between kills and the washing up.

The only development that gave Beatrix cause for
worry was the marked absence of Dunstan from the
inn. At first, she attributed the brutish woodsman's
avoidance to the humiliation Alder had dealt him
the day he'd rallied the folk in the clearing. But Dunstan was never one to stay away from merrymaking
for long, and even the Leamhnaigh were expressing
concerns for him and his meek wife.

"He's nae left his house in days."

"Freda willna let anyone in—she says Dunny's
feelin' poorly. Sleeps the day away."

"The poor woman is worrying herself to naught."

Although Beatrix held no great affection for Dunstan, she was still the Levenach, and she had decided
that before she and Alder began their hunt in earnest
that night, she would answer her responsibility and
at last make a personal call on Dunstan and Freda's
cottage and inquire as to their welfare. Once that chore
was done, she could give in to her wild desire to hunt
down the bloodsuckers, with the bold and mysterious, amorous and dangerous Alder at her side.

What she was to do about *him*, Beatrix had no idea.

*  *  *

Alder was uneasy. Their hunt that night had been unsuccessful, but he had feared as much as soon as he and the Levenach had left the dark and seemingly deserted abode belonging to the forest man, Dunstan.

To Alder, the timber and mud house had reeked of vampire.

Beatrix'd had little comment on the absence of the mortal man, save to speculate that perhaps he and Freda had left the Leamhan forest for good. Alder did not think that was so, and he was darkly certain that Laszlo had a hand in whatever evil was afoot.

After all, Alder knew from personal experience that it was the king of the vampires' nature to use those he considered beneath him for his own gain.

Alder remained more alert than usual throughout the deep hours of their hunt, but he neither sensed nor smelled any further sign of the bloodsuckers. They were obviously in hiding, and that worried Alder more than Dunstan's mysterious disappearance. A trap was being laid, and Alder used every shred of his keen abilities to try to keep himself and Beatrix from falling into it.

They returned to the White Wolf Inn the hour before dawn, tired and dirty and frustrated. Alder was hungry again, but his need for blood was not yet so great that he felt the Levenach's life was in danger.

Her breeches, on the other hand, were in grave peril.

A thorny bush had snagged a seam of the heavy woolen pants just under Beatrix's hip early in the hunt, and ripped a wide gash beneath her right buttock. She'd given the damage little comment, and Alder knew it was because she thought him unable to see the crescent-shaped slice of white flesh flashing at him with every other step. But seen it he had, and imagined a great deal more. He was shaking for her by the time she pushed open the back door of the inn and Alder followed her into the darkened kitchen.

Before she could lay hand to a candle, Alder seized her around her waist from behind, causing her to gasp and clasp both of his forearms with her hands. He nuzzled her hair—the scent of the midnight forest clung to her, damp and dark and cold, mingling with her own sweet sweat like a cologne. He felt his fangs growing behind his lips.

"Alder!" she half-laughed. "I'll step on the cats. Loose me so that I might give us light."

"I don't want light," he murmured against the shell of her ear. "I want you. In the dark. I can't wait any longer, Levenach. You're driving me mad."

Then she did laugh. "You're only bothered that there was nae kill tonight. But you'll nae take it out on me." She tried to pry his arms from about her torso.

He held tight. "Why not?" he cajoled, beyond reason now. He didn't care about Laszlo, didn't care about his soul. Beatrix Levenach's magic had enchanted him, and his flesh wanted hers. Needed it. Hungered for it. He had never felt so strong and yet powerless in the face of this foreign desire. "You, too, feel the frustration of our wasted efforts. You have no man save me. When I am gone, we will both be alone."

She grew still. "You would talk of leaving already? We have not yet found Laszlo."

"We will. Soon. Or he will find us." Alder had heard the hurt in her words and it cooled his lust somewhat. "Levenach, I spoke true when I said that I was dangerous to you. After Laszlo is dead, I cannot stay. You wouldn't want me to, if you only knew—"

"That you are using me?" Beatrix interjected, and Alder knew a cool stream of fear in his spine. When he did not answer her, she gave a chuckle. "I'm nae the Levenach for lack of brains, Alder de White. I ken that you've nae come here out of the goodness of your heart, if even you possess such a tender thing."

Alder's breath caught behind his fangs.

"I know verra little about you," she continued. "But I do know that our lives are intertwined for the time being. If one of us should die before Laszlo is destroyed, so will the other perish. You need me as much as I need you, and that is why I doona fear you."

"If you don't fear me, then lie naked with me tonight."

She turned her head slightly, as if trying to look into his face. "So that I can bear your bastard?"

Alder shook his head. "You won't." It was impossible. "I swear to you."

She was still for a long moment, and Alder turned her in his arms. "I want you, Beatrix Levenach. I have not lain with a woman in longer than you would believe. Not because I've had no chance, but because I've not had the desire. My desire for you is destructive, it's eating at me. It makes me think of doing things you would not like. Violent things."

"You wouldn't hurt me, Alder," Beatrix said softly.

"Don't be so certain." He could feel her pounding heart against his chest, pushing the current of warm and rich blood beneath the creamy skin of her breasts like a dangerous tide. He dropped his lips to her neck, fool that he was, to taste her skin. He murmured his dark fantasy against her silkiness. "I want to feel your power mixed with mine while I take you. It would be . . . spectacular. I want to hear you scream."

She jolted slightly as her knees buckled and her head fell back. "You're mesmerizing me."

"Perhaps," he conceded. "But I could not if you weren't willing—you're too powerful, Levenach. And you want me, as well, do you not?"

"Of course I do," Beatrix insisted in a fierce whisper. He felt her fingertips crawling up his stomach, her nails digging into his skin, leaving welted crescents as her brand on him. She reached into the V of his shirt and slid her hand behind his head over the pucker of his scar, pulling his mouth against her pulsing neck until Alder's fangs dug into his own lips. It was as if *she knew* . . . she knew he wanted to feed from her, and she was teasing him, daring him. "And it *would* be spectacular."

He thought he heard a whimper, and he realized it had come from his own throat. Beatrix crooked a knee and hooked her calf behind Alder's buttocks, pressing herself into his erection. He bucked. She moaned.

"I have to take you," Alder said, although the statement was more a plea. He ran his tongue down her neck, across the front of her throat, and up the other side to the opposite ear. His fangs may have skimmed her skin, but he could not care. "Beatrix, Beatrix . . ."

Her hands left his neck and pushed between their bodies to jerk open his breeches. She plunged her hands between the fabric and his hair and seized him. Alder whipped his face away from her neck and hissed as his fangs erupted fully.

Dropping his own hand to the rip in the seat of her pants, Alder tore the backside of her breeches away in one vicious motion. He lifted her under her buttocks and sat her down hard on the edge of a worktable.

"Not here," she gasped.

"What?" Alder demanded.

"I *cook* in here." She seesawed against his groin, trying to scoot off the table.

"I can't wait to go upstairs."

"I canna, either—take me to the common room."

He lifted her again and she locked her legs about his middle as he carried her into the large dark room and deposited her onto a table before the hearth. She fell onto her back and Alder wasted no time creating a seam in the front of her shirt where none had been. Her breasts fell free. The sight of her, her clothes hanging in shreds from her body, with only the most erotic parts exposed, caused Alder's hips to pump once reflexively. He felt wild and evil and hungry, and like he would tear her to pieces.

As if she could hear his thoughts, Beatrix demanded, "Don't hold back."

It was madness he felt, and Alder gladly embraced it as he pushed his breeches down fully. His vampire eyes could clearly see her sex as he positioned himself at her entrance and he gave an openmouthed sigh at the slick, fiery contact. It had been one hundred years since he'd lain with a woman, but never had he been blessed with such a one as was bared before him now. The Levenach, the most powerful witch in all of the highlands, the most beautiful, the most pure, the—

On the table before him, Beatrix writhed and panted, her eyes flashing witch fire at him. "Do it!" she shouted at him. "Do it now!" She reached up with one long arm and grasped his shirtfront, jerking him forward and atop her with amazing strength.

Alder fell, catching himself with one palm on the tabletop, his other hand seizing one of the Levenach's breasts, and he thrust his hips forward. She cried out and pulled him more fully into her with her legs, bucking up against him with another ragged cry.

Alder was blinded with sensations as he rocked into Beatrix, causing the table legs to screech on the floor. He wasn't worried that he hurt her, for the more he gave, the harder, the more she demanded from him. She urged him on mercilessly, heedless to the fact that Alder was on the brink already. With each greedy command she gave, he swelled, ached. His ears rang and he heard strange sounds, smelled odors that didn't belong—oil and smoke. The heat . . .

"Fire," Beatrix gasped.

"I know," Alder panted back. "I know, I—"

She shoved at his chest. "Nay, Alder—*fire!* The inn's afire!"

She rolled from beneath him and Alder struggled to come into reality and see the yellow flames bubbling over the wooden walls only steps away from where he had been crudely taking the Levenach. The dried mud between the timbers cracked audibly in the heat and the entire room rippled with fire, roiled with oil-laced, choking black smoke.

His passion doused by actual flames, Alder yanked his breeches around his waist once more and spun away from the smoke.

The Levenach had vanished.

"Beatrix!"

Alder turned the other way and saw the front door outlined by the sunlight showing through its frame, brighter than the flames that were now creeping across and gnawing on the wide timbers on the ceiling over his head.

Dawn had come.

Alder was trapped.

# Chapter Seven

Beatrix swam through the thick smoke, treading the black to the kitchen. She felt blindly for the long, heavy apron hanging on a peg inside the doorway and pulled it over her head to cover herself and scrunched the bodice up over her nose and mouth to filter the choking smoke.

"Bo! Era!" She knew she would not be able to see the cats in the burning fog, but she hoped that they would hear her voice and come to her. When she jerked open the back door, she thought she felt a soft swish past her calf and she left the door swinging wide. She turned back to the kitchen.

How had the common room become engulfed so immediately?

And why wasn't Alder behind her? She heard a ripping crash from the large room beyond—the sound of wood past its breaking point—then a hoarse cry.

"Alder!" she half choked. "Alder, this way!" It was impossible to see through the smoke—the daylight pushing ineffectively through the back door did little but reflect from the wall of roiling black. Beatrix raised a warding palm at the raven barrier.

"Black as night, flee from my sight! To banish this bane, I call the rain!"

The choking curtain parted and a low white shape began to materialize—larger than Bo or Era, but slinking through the smoke on four legs.

A white wolf, his black eyes rimmed with red, his snowy coat dusted with soot, came at her muzzle first, streaked past her hand, and leapt through the open kitchen door. His big body bumbled into her, and Beatrix felt a slick wetness on her fingers, and the back of her hand. She followed without hesitation.

A crack of thunder heralded their arrival at the front of the inn, which was already coughing smoke from under its thatched eaves, and the first cold, heavy raindrops felt like ice chips on Beatrix's face. She could hear shouts coming from the woodland path and muffled by the trees as the white wolf bolted into the cover of forest, his left flank a smear of red.

Beatrix spun back to face her home as the rain fell harder around her, sizzling on the coaling timbers and cracking mud. The footfalls of arriving woodland folk pounded into the clearing behind her as she at last saw the two people slumped against the inn's door.

It was Dunstan, and his wife, Freda, shoulder to shoulder as a companionable married couple should be, only with their severed heads resting neatly in their laps.

Beatrix brought her hands to her mouth to cover her scream and felt the wolf's cool blood against her lips as the first outraged cries from the Leamhnaigh pierced her core.

"Have mercy, she's killed Freda and Dunny!"

Beatrix spun around again to face her mistaken accusers, and the rain washed her hair into her eyes. "Nay! I didna! He . . . they—"

"Look—their blood still on her hands!"

Beatrix stood anchored to the sticky mud before

the semicircle of horrified folk, expecting to be rushed at any moment, but they only stood staring at her wide-eyed. Behind her, the inn sizzled in the rain, the flames in retreat, surrender moments away.

"Ye'll pay for this evil, Beatrix Levenach," one man said to her, almost sadly. Thunder rumbled over the treetops. "We trusted you. Trusted yer man. Where is he, now? Have you had done with him, as well?"

At this suggestion, the spray of people started like a herd of frightened sheep and began backing away toward the sheltering trees once more. Lightning struck deep in the forest, although the rain was little more than mist now.

"Ye'll pay," the man promised again. "And when next we come for you, there'll be none who will stop us."

With that dire promise hanging in the humid morning, the Leamhnaigh melted into the tree line like the smoke from the inn's rooftop and were gone.

A flash of white caught her eye and Beatrix turned her head to see the white wolf limp from the wood and stop, staring at her, his sides heaving, his head down. He regarded her warily, and Bea could see that he was holding his left rear leg slightly aloft.

She sighed. "Come, Alder. Let's get you inside where I can look at your leg."

Beatrix turned and began to walk once more toward the back of the inn, not bothering to wait and see if the wolf would follow.

When Alder limped into the kitchen on two legs, the Levenach was already gathering a collection of supplies on the table to tend him. Her torn shirt and breeches were largely covered by one of her innskeep aprons, revealing only her wool-clad calves and the sleeves of her shirt. She glanced over her shoulder at the shuffle and drag of his boots on the stones but then quickly returned her attention to the task before her without comment.

She knew he was the wolf. His cold, heavy heart pounded and he could not bring himself to step closer to her. Perhaps even now the ingredients she readied were the poisons that would kill him. She was strong, she was smart, she was a hunter. She was sworn by her very nature to battle bloodsuckers, of which surely she now suspected he was one.

Beatrix picked up the small tray with one hand and strode to a far corner of the room. Bending at the knees, she pulled aside a heavy woven mat, revealing a square wooden door set in the floor. She pulled on a metal ring and the door rose. She glanced at him, and for a moment Alder thought he saw a flash of doubt in her eyes.

It was gone with her next blink. "Come into the cellar—there willna be as thick of stench, and we will be safe down there should the Leamhnaigh return."

Then she was descending a set of steps invisible to Alder from where he stood.

He knew his own moment of indecision. The Levenach could very well be leading him to his death. Then he remembered her face, her demanding passion as they had made love in the common room. Alder had known from the beginning that his strange relationship with the Levenach would end in death, and as of this day, he would rather it be his own than hers. He would not drink from her. If she wished him dead for what he was, so be it. He followed.

He was only halfway down the steps when he heard her soft command of *"teine,"* and yellow light bloomed beneath his feet like a magical lake. As he stepped onto the lowest level of the White Wolf Inn, he saw that he was not only in the cellar, but Beatrix Levenach's bedchamber.

She had secreted herself away from him, he realized, in an area of the inn Alder had never suspected existed. All along, he had thought her just within his reach while he slept, but the Levenach had wisely protected herself.

She walked to the bed pushed against a stone wall, and set the tray of supplies on her woven coverlet. The room was lit by four tall, standing candelabras, each holding seven thin, yellowed tapers. A small wooden table held a wash bowl near the head of the bed, a bright rug covered the oddly fashioned dirt and black stone floor, and pegs along the diagonally ascending risers of steps held a collection of clothing. Mundane furnishings, certainly, common to any simple sleeping room.

But the hair on Alder's nape prickled and his fangs throbbed instinctively at his folly. He was in the magical lair of the Levenach, and Alder had never felt so vulnerable.

"Lie down," Beatrix ordered as she strode past him to the hooks on the steps. She selected a long, shapeless gown and then ducked into the shadows under and beyond the stairs.

Alder limped to the bedside and lay down, careful to avoid jostling her supplies. His left leg throbbed and burned. He could feel his fangs semi-erupted in response to the pain.

Beatrix emerged from under the stairs a moment later, retying the apron over a long gown, and she came swiftly to the bed, her eyes averted from him.

"I suppose you saw Dunstan and Freda," she said as she took hold of the two ragged edges of pants surrounding his wound. She ripped the tear wide, revealing the whole of his leg.

Alder nodded. "Laszlo's work. I could smell his evil stench at the cottage earlier." His words sounded awkward to his own ears, his lips trying to shield his elongated eyeteeth.

Beatrix turned a bottle of some unknown liquid onto a wadded-up rag and then began to blot firmly at the gash alongside Alder's knee and thigh where the falling timber had torn his skin.

"He's nae playing with us any longer," the Levenach observed.

"Nay."

She set the rag aside and picked up a needle threaded with thick gut. Alder's leg twitched in anticipation of the stitches. His leg would heal well enough without them, yet he did not stay the Levenach's hand, relishing even this opportunity for Beatrix to touch him while she continued to speak.

"He'll end it soon, then."

Alder nodded. "If he does not, then I must. Beatrix, the sun's dawning means that today is All Hallow's Eve."

"I ken that, Alder. The day of the dead is an important one to witches, as well."

What she meant by that statement, Alder could not discern.

"I'm sorry should you feel any pain," she said quietly, not meeting his eyes. Then she bent over his leg and poked the needle into his flesh.

Alder's leg stiffened reflexively, but the discomfort was slight. He spoke through clenched teeth. "The next sunrise must find Laszlo destroyed and me far from the Leamhan forest. When I seek him this night, you must not follow."

She did not respond, only continued her ministrations with her brow knotted in a heavy frown. Her stitches were small, quick, expert.

"Best that you leave the Leamhan forest, as well," Alder suggested. "Before nightfall. The folk will not be denied now."

"I willna flee," Beatrix said distractedly. "My family's oath forbids it."

"Then you will *die*," Alder hissed and reached down with one hand to still her wrist and force her to look at him. "Either by the folk or by the fang. Beatrix, you cannot stay in this place alone."

"I'll nae be alone—I'm going with you." She pulled free from his grasp. "Be still," she commanded. "I'm nearly through."

He let her finish the stitches in peace, although his mind raced with how to convince her she could not accompany him to Laszlo's lair. Once she had knotted the string and cut the needle free with a short blade, Alder grasped her wrist once more.

"Heed me, Levenach," he implored, the effort of concealing his fangs making his words slurred. "I ken that you have a duty to your family, and already you have fulfilled your promise—you've held the beasts at bay until my arrival, and now it is I who must finish it. Alone. I am also being hunted, by a creature that is not vampire, but neither is he mortal. If he finds me this night—and you with me—we are both damned. And even if he does not—" Alder swallowed. "Beatrix, I told you no falsehood the day I arrived. *I* am your greatest threat. You don't understand."

"I *do* understand!" she snapped in a low voice and held his gaze steady with her eyes. "Alder, I know you are a vampire."

Beatrix let Alder keep hold of her wrist while her confession of knowledge of his true nature hung in the cool air of the cellar. She saw his throat work as he swallowed, the warm candlelight playing over his pale face.

"You knew before I came?"

"Nae before you came," she admitted. "But as soon as you touched me, came near to me in the clearing." She let a smile come over her face, although the last thing she felt was merry. "I am a hunter, Alder. 'Tis in my very blood. Think you that I could not sense what you are just because of your handsomeness? Or because you were prophesied to come by my family's oldest legends?"

"You knew, and yet you did not slay me," he observed, and his hand tightened around her wrist.

Beatrix twisted her arm until she could pull her fingers through the tight circle of Alder's palm and lace their fingers together. She had made up her mind.

"Nay. You've already saved me once, Alder. I hold nae fear of you. I trust you. With my life, and with my soul."

His face took on a pained expression. "Beatrix, no. Listen to me, on this day when the veil between earth and eternity is thinned, once Laszlo is dead I—"

She leaned over him quickly and placed a finger over his mouth, stopping his confession, whatever it might be. She did not want to know. She let her fingertips bumble over his lips, feeling the raised outlines of his fangs, and shook her head.

"I have lived in the Leamhan forest the whole of my life, and knew from a young age that I was to be the Levenach. I am sworn to give my life in protection of the Leamhnaigh, and that duty I willna shirk. But, Alder, you are the first man, the first person nae of my blood that I would willingly die for. I canna explain it, I doona understand it myself. And I doona care. If I must die tonight, then let it be by *these* hands, by *this* mouth."

She leaned closer to him, her hunger for his body inflamed now that she knew with certainty that their hours together were few and dwindling fast.

"I don't want to harm you, Beatrix," Alder whispered.

She smiled at him again. "Could it be that you love me, Alder?"

He frowned, looked away from her face as if shamed. "It is not in my nature to love."

"Oh, but I think it is," she argued, and drew her body alongside his on her narrow bed. "I've never wanted a man before you, and now that you know I am not ignorant of who or what you are, you may take me with a clean conscience."

"I have no conscience, either," he nearly growled, and Beatrix could see his black eyes dilating in the flickering light, could hear his accent thickening as she ran her free hand up his chest and neck to caress his face.

"Then take me," she said simply. "Give me what I ask for and let us have these last hours together." She kissed his mouth lightly. "Alder, I am inviting you in once more. Doona refuse me."

He took her mouth in a rush, plunging his tongue between her lips and pulling her roughly to him with both strong, lean arms. They were facing each other on the mattress now, and Beatrix drew one leg up to hook around his hip, careful of his injury. She longed to feel him inside her once more, to at last gain the release of desire he had built in her while the fire had sprung around them in the common room.

At her encouragement, Alder pulled her beneath him fully and reached down to drag the long skirts of her apron and gown up around her hips. He buried his face in the crook of her neck and she turned her jaw away to give him access.

"Don't allow me to do this, Beatrix," he said, his voice strained.

"I am *making* you do this," she said, and arched her hips, pressing into him, taunting him. "You must. I command it. Make love to me, Alder."

Then he did growl, sounding like his other four-legged self, and he snaked an arm between their bodies to free himself. "I will obey, Levenach," he threatened hoarsely. In a blink, he slid inside her, and Beatrix cried out, matching Alder's moan.

He drove into her rhythmically, firmly, steadily, filling her and more as he jarred her body with his length and his power. She panted up into his face, saw the gleam of his bared fangs, and the sight of them set loose her forbidden climax like an explosion. She cried out over and over as he pumped his hips faster, relentless in his pursuit, and when he dropped his open mouth to her throat, she cried out again, partly in fear, partly in anticipation.

She felt the initial prick of his fangs as he climaxed deep within her, felt them threaten and then abruptly withdraw as he screamed with his release. Beatrix's head swam as if she was drunk, Alder's cries sounding distorted, her own body quaking, her eyes blind with silver and white starlight in the cellar, and she took his vampire seed hungrily, willingly, gratefully.

They slept tangled together while the sun rose slowly to its pinnacle outside the crippled White Wolf Inn and hiked across the dome of sky, then began to sink over the treetops once more.

Neither roused when the stone slabs in the floor slid apart with a scrape, and the soot-dusted cats paced agitated circles around the bed legs. Bo and Era yowled mournfully, but neither their cries nor the light escaping the Levenach well caused the slumbering pair to wince in their sleep. The well's single black eye shut tight once more before dark had fully fallen.

# Chapter Eight

The bodies were gone.

Beatrix squinted through the thickening gloom of dusk at the front door of the White Wolf Inn, but the corpses were not just hidden in shadow. The mortal remains of Dunstan and Freda were no more.

In the place where the bodies of husband and wife had leaned together was a pile of herbs, bent twig talismans hastily assembled by the looks of the ragged knots, and bowls of coarse salt. A ragged X was scratched in the charred soot of the front door.

The folk had returned to claim the couple, and left the warding objects for Beatrix, perhaps thinking the charms to keep them safe from her. The knowledge caused a pinch in her heart. The people her family had protected for generations were using her own talismans against her. The symbol on the door was clear. They thought her a killer of the innocent. A murderer.

And now they would kill her if they had chance. Alder was right—she was no longer safe here.

As if the thought had summoned him, she felt his hand upon her shoulder. She'd not even noticed that night had come.

"Will you heed me now?" he asked quietly, the

dark snuggling around them both like a cold blanket.

Beatrix shook her head. "Naught has changed. I still have a duty to fulfill."

"How can you feel you owe them anything when they would kill you?" His words were gentle, yet demanding of an answer to his cool, vampire logic.

"I doona owe the *Leamhnaigh*, Alder—I owe my *family*. My *father*. If my oath was only of my blood and nae by my lips, mayhap I could flee. But I knew what I promised when I took the vow of the Levenach years ago. And I will honor that vow."

His hand fell away, and if it was possible for one of his nature, his tone grew even cooler. "What will you do, then?"

"I will go with you to find Laszlo, and kill him."

"I won't take you with me, Beatrix, I've told you already—"

She spun around to face him, at last dragging her gaze from the pile of damning evidence against her. *"Then I will go alone!* Your reasons for revenge against Laszlo are your own, Alder, and you may keep them if you wish, but mine are clear and not to be denied. I have nae choice. I may have shared my body with you, but it doesna make you my laird. *I am the Levenach,* and in this place, I rule. You are a *vampire*, and you have no power over me, tonight of all nights."

"No power?" Alder challenged, seizing her shoulders and pulling her to him. "Not even over your tender, mortal heart? I don't believe you, Levenach. You would have killed me long ago."

She shoved him away. "What of your own heart, Alder, white wolf of vampires? Does it beat for me? Would you shirk your vengeance upon Laszlo to flee the Leamhan forest with me and be my man?"

"My heart is not tender, nor is it mortal," Alder replied quietly, stiffly. "Our future together would be a sad one, Levenach. And for you, very brief."

"Perhaps not," Beatrix argued. She looked into his eyes for a long moment, contemplating the gravity of what she was about to suggest. "If we succeed—if we seek Laszlo together and slay him, you could make me one with you."

"Make you a vampire?" he asked in disbelief and then shook his head. "Never."

"You would rather leave me?"

"Than to condemn you to a soulless eternity, hunted like an animal for your evil thirst? Yes, I would rather leave you!"

The black woods around them were eerily silent as they stood in the midst of their heated emotions. No wind stirred. And yet Beatrix could feel an impatience radiating from the elm trees on this night of magic, urging her, but she could not discern its intent.

"Then we doona have much time," she said quietly. "This night, and only this night, which is already upon us." She cocked her head and looked slightly over her shoulder as she heard the muffled voices of the crowd of forest folk coming through the thick wood for her. Her eyes found Alder's again. "Go inside and collect our weapons. I have visitors to attend and 'twill nae aid my cause for them to see you in a temper."

"Are you so foolish as to have forgotten the feel of the noose around your neck?"

"That was a different day, Alder," Beatrix said and smiled in the dark. She knew she would never convince him with words.

Beatrix left him and walked to the inn's door, bent down, and raked a handful of chunky salt from a wooden bowl on the ground. She stood and turned, crunching the mineral tightly in her fist until it burned and bit into her palm.

"Tonight, I am truly the Levenach. On this night, I am"—she swung her fist, spraying most of the salt in a wide arc over the clearing. Where each tiny grain landed, a white spark of light sprang up, until the clearing seemed alight with a mirror image of the starry, black sky above them—"a witch," she finished simply. The sounds of the approaching folk grew louder. "I canna die at the hands of the Leamhnaigh tonight."

Alder looked at her display of glamour sparkling on the ground for a long moment but said nothing. He turned and began walking back to the inn.

Beatrix now faced the wood alone, the bright orange glow of advancing torches blinking through the trees at her like malevolent eyes.

The kitchen had fallen pitch with the outside, and Alder laid a trembling hand upon the old quiver that had once belonged to Gerald Levenach. Then he picked up the sling that held Beatrix's weapons. He held these things before him, studied them both with his vampire eyes. These were the tools that had allowed the Levenachs and the Leamhnaigh to survive these one hundred years since the slaughter that Alder had helped instigate. One hundred years ago this night, he had stood in yonder clearing a mortal man, an ambitious, power-hungry man, unwittingly unleashing an evil over this land and these peoples.

And Alder had sacrificed his own soul in payment, been sentenced to one hundred years of servitude to the hellish band of monsters led by a vengeful archangel who had used Alder like the animal he had become. Soulless, heartless, a cold shell of a body housing the rotten remnants of his memories of life and warmth and love. A killer.

It was supposed to end tonight. He was supposed to kill Laszlo and then take the lifeblood of the last living Levenach witch, regaining his soul and his human nature for the rest of a natural life. Setting to rights those old, evil wrongs. Ridding the land of both vampire and witch, forever and ever, amen.

A breath of mirthless laughter escaped his lips.

Alder let the quivers of stakes and magical talismans fall back to the worktable with a startling clatter and squeezed his eyes shut, his fists clenched before him. Beatrix's lovely, mortal face was clear in his mind.

He would get at least part of it right.

The hair on the back of Alder's neck prickled as the first inhuman howls reached his ears. He turned his head toward the back door of the inn, and the rotten, burned stench of old vampire wafted in on a frigid breeze. Alder's fangs erupted, and he felt his eyes dilate as screams of the Leamhnaigh fell like stones through water.

*Laszlo.*

Alder moved through the door once more, this time as if in a dream. The Levenach's weapons lay forgotten on the table.

The clearing beyond the inn was still lit by the Levenach's white witch fire, and enhanced by the score of torches carried by the woodland folk gathered in a mob some distance away from her. The light burned the images onto Alder's vampire eyes and he reflexively hissed, his anger, his bloody hunger ignited like an oil-soaked cloth. He swung his gaze to the sky, to the tree line, to the shadows that stalked the mortals in the clearing. He could see no sign of Laszlo.

But he could *smell* him, *feel* him and his minions.

He barely registered the Levenach commanding the forest folk, who clutched at one another and scanned the cold sky above the clearing before turning their attention back to Beatrix.

"You must flee now," her voice called firmly. " 'Tis nae safe for you here—there are killers afoot, and soon, this place will be awash in your own blood do you not heed me!"

"The only killer afoot is you, Beatrix Levenach!" a Leamhnaigh man accused, angling his torch at her, but fear was bright in his eyes. "The claim that you and your kin were the protectors of our people was naught but a lie! We were your own herd of sheep, were we nae? To cull and have sport with as you saw fit?"

"That's nae true, and you well know it," Beatrix said.

"It is true!" The man shook his torch at Beatrix again. "You're evil! *Evil!* Ev—"

The man's words were abruptly cut off as a black skeletal shadow swooped from the night sky and snatched him off his feet, leaving his torch to fall and roll on the dirt.

The crowd gasped and one by one the faces of the Leamhnaigh turned upward once more, their eyes as big as their fists, and they saw the swarm of vampires circling like the birds of prey they were.

Screams broke out as two more vampires broke rank to dive into the mob of mortals and, like herons at a lake, snatch up their food from the depths.

"Behind me!" Beatrix shouted, her own face turned skyward, keeping a wary eye on the hungry flock above her clenched fists held high. "Leamhnaigh, come to me!"

"Do it!" a woman shouted. "The Levenach is our only hope!"

Alder watched from the corner of the inn as nearly two score of woodland folk crowded between Beatrix Levenach and the front of the White Wolf Inn. He was deep into his own hunger now, so much that he could not help the mortals being preyed upon by the swooping and diving vampires. But he could feel clearly the glow and power of the Levenach, and his hunger trebled as she spoke.

"Ancient light, rid evil from my sight! As I command it, so it becomes!"

The roiling cloud of evil rippled and perhaps five of the vampires heeded the Levenach's spell. After only a moment, though, they rejoined the flock.

Their numbers were too great, their power too strong, Alder realized coolly. He could not care. He had to feed soon, and the only sustenance that would do was Laszlo . . .

Or Beatrix.

She seemed to move slowly closer to him as he watched her hungrily, and Alder heard his own feral whine as if from far away. His vampire eyes could see every strand of her fiery hair, every pore in her creamy skin, and the vibrating light that surrounded her. He could remember the feel of himself buried inside her, the tiniest taste of her blood that had been left in his mouth when his fangs had scraped her neck, and he was ready to take her again. He would fly down upon her, knock her to the ground, and take her body and her blood in the same moment. Before her precious Leamhnaigh, where they could watch as he destroyed her and know the truth of her goodness as he drank it, used it up. And then he would destroy them all. . . .

And then the most vicious scream shook the already trembling night air, announcing its owner's arrival like wicked royalty, and Alder felt its vibration to his black, cold core.

"Beatrix Levenach," the voice called, loud enough for the mortals in the clearing to hear, but also whispered like a lover into Alder's ear. "You *do* look delicious."

The sight of Laszlo le Morte strolling from the woods into the clearing like a dandy mortal caused Alder to go temporarily blind with madness. At last, there was the face that had haunted Alder these one hundred years—the pointed, bearded chin, the long, bony nose, the sharply slanted, black eyes. His arms were clasped behind his back, hiding from view the unusually long palms and fingers Alder knew he was so proud of. Alder could still remember the feel of those fingers digging into his shoulders, holding him down while his soul exploded from his being, his blood flowed out of his veins. . . .

Alder crouched and then sprang, flying over the clearing in a single leap toward his unnatural maker.

But Laszlo was older, faster, and not even Alder's supernatural vision saw clearly how fast the dark-haired devil flashed to Beatrix, bending her against his body, one impossibly long hand over her face, pushing her head away to expose the hump of her throat.

Alder fell to the dirt with a thud but then quickly sprang to all fours, ready to fly at Laszlo again.

"Alder," Laszlo said mildly. "Why, it seems a hundred years!" The demon chuckled. Beatrix did not so much as twitch.

"Let her go, Laszlo," Alder growled. "And put me off no longer. I will have your blood this night."

"Perhaps. Then again, perhaps not," Laszlo said

thoughtfully. He looked down at Beatrix, leaned a mite closer to her neck and took a long, exaggerated sniff. A greasy smile slid across his thin lips. "Well, well—fucked her, have you? And—oh my!—what are these here? *Fang marks?*" Laszlo nuzzled Beatrix's skin and laughed. "Tsk-tsk, Alder. Sampling the goods overmuch, I daresay. Perhaps you've already drank enough of her, then, for me to end your life once and for all."

"Test me," Alder dared him.

"I think I shall," Laszlo conceded. "Just as soon as I've had a taste of the Levenach's fabled blood myself. I, too, have longed to savor witch blood again, and once again it is you who has given me chance, so I'm certain you won't mind at all. . . ."

He began to lower his open mouth, long, stained fangs protruded, and Beatrix's right fist swung up from its dangle, smashing the remains of salt into Laszlo's face.

# Chapter Nine

Laszlo's claws fell away from Beatrix and he hissed as he flew backward from her. Beatrix staggered aright and spat in the dirt, trying to clear her mouth of the close taste of his stinking flesh.

The vampire swiped at his face, and in the glow of salt fire and torch, Beatrix could see the melted pockmarks the mineral had left in his skin, like a sheet of candle wax onto which hot embers had flown.

The salt would not kill him, of course, but it had bought her time to escape. And it had shown Laszlo that the Levenach would not make easy prey.

"Not nice, Levenach," Laszlo tsked, smiling through his pitted skin. He wagged a finger at her, and to Beatrix the digit seemed as long as her forearm. "Your determination is to be admired, but I do take offense. I would have taken you quickly. Now, I fear 'twill be much more painful if only because of your poor manners."

"Test me," Beatrix said, borrowing the phrase from Alder. "You die this night, devil."

*"Die? Me?"* Laszlo began to chuckle. The chuckle grew into rolling laughter as, with swishes and soft thuds, vampires began to drop to the ground behind him, like a demonic army.

"Going to put end to us all, are you?" he guessed in a condescending tone. "That's quite an ambitious task. I do hope you brought your supper along, Levenach. There is no mortal—or witch—who can match me. Your poor pet, Dunstan, discovered that too late. Smart enough to align with me, but too stupid to realize I had used him until he sat with his fat head in his fat hands." Laszlo looked to Alder. "Remind you of anyone?"

Beatrix felt the crowd of Leamhnaigh gather closer to her, eventually flanking her. She let her eyes dart to the sides and saw that they had collected the talismans once piled against the inn's door and were now clutching them defiantly in the face of Laszlo's fiends. The folk now knew the truth, and Beatrix felt her ancient blood, her magic blood, shooting impatiently through her veins.

"Stay behind me," Beatrix warned the folk in a low voice before addressing Laszlo once more. "It stops tonight," she said to the vampire leader, realizing at once that Alder stood between the two groups—Beatrix and the Leamhnaigh on one side, Laszlo and his vampire offspring on the other.

In that moment, she did not know with which side he would stand.

But she could not allow herself—or her heart—to dwell on the repercussions of whichever choice he made. Tonight was All Hallow's Eve, Beatrix was the Levenach, and she would honor her family's vow to its ancient and unknown resolution.

Laszlo's keen and evil senses must have caught her quick glance at the white wolf, for he homed in on it like fresh blood.

"You fancy he's in love with you, don't you?" Laszlo taunted, his children pacing and gnashing their fangs impatiently behind him, scraping at the dirt like beasts mad for the kill. "Perhaps he'll take you with him when you've put through with me, eh?" He belched his despicable laugh once more. "Alder might be here to destroy me, true, but he also has another motive, do you not, Alder?"

Beatrix could not help but glance to where Alder had been crouched. He was no longer there. Her eyes flitted about the clearing, but she saw no sign of him.

She knew a blink of panic at the thought that he had abandoned her, but dismissed it. It did not matter. Alder was what he was, and naught Laszlo could say would deter Beatrix from her duty.

"Hmm, wonder where he's flown off to?" Laszlo mused with a smirk. "Well, *I'll* tell you why Alder is here, and why he's kept such close company with you, Levenach—he needs you."

"Alder doesna need me to kill you, Laszlo."

"Oh, no, no, no," the demon insisted, wide-eyed. "You misunderstand. He doesn't need you to *kill me*, he needs your *blood.*"

Beatrix froze. "My blood?"

"Alder seeks his revenge on me, true, but do you know why?"

"Because it was you who made him a vampire," Beatrix said boldly.

"Oh my, yes. And I must say he is still quite put out with me for that. He wants his pathetic little soul back, for what reason I can't possibly fathom. He has come back to this place, on this night, one hundred years later, to try to regain that sorry scrap of humanity which I so graciously liberated him from." Laszlo paused, looking at Beatrix with unconcealed glee. "Did you hear that, Levenach? *One hundred years.* Alder is no stranger to the Leamhnaigh. He has been here before. Think on it for a moment, if you must—what happened here one hundred years ago, tonight?"

"The massacre," Beatrix whispered.

"Correct!" Laszlo smiled. "The massacre, exactly! One hundred years ago, I was led into the Levenach compound by . . . ?"

"A mortal," Beatrix choked out.

"Right again! And that mortal was none other than Alder the White, ruler of a small English settlement just beyond the border. He was hungry for power, and it was power I promised him. Drunk with the idea of it, he couldn't get here quickly enough! He was so very offended when the truth came out." Laszlo showed his fangs.

"I care not if 'twas Alder," Beatrix said, trying to overcome her shock and not let Laszlo see how it affected her. "You tricked him. He's nae to blame."

"No?" Laszlo challenged, amused. "Well, perhaps not. But I do doubt you'll feel so charitably toward him when I tell you that he's returned for a purpose more dear to him than my destruction." Laszlo took a single step forward and the folk around her bristled, readied for his charge. But the devil stopped his advance and only brought a grotesquely long palm to his mouth, as if imparting an aside.

"In order for Alder to regain his soul, he must drink from the Levenach's lifeblood." Laszlo straightened. "Of which you, my desirable little witch, are the last defender."

Beatrix's blood pounded in her ears. "You lie," she whispered.

But Laszlo only shook his head with a knowing smile, and in that moment, Beatrix recalled all the warnings Alder himself had given her.

*Laszlo stole something from me, many years ago. I've come to get it back, and destroy him. And for both those tasks,* you, *Beatrix Levenach, are the only one who can help me.*

*You're not safe with me, Beatrix . . . You're in more danger than you have ever been, the whole of your life.*

*After Laszlo is dead, I cannot stay. You wouldn't want me to, if you only knew—*

And just before they had made love this morning: *I don't want to harm you, Beatrix.*

She at last completely understood Alder's coming, and the point of his mission.

"Make sense now, does it?" Laszlo's grating voice burst the poisoned bubble of Beatrix's thoughts. She didn't know how he had managed to move closer to her, but now Laszlo was perhaps only five paces away. The folk around her were frozen, as if mesmerized by his evil presence, and the vampires behind Laszlo also held their places. It was as if time stood still in the clearing, frozen like the cold night stuffed between the trees.

Laszlo's black gaze, the color so like Alder's but colder than hell itself, bored into Beatrix's mind like frozen talons. His words were a sick caress. "Poor little Levenach—you asked him to make you vampire, but he refused. Didn't he?"

Beatrix nodded. She seemed unable to do anything but.

"*I* won't refuse you, Beatrix," Laszlo whispered, and now the vampire stood before her, over her, although she hadn't seen him move. "I will do it . . . right now, if you wish. Be done with these stupid mortals herded about you. Taste the true meaning of power, eternal power! Then you may chase after Alder the White forever, if you wish . . . only take my hand and it is done."

Beatrix looked down and saw Laszlo's unnaturally long and misshapen palm held open before her. The grotesque image wavered as hot tears filled her eyes. She wanted to scream "nay!" but her throat, her body, were frozen.

Except for her right hand, which was rising toward Laszlo's, as if of its own accord.

Alder charged Laszlo from the darkness just as Beatrix's fingertips hovered over the old vampire's palm, and locked together they flew across the clearing into the dirt with matching screams of rage.

"Feed!" the ancient bloodsucker screamed to his minions as he struggled to throw Alder off.

Laszlo had mesmerized the Levenach, but at Alder's interruption, she came to her senses and now rallied the Leamhnaigh as the howls of the vampires shook the very forest.

Alder wrapped his hands around Laszlo's throat and slammed the vampire's head into the dirt, but a moment later, Alder himself was rolling head over heels, his prey deftly escaped. Alder had barely come to rest against a tree when Laszlo was upon him once more, using his long fingers to scramble up Alder's chest, a hissing squeal ringing off his fangs.

Alder rammed his palm into Laszlo's nose and cheek, knocking the old one off balance long enough to throw him to the ground. Their heads lunged and bobbed at each other, mouths open, fangs elongated to battle length, each seeking an opening to rip and feed from his enemy.

Around them, Beatrix led the Leamhnaigh into battle against the other vampires, mortal screams mingling with hungry cries. The smell of blood was everywhere, the air was thick with death and magic and Alder could feel Laszlo's black blood so close for the taking, could feel the greater storm building around them.

"Your evil ends tonight, Laszlo," Alder growled, coming close enough to the vampire's face to rake a gash along one bony cheekbone with his fang.

Laszlo howled in pain, but then drove his fist into Alder's eye, dazing him for but a second. Alder felt the sting of fangs on his shoulder and rammed his knee into Laszlo's stomach, sending the black one rolling away.

The ground beneath them began to hum.

"You will never best me, pup," Laszlo said, staggering to his feet. He crouched down, at once at the ready, and Alder mirrored the pose. The two circled each other.

The ground began to shake, as if a thousand horses raced toward the clearing.

Baying hounds added their whispering song to the cries of both mortal and vampire.

"Do you hear it?" Alder taunted, even while the scar around his neck began to burn. "Does it sound familiar to you, Laszlo? It does to me, for I have had one hundred years as its companion. Its slave."

Laszlo's face, already the color of old bones, paled further. "Then you know that sound means your death." Laszlo glanced around the clearing quickly, and Alder knew he was seeking a way to once more escape.

"After you," Alder invited and then launched himself at Laszlo once more.

It was clear now that Laszlo was no longer fighting to kill Alder, but to keep his own blood in his veins and escape before the hellish band was upon the clearing. Alder's fury gave him the strength to contend with the ancient one, and indeed, overpower

Laszlo until the black one was facedown in the dirt
and scrambling to get away from Alder. Alder opened
his mouth wide and let his fangs scrape down Laszlo's
back, shredding his tunic and revealing scored and
seeping fish flesh beneath the thick material. Laszlo
howled and writhed on the dirt.

And then Alder felt the silver and gold glow of the
Hunt's light strike his face. The deep scar around his
neck began to throb, as if crying out to be reunited
with that golden tether.

Alder's time was slipping away.

"Release me!" Laszlo begged over his shoulder.
"The pair of us might yet escape! Let the Hunt take
the rest—you and I will build a vampire empire else-
where! We have the power—join with me!"

"I may join you, Laszlo," Alder conceded and he
stared down into those ancient, black eyes as the
screaming, winged horses stirred the blood-scented
air in the clearing. "But it will only be after I have
sent you on to hell!"

Alder dropped his mouth to the back of Laszlo's
neck as the vampire raised his face in a final howl.
Alder's fangs crunched into that decrepit old neck,
and he drank his revenge to its long-delayed fill.

# Chapter Ten

The vampires were retreating.

Beatrix heard the stomach-churning cry of Laszlo le Morte, tangled in battle with Alder somewhere beyond the loopy ring of torchlight, but she could not see them. And, one by one, the lesser bloodsuckers sprang from their toes into the sky, some taking prey with them, others delaying flight to finish their meal hastily on the ground.

Was Laszlo's scream one of triumph? Had he killed Alder, and was he now calling his minions away?

Beatrix's breath caught in her chest at the thought of Alder lying dead on Leamhan ground.

"Alder!" she cried, her eyes straining against the glare of the—nay, 'twas not only the dancing flames that lit the clearing now, but a cleaner light, both silver and gold at once, coming in rolling waves from the forest. The ground vibrated beneath her feet and the screams of horses rent the heavy air, now scented with perfumed smoke and the misplaced odor of wet iron.

The Leamhnaigh were shouting, running about the clearing with no real purpose, trying to gather up the bodies of the fallen, crying out names of those who had disappeared.

"It's hell coming! It's hell! It's come!" a woman shrieked from her place on her knees in the dirt, her fingers raking her cheeks.

Beatrix stood in the midst of it all, unmoved.

Sharp baying of hounds chased a rushing wind down the path, bending the thick trunks of the closest trees with woody screams. And then with a trumpet blast that sounded as if it came from the body of some beast, the gold and silver light exploded fully into the clearing.

And on that wave of light arrived a band of riders and monsters, the likes of which Beatrix could have never conjured in her worst vampire nightmare. Behind her, the Leamhnaigh fell prostrate to the dirt and were at last silent, only weak, muffled sobs breaking their terrified stillness.

Black dogs, some as large as foals, led the charge, loping and circling with their red eyes like beacons beneath the horses' hooves. But those fantastic creatures could only politely be called horses as they appeared only partially equine, with elongated heads like fabled sea creatures, their long, scaly legs churning the air above the ground, their glinting hooves only touching the dirt as the band came to a halt.

The horrors astride the horse-beasts were worse. The leader seemed the height and breadth of two men, matching the impossible size of his unnatural steed. His chestnut hair was long, thick, and fell down his back onto the horse's rump. He wore no shirt save a chain-mail vest, and carried a broadsword that looked as though it could fell a tree with one swing. The leader's eyes fell upon Beatrix and she winced, brought up one palm as if to ward off his penetrating and too-bright gaze. It seemed his eyes pierced her soul like a blade, and Beatrix felt naked before him, her faults, her misdeeds, written plainly in the rippling, golden air that hung between her and the massive creature.

In the shadow of her hand, she could make out the leader's companions: a menagerie of demons and corpse-like human monsters so vile that Beatrix felt dizzy. The reanimated dead rode with beasts from hell's darkest legends, bloody and wounded, with horn and scale and claw where human appendage should have sprouted.

The leader's horse snorted, danced, jarring the dirt and bringing Beatrix's attention back to the commander of legion. His broadsword was sheathed now, and in its place in his palm was a coil of sparkling, golden rope.

"Beatrix Levenach," the leader said, his voice like two boulders rubbing together, and Beatrix gasped that the giant knew her name. "I have come for the wolf. Where is he?"

"I doona know," Beatrix said, her voice breathy and dazed to her own ears. "He battled a vampire. I doona—"

"Alder *is* a vampire." He looked her up and down. "*My* vampire. And I want him returned to me. You of all people should be of little mind to protect the thing who once ravaged your ancestors."

"He came here for his own revenge," Beatrix argued, even though her voice cracked. "He fought the vampire who—"

"I well know Laszlo le Morte," the leader interrupted. "And why Alder escaped his servitude to seek the bloodsucker." Beatrix's knees grew watery under the leviathan's weighty gaze. "He has come for you as well, Levenach. You know this, yes?"

Beatrix nodded. "Yes," she whispered.

"Hmm," the leader said thoughtfully. His head swung away and where his gaze went, also went the brilliant light that surrounded him.

Beatrix dragged her eyes from the man's fierce countenance to that which he sought, and in that moment, she saw Alder.

He stood over a pile of glistening clothing, and Beatrix knew at once that Laszlo le Morte was dead. Alder's mouth as well as all his face from the nose down and onto his shirt was tarry black with vampire blood. His arms hung limp at his sides and his eyes were . . . resigned. He stared at the great leader with no fear.

"Most holy Michael," Alder said, his voice flat, and then he stepped over Laszlo's slimy, rotting remains and fell to his knees. "Have mercy on me."

Beatrix's eyes flashed up to the archangel. "Doona harm him," she whispered. "And doona take him. Please. He was trying to make it right. He saved my life, and Laszlo is dead."

But Michael behaved as if she'd not even spoken.

"Alder the White, you have broken your covenant." Michael swung the coil of rope over his head once, and then let it fly. A perfect loop snaked across the clearing and landed around Alder's bowed head, sealing itself over the deep scar circling his throat. "You will take your place in the Hunt once more."

"Nay!" Beatrix cried.

Alder raised his head to look at Michael. "I made no covenant with you, holy one."

"Indeed, I took you as my hunter rather than send you on to the hell you so deserved in your mortal life. That was our covenant." Michael paused. "But now that Laszlo le Morte is dead, I suppose you may choose your fate. Join with me again, or meet your final eternity."

"Nay!" Beatrix cried again and, heedless to the danger she put herself in, ran toward the archangel.

"Beatrix, stay back!" Alder shouted.

Rather than dance away nervously at her approach, the horse turned toward her aggressively, but Beatrix did not stop until her palms pressed against the horse's burning side, near Michael's calf. She hissed as her hands made contact and then screamed as Michael reached down and seized the back of her gown with one fist and pulled her from the ground.

He held her before his face, as a man might dangle a mouse by its tail.

"You try my patience, Levenach," Michael said pleasantly.

"Please doona take him," Beatrix pleaded, her fear causing her to shake in the grip of the angel. She could feel his power like the sun, penetrating her clothes, her skin, her very being. "I love him."

"You would love a damned creature?" Michael challenged. "One who helped destroy your entire family and even now needs you for his own selfish desires?"

"He need not stay damned," Beatrix said. "I know the price that must be paid for the return of his soul."

"And you are willing to pay that price," Michael observed.

"No!" Alder shouted and Beatrix heard his approaching footfalls. "I will not do it, Levenach."

Beatrix was afraid to look away from the archangel. Keeping her gaze steady, she nodded.

Michael gave the rope in his other hand a jerk and Beatrix heard Alder's strangled cry.

"Approach me not, wolf," the archangel warned. His next words were for Beatrix, still suspended before him in his tireless grasp. "Are you certain you understand what must be done?" he asked. "You cannot swear it and then leave it unfinished. I will not allow the wolf to exist in his present form."

"I know that Alder must partake of the Levenach's lifeblood, and I swear to you that I will see it done." Her voice was steady now with her vow.

"If you fail in this"—Michael's eyes flicked over Beatrix's shoulder—"I will return and kill you both. Evil begets evil. He will not be allowed to exist, and neither will you should you aid him in his depravity."

"Before the night has found its end," Beatrix promised on a whisper, "he will be whole once more."

"Beatrix, you know not what you vow," Alder choked.

"Very well." Michael lowered Beatrix to the ground.

As soon as she was freed, she felt Alder rush past her toward the archangel.

"Take me with you," Alder demanded. "Or send me on to hell. Only don't leave me here with her. I won't take her lifeblood."

Michael snapped the golden rope and it came over Alder's head, untethering him. "Should you not do as the Levenach promises, I'll return and I will kill her for her lie," Michael said simply and then coiled the rope with a flick of his wrist. "You are beholden to her vow—I make no covenants with vampires." The archangel smiled slyly.

Beatrix approached Alder's back, reached out a hand to touch him.

He spun and flung her hand away and Beatrix was horrified at the anger coming from him, almost as much as the tears in his black eyes.

"You don't know what you've done, Levenach," he choked. "You will destroy us both."

Beatrix shook her head. "Trust me," she begged. "Alder, you must trust me. 'Tis the only way."

Michael's horse-beast pranced again as the keening trumpet blasted through the clearing. The band of monsters that followed the archangel began a chorus of agonized screeching, as if eager to be away, but Michael had more to say to Beatrix.

"You have done well, Levenach, in caring for your charges, and I pray you succeed with this one as well," he said, gesturing to Alder. He looked over the clearing before the White Wolf Inn, at the bodies, living and dead, scattered on the ground. "Once I depart, the Leamhnaigh will return to their homes. They will have no recollection of the events of this night, the dead attributed only to sickness. Do I not return to kill you, it will be your duty to protect the people from Laszlo's leavings. Do you understand?"

"I do," Beatrix choked.

"So be it," Michael intoned. As the words left his mouth, a mighty gale rushed through the clearing, and Beatrix saw for the first time the massive span of wings unfold from the archangel's back. The hounds took up their mournful cries once more as Michael tilted his head back and commanded, "Hunt!"

The gust from his departure from the ground knocked both Beatrix and Alder to the dirt, and the band swooped into the black forest with a deafening roar. In a moment, the clearing was nearly pitch, the forest folk's torches and Beatrix's witch fire having long since suffocated in the dirt.

They watched as the Leamhnaigh began to stir. They paid Alder and the Levenach no heed, but only gained their feet as if in a deep sleep, some working together to take up the bodies of the dead, and slowly dissolved into the night of the forest path, in the opposite direction of Michael and his Wild Hunt.

Now alone, Beatrix looked to Alder and found him studying her with barely concealed rage on his drawn and bloodstained face. He did not attempt to hide his fangs when he spoke.

"You've damned the pair of us."

"Nay," Beatrix insisted, her voice still aquiver from the night's events. She rolled to her feet and held out a hand to Alder, trying to give him a smile.

Alder ignored her hand, gaining his feet on his own. He stood before Beatrix for a long, silent moment before walking toward the inn alone, his shoulders hunched, his head bowed.

Beatrix wondered if, when it was all over, he would leave her forever.

# Chapter Eleven

Alder stood in the smoke-ravaged kitchen of the White Wolf Inn, the darkness not inhibiting his wicked sight, and he waited for the Levenach to follow, as surely she foolishly would.

The stupid woman. Stupid and foolish and . . .

*I love him,* she'd said to Michael. To the most powerful and deadly of all of God's justifiers, Beatrix Levenach, witch of the Leamhan, had defended Alder the White, a vampire, and for him had wagered her life and her soul.

Alder's eyes squeezed shut, as if denying himself of his sense of sight might lessen the burden of anguish he felt. It did not. His chest and throat tightened painfully, sensations he'd not felt in more than a century, and the cold fire of vampire tears leaked onto his cheeks and cut the black muck that was all that remained of Laszlo le Morte.

He could not damn her, would not. Should he take just enough of her blood to redeem his own wrecked soul, Beatrix Levenach would turn from huntress to hunted, with a depraved thirst that would last an eternity, or until someone drove a stake through her heart. Her pure, magical heart that now held mortal love for an unclean creature such as Alder.

And as much as the coward in him wanted to, Alder could not simply walk away from the inn, leaving the Levenach untouched. The vengeful archangel spoke true—he would hold to Beatrix's oath, and return did she not succeed in redeeming Alder. Alder had seen Michael's wrath played out for one hundred years, and he could not allow himself to think of the myriad of torturous ways Beatrix might be punished for her failure. Perhaps the archangel would even do as he had with Alder, and enslave Beatrix as a hunter in his vengeful band. The only certainty was that if Beatrix was either made vampire or left whole, Michael and his Wild Hunt would find her.

There was only one other choice, the single thing that would ensure the salvation of Beatrix's soul, as well as her safety from the Hunt. And that meant that Alder had only a few short hours remaining to be with the only woman he had ever loved in one hundred and thirty years. A few short hours to make up for several lifetimes. To be worth eternity in hell.

He opened his eyes as her quiet footfalls scraped over the threshold of the doorway, and he turned to face her.

Even after his earlier rebuff, Beatrix came to him without hesitation, and Alder took her fiercely into his arms. "I love you, Beatrix Levenach. I don't know how that is possible, but I do."

The Levenach stilled in his embrace and then her arms tightened around his waist. "And I love you. That is why you must trust me, Alder. *Trust me.*"

Alder said nothing. She turned her face up as if she would kiss his mouth, but Alder averted his head.

"Let not your lips touch mine—I am soiled with Laszlo's filth."

"Very well," she said lightly. "We'll go below and wash you clean." She spoke as if Alder had but been toiling in a field under honorable labor, rather than dirtied by the deepest evil under God's heaven. As if mere water could wash away his sins.

She stepped away then but took his hand, leading him to the corner of the floor where the trapdoor to the cellar lay. Alder followed, every footstep drawing him closer to the moment when he would kill Beatrix Levenach.

Beatrix was atremble with fear and anticipation as she led Alder once again into the inn's cellar. The candles still stood bright sentinels in the corners, but the glow they emitted seemed different in those last hours of All Hallow's Eve—brighter, more pure, and sparkling with silver magic and mystery. The smell of stagnant damp was no more, having been replaced with the scent of a clear running stream in a quiet forest glade, a cool breeze chasing over the stones and making the candle flames sway sensuously.

Again she led him to the bed, this time to treat a wound more dire than the one he'd suffered from the falling timber. Alder sat without direction or comment, his long, white hair shielding his face, his shoulders hunched as if his physicality was at last catching up with his old, old age. She laid her hand against the side of his head briefly, her heart paining for the struggle she knew he felt.

"Trust me," she whispered again.

He said naught.

Beatrix let her hand fall away and then removed herself to the shadows of the cellar to gather her supplies. He had not so much as shifted his weight in the time she'd left his side. She sat on the edge of the bed and dipped a rag in the bowl of blessed water.

"Take off your shirt," she commanded gently. When

he delayed, Beatrix let the rag fall into the bowl and reached both hands for the ties over his chest.

Her action moved him from some trance, for he raised his arms and pushed her hands aside before they could touch him.

"I'd not have you serve me," he growled. "I am not worthy, Levenach."

Beatrix could not keep the bittersweet smile from her mouth. "Oh, I think you are."

He raised his eyes to her for only a moment, and Beatrix glimpsed such pain in those black, bottomless depths that she was forced to swallow before she could speak again.

"Throw the shirt on the floor. We'll burn it in the morn."

She was saved from his hopeless gaze as he pulled the blackened and stiff garment over his head and let it fall to the cold stones, his wrists dropping to his knees, defeated.

Beatrix kept her silence as she once more took the rag in hand and reached out to take a tentative swipe down Alder's right cheek. The sticky black demon's blood disappeared beneath the blessed water as easily as wind dispersing a pile of dry, dead leaves. Encouraged, Beatrix scooted closer on the mattress.

He did not look at her as she washed him, only continued to stare at the space between his soiled boots, but Beatrix could not help the welling of emotion she felt as she smoothed the rag over the white skin of his face, neck, and chest. How had she come to care so deeply and so quickly for a creature she was sworn to destroy? Did Alder's coming to the Leamhan forest mean that they were fated to be together?

Or would her ancestors exact a high penalty for her blood betrayal?

Beatrix could not yet know. She would continue to fulfill her obligation—now that the king of the vampires was dead, it was her duty to care for those touched by his evil. To Beatrix's mind, no one more deserved mercy and reward than Alder the White, who had not only saved her life, but perhaps her soul. She loved, when she had never thought that emotion to be in reach of the Levenach. The fear that ran through her was not because the great well might witness her act of mercy as an abomination, but because once Alder was whole again, he would leave her at the inn as he had found her—alone.

"There," she said quietly, setting the bowl and rag on the floor and sliding them under the edge of the bed. She waited a moment and then took a deep breath. "Are you ready to have done with this, then? We only have a little time left."

He turned his head—still bowed—slowly, slowly to look at her. "I cannot do this, Levenach. I have not the strength. The courage."

"I doona—" *understand* had hovered on Beatrix's lips until she once more looked into his eyes. The cellar around her seemed to fade to black night, making a tunnel of clarity from her eyes to Alder's, and in that narrow corridor, Beatrix *saw*.

She saw herself in Alder's embrace, similar to the way Laszlo le Morte had held her captive in the clearing. Alder's face was buried in her neck as a lover might do, only Beatrix's own expression was not one of passion, but of horror.

He drank from her, and she watched as her life flooded out of her body, her skin tightening and going gray over her decimated flesh, her limbs falling limp; her eyes widening, blanking. Alder raised his head, his own skin now a healthy pink beneath the tears on his cheeks and her blood on his lips. He laid her dead body gently on the ground, stood aright with a ragged yell . . .

And burst into flames.

Beatrix started, gasped, on the bed, and the cellar once more came into reality around her.

"You would kill me?" she whispered.

"I would not make you what I now am by only taking enough of your lifeblood to retrieve my own soul. It would damn you, Beatrix. But do you not fulfill your promise to Michael, he will come for you, and his punishments are worse than death, many times over. I care little for my life now, but you—Beatrix, you are yet pure."

Beatrix's head spun with the madness of what Alder was telling her, and he continued to speak as she tried to make sense of it all.

"I love you and would suffer the rest of a mortal or unnatural life for you, but we cannot share the same eternity. I must do what I can to save you. Out of my love. Can you understand?"

And then the crazy pieces slid into place and at last, Beatrix did understand. She smiled at him.

"You would spend the rest of your life suffering for me?" she repeated.

His frown deepened. "I would. But it matters not. We—"

"I'm nae certain that's at all flattering, but I will hold you to your word, Alder the White," she said, cutting him off and rising from the bed. She walked to the center of the cellar, facing the giant slab of black stone.

"Beatrix, what are you doing?" Alder asked from behind her, alarm sharpening his tone.

The Levenach stretched out her arms to either side, her palms facing the stone. She could not answer

Alder's question because, in truth, she did not know what she was about to unleash on them both. But she trusted that the power that had brought Alder to her would not forsake them now.

*"Fosgail,"* she commanded.

*Open.*

# Chapter Twelve

Alder's body began a queer trembling as Beatrix stood with her back to him, her hands raised, her red hair tossed by an impossible breeze in the close space. At her commanding word, the black floor itself, made in part from shining black stone, began to crack and slide apart.

Was the Levenach summoning hell for Alder? Something about her actions struck a fear in his heart colder than the vampire blood that coursed through his veins, and Alder wanted to flee.

Instead, he stood. He would not leave Beatrix.

As the gaping blackness that was the void beneath the stone widened, the candles in the corners of the cellar winked out, allowing first only night to flow from the crevasse, then shooting rays of silver light. Alder threw up a forearm to shield his eyes from the bright blades, sparkling like stars shooting across a midnight sky.

Beatrix dropped her arms to her sides and stepped back one pace, then a pair, until she stood next to Alder. When she turned her face and looked up at him, he saw that Beatrix, too, was more than a little frightened of what she had done.

"What is happening?" he asked.

She swallowed. "I doona know."

Alder drew his arm across Beatrix's shoulders and together they looked to the sparkling hole in the floor once more.

The first phantasm swooped out of the black like a streaking swath of fog, whistling a circuit around the cellar walls, tossing both Alder's and Beatrix's hair—white and red, tangled together. She turned into him slightly, and gripped his sides with her fingers.

The swirling apparition was soon joined by another, and another, and then what seemed an endless river of white erupted from the floor and turned the air in the cellar into a storm cloud, nearly deafening in its power. A cyclone of gauzy white, glowing, radiating energy and light, and seeming to push Alder and Beatrix even closer together.

Then, as suddenly as the storm had formed, it ripped into separate sheets and fell to the stone floor like giant raindrops, splashing into hazy, white shapes of . . .

*People.*

In the blink of an eye, the cellar of the White Wolf Inn was choked with scores of the spectral images, standing five and six deep against the walls in some spots.

Beatrix gasped beneath Alder's arms and pushed away.

"Da," she choked, running to one of the ghostly figures.

Although Alder could clearly see through their forms as if made of little more than smoke, the shimmery image that Beatrix ran to met her in a solid embrace.

"Honey Bea," Gerald Levenach said with a smile. "How foine it is to hold you once more."

"Oh, Da," Beatrix cried, and began to sob against her spectral sire.

Alder let his eyes skim over the crowd of figures openly staring at him, and he felt his fangs erupting behind his lips in instinctive fear.

He recognized several of the faces. Even after one hundred years, he could not forget. These were the Levenachs of a century ago. The victims of the massacre.

Alder's judgment was at hand.

"Is this him, then?" Gerald Levenach said to his daughter, and Alder forced his eyes away from the damning gazes of the ghosts in time to see Beatrix nod and swipe at her eyes.

"He did it, Da, as was foretold—Laszlo le Morte is dead."

Gerald nodded and his eyes pinned Alder. " 'Tis well. And what will bring the end of this evil, once and for all?"

"He needs us, Da," Beatrix said. "In order to regain his soul, he must drink of the Levenach's lifeblood."

Gerald Levenach's ghostly eyebrows rose. "Must he now?" He looked pointedly around the cellar at his otherworldly companions. " 'Tis nae only up to me, Honey Bea."

"I'll not do it," Alder said. "I love Beatrix. More than anyone I ever have in my mortal life or the unnatural one I have now. Better that you take me back into the depths with you than leave me, a monster, here alone with her. I will not damn her as I have been damned."

"Damn her? I should hope nae, if you love her as you say you do," Gerald observed with amusement. "Our clan will decide, as it always has."

Alder did not understand the cryptic answer, but

ignored it, dropping to his knees on the cellar floor. He now addressed the audience of spirits watching him keenly.

"I have done your family a grave and ancient wrong, and for that I am sorry. My greed and my thirst for war when I was still a mortal man led to the massacre. I was turned into what I am by Laszlo le Morte, but he is no more. I have hunted him for a century, a slave, and soon I will be condemned to an eternity of hell. Perhaps only what I deserve. But I will not sacrifice the last Levenach, the most good and noble human I have known in all my many years, to save myself. I love her, and I will not do it. I ask not for your blessing, only for your forgiveness."

He turned to look at Beatrix; silvery tears ran down her cheeks. "I will say again to you, Beatrix: I love you. And I also ask you to forgive me for not being the man you deserve."

"There is nae need to ask my forgiveness, Alder," she choked.

Gerald Levenach turned his head to appraise his companions. "What say you, kin? What is your judgment upon this creature?"

"Guilty," one phantasm intoned in a grinding voice.

"Guilty," added another.

"Aye, guilty."

And so it went, until all the spirits had voiced their damnation of Alder. When they were silent once more, he felt almost relief. He was guilty in their eyes. They would not allow him to take Beatrix.

"Thank you," he whispered.

"We're all agreed then, White Wolf," Gerald announced. "You are guilty."

"I am."

Gerald looked down at his daughter. "Let him be healed, Honey Bea. Give him the lifeblood."

"Truly, Da?" Beatrix whispered.

Alder frowned, confused. "No."

Gerald continued as if Alder had become less substantial than the ghosts populating the cellar. "You have fulfilled your oath. May our family's lifeblood sustain and protect you both. The highlands need you."

Beatrix threw her arms about her father's neck. "I love you, Da."

The spirits standing along the walls began to howl. Alder did not understand what was happening, but the cellar had started to cant queerly to one side. He blinked, and his vision blurred.

He blinked again and his eyes opened on blackness.

"I love you, Honey Bea," he heard Gerald Levenach call from the void.

And then the whirlwind started once more, this time invisible in the endless pitch of the cellar, and Alder felt himself falling, falling. . . .


"Drink, Alder," Beatrix whispered into his ear. It was still so black . . . but it was warm, and Beatrix was pressing her naked body against his own cold flesh.

"No," he mumbled, trying to turn his head away.

"Aye, drink. You must. The sun will soon rise."

He could hear the first tentative calls of the forest birds, rousing from their nests and announcing the day. Alder could smell earth, the moldering leaves. He could feel the hard ground beneath his bare skin. Were they outside? But how had Beatrix . . .

"Alder, drink," Beatrix insisted from the blackness again. "We have only moments."

If the sun rose upon him, touched his skin, Alder was finished. "I will not damn you," he insisted, feel-

ing with his every sharpened sense the impending
sunrise. "Let me be destroyed."

"Do you love me or nae, Alder?" she asked urgently, her breath feathering his cheek.

"More than my own soul."

"Then you must trust me. And you must drink
now! *Now!*"

Alder felt the hellacious burn on his skin, and as
he opened his mouth in a hiss, his fangs springing
free, a warm, thin liquid flooded his mouth.

Beatrix pulled the cup away slowly, watching with
frightened tears in her eyes as Alder writhed on the
ground before the inn. She hoped she had not been
too late.

She stood, her legs feeling like limp ropes, and
faced the rising sun, reaching its arms over the treetops as if to seize the man on the ground behind her,
who thrashed and gasped.

"Eternal Mother, I thank you for your bounty," she
choked. "The legend is fulfilled. Blood for blood,
right for wrong. Let peace come over your land and
peoples, and we will guard it well. Bind and banish
the evil, as my man pours out his sacrifice on this sacred ground. I, too, make my own sacrifice."

Beatrix emptied the cup of the remaining water
from the Levenach well onto the dirt. It pitted the
loose soil and turned it into a siphon, spiraling deep
into the earth with a whisper and a shudder.

Behind her, Alder screamed, and his cry echoed
one hundred years of pain and remorse.

The sun burst over the Leamhan forest like a fireball, tenfold as bright, burning Beatrix's already watering eyes. The morning wind took up a march
through the clearing, moaning with the satisfied voices

of her ancestors, the final trumpeting end of a century of evil, come full circle at last.

And then all was very, very still.

She stood for a long moment facing the wood, too frightened of turning and seeing Alder's body lying in a pool of nothing. Perhaps she had been too late, they had all been too late.

"Beatrix?"

At his weak and pleading whisper, she spun.

Alder lay nude on the ground, staring up at the streaked sky with wide eyes. She rushed to him and dropped to her knees at his side.

"Alder," she choked, running her fingertips down his cheek. His skin, once so white it nearly glowed, was now pinkening, his black eyes lightening before her disbelieving gaze to a blue that reflected the morning sky above them.

He turned his head to look at her, and those blue eyes roamed her face wondrously. "You're still alive," he whispered.

Beatrix nodded. "And so are you."

"But . . . your lifeblood?"

"It was in the well, Alder. The lifeblood of the Levenach clan is the blessed water that has protected my family these many years. You only needed permission to take from it."

Alder huffed a laugh. *"Well water?"*

*"Magic* well water," Beatrix clarified.

Alder's chuckle deepened. "I'm alive," he said, and held his palms before his eyes, turning his hands front to back. "Truly . . . *alive.*"

Beatrix also laughed, and when she saw Alder's teeth—white and even—her heart clenched.

He *was* alive, and he was mortal once more.

Alder suddenly shot up into a sitting position. He seized Beatrix by her shoulders, turned her onto his lap, and kissed her, his mouth warm and wet and aggressive.

In but a blink, her desire for him was raging, and she drew her arms about his naked body.

He pulled his mouth away from hers and stared into her eyes. "I want a family with you," he announced.

She laughed. "Very well."

He dropped his lips to hers once more, but only for a moment. "And you will marry me."

"Straightaway."

He turned her onto her back in the dirt and she shrieked with laughter.

"Are you cold?" he asked. "Shall we go inside?"

Beatrix shook her head and then framed Alder's face with her palms. "I'm nae cold, and I doona want to wait."

Alder grinned. "Neither do I."

And in that clearing on that morn, a new dynasty was planted, a magical and wide-branching tree that would grow and spread to protect not only the Leamhnaigh, but all of the highlands.

The following summer, the first white witch of the Leamhan forest was born.

# LAIRD
# OF
# MIDNIGHT

Victoria Dahl

*This story is for my boys, who are not impressed with love stories but might be impressed with vampires.*

# Chapter One

*Larmuir, Scotland—1595*

He was back again.

The man. Every eye in the inn slid away from him as soon as his foot crossed the threshold. Kenna watched him mark each face with his gaze before he made his way toward the table in the farthest corner. Not one other person had dared to sit there since the man's first appearance five nights before.

The MacLain, Cousin Angus had called him, his voice a whisper of warning. When Kenna had asked questions, Angus had shaken his head and stared hard at the ground.

But others had whispered. The last of his clan, they'd said. A curse handed down by the Devil himself. The MacLain's great-grandfather had killed his whole family, and been punished in turn. Each MacLain chief could have one son and nothing more. No daughters. Not even a wife. Just a son delivered of a banshee woman whose ghostly form was torn apart in the violence of the birth. When the son came of age, the father died. The solitude of the MacLain men was inescapable.

For five days Kenna had pieced together these

whispers, hungry to know why others seemed so frightened of him. He looked powerful, to be sure. Wide shoulders and muscled arms, and eyes that carefully measured each man in the room, as if he were walking into battle instead of sampling the ale.

He was neither handsome nor ugly, she thought as he shifted his chair to face the door. But his eyes . . . his eyes could capture souls. They were the pale green of drying leaves, cool and removed.

A hand closed over her breast. "Bah!" Kenna barked and slapped the head of the man closest to her. An explosion of laughter erupted from the table as the man protested his innocence.

"By God, she's bonny," the man next to him sighed.

"Keep your hands to yourself, peasants."

They all laughed, taking none of the offense she'd intended. She was a peasant now, too. Or something even lower. The local serving wench. The woman who brought the peasants their ale.

The inn was growing more crowded. Peat smoke mixed with burning fat from the spit, thickening the air with an acrid haze. Already, it had grown busy enough that she would no longer be able to defend herself. Once her hands were crowded with the handles of heavy tankards, there'd be no batting away the eager fingers of the patrons. They'd caress her breasts and slap her arse and even sneak an occasional hand up her leg.

Kenna wanted to slump with weariness. She wanted to retrieve her next load of ale and dump it over the heads of the nearest drinkers. She wanted to spit and scream and drive them all away.

But it was either tolerate the hands that groped her bottom or starve. And she was done with starving.

"Wench!" a red-faced man called, jowls quivering with the movement of his jaw.

Kenna ignored him and carried her last tankard toward the far corner. The MacLain might be cursed by the Devil, but his corner was peaceful, and he never tried to pinch any part of her.

In truth, she liked being close to him. He was . . . dignified. Charming in a quiet way, like the gentlemen of her youth had been. Whether he was in league with dark forces or not, the MacLain was a gentleman, and she felt pulled toward him, as if he carried a scent of her childhood home.

"Sir," she murmured as she slid the ale across his table.

He inclined his head. His strong brow cast a shadow over his eyes.

"Will you take supper this evening? We've bean stew and a leg of venison."

"I will," he answered. He rarely spoke, and Kenna found herself leaning slightly forward at the sound of those two words.

"And some bread perhaps?" she asked, as if there were any question she would bring it.

"Yes, thank you."

She didn't move. For just a moment, Kenna stood in front of him, waiting for him to say more and knowing he wouldn't. But then his wide mouth quirked up into a crooked smile. At the sight of that smile, she lost her nerve and spun away.

What was it she wanted him to say? *Would you honor me with a stroll about the inn, lass?* She knew full well how a stroll about the inn with a serving wench would end.

"Fool," she muttered and made herself keep moving even when she heard MacLain call out, "Wait."

She had no time for mooning about, staring at a man who could offer her nothing more than a tumble. She was busy and tired, but she didn't mind that so much. If only the men would keep their hands to themselves.

"Kenna!" Angus shouted from behind a barrel he was tapping. "Stop hitting the men!"

"They've no right to put their hands on me."

"'Course they do. Don't act so proud."

"I am your cousin's widow," she hissed. "How can you suggest such a thing?"

"I'm well aware whose widow you are. Why do you think I haven't sent you abovestairs with anyone? 'Tis not for lack of offers."

Tears of frustration welled in her eyes. "Well, thank you for your kind consideration, *cousin*. And you needn't worry over the men. My resistance is free entertainment for them."

"I know that. God's bones, I'm trying to help. If you stop fighting, Kenna, they won't be so rough with you. All they want is a tickle."

A tickle. Yes, just a friendly rub or curious squeeze. And if a hand slipped beneath her skirts on occasion, what did that take away from her?

Kenna picked up the heavy tray of trenchers and turned slowly back to the smoky room.

She'd done this to herself. Her parents had warned her, but she'd been young and headstrong and fancied herself in love. Alas, it had only been reckless lust that had driven her into the arms of John Graham. They'd married, and after a year of living off the charity of his widespread family, traveling from home to resentful home, Kenna had fallen out of love with him. After two years, she'd fallen out of lust. And after three, he'd died, and she'd had nothing. Not even pride.

Now she had food, at least.

When she set a serving of stew before the red-faced drover who'd shouted for her earlier, his thick fingers crept beneath her arm to twist her nipple. She only halfheartedly banged his knuckles with the tray before turning away.

"Well worth the punishment," he crowed to his chortling friends before giving her rump a painful squeeze. Kenna ignored him and served the next table. Two pinches and one rub later, she was down to her last trencher.

For the first time since he'd started coming to the inn, Kenna didn't look at the MacLain when she approached his table. She only pushed the stew toward him and turned away.

From the corner of her eye, she saw a movement of his hand and jumped forward. If even MacLain began to paw at her tonight . . . Kenna blinked back tears and fled toward the narrow passage that led to the yard.

This wasn't the first time that regret had overwhelmed her. She just needed a moment. Just a moment of quiet in the clear air of the corridor. Cold wind sneaked beneath the crooked door that led to the horse yard and stable. It carried the faint scent of manure, but the air was crisp and smelled of rain, and she dropped down to her haunches and laid her forehead to her knees to draw a deep breath.

She'd long ago ceased to imagine that her life was simply a bad dream from which she'd awaken. No, she no longer hoped to open her eyes in her fine, warm feather bed and go downstairs to break her fast with her family. Her father had disowned her for running off with a wastrel. So now she was only Kenna Graham, serving wench, and sometimes the reality of it was too much to bear. But only for a few moments. Even regret was a luxury now, and best saved for those moments before sleep overtook her.

A footstep whispered against the packed earth at the start of the passageway. "Lass?" a voice said.

Kenna cringed and took a deep breath. Time to get back to it.

"Mistress Kenna?"

That brought her head up. In this place, only Angus called her by her Christian name, and that was not his voice. She squinted against the dim. The faint light of the great room was blocked out by the man. When he shifted, the firelight caught his profile, and Kenna gasped and scrambled to her feet.

The MacLain.

"You did not look well." His deep voice rumbled over her as he stepped closer. His shoulders brushed the rough wood as he walked. His body did not quite fit here. "Is aught wrong?"

"Nay," she whispered. "I'm well."

"You seem troubled."

She could smell him now, a scent that reminded her of snow, it was so cool and pure. "How do you know my name?"

He stopped only a foot from her and frowned as if she'd said something odd. "I've heard it spoken by the innkeeper."

Simple enough, she supposed, but why would he remember it?

"Why are you weeping, Mistress Kenna?"

She shook her head to deny it even as she raised the apron to swipe at her face. How embarrassing to be caught here like a moody child denied a treat. "I must return. I'll be missed."

Though she started to push past him, there was no easy route, and when he turned to give her room, Kenna found herself pushed against the wall and facing a very warm man. His hand rose and he set his fingers lightly beneath her jaw.

"Why are you not afraid of me?"

Pleasure seemed to emanate from his fingertips and spread down her throat like droplets of water trailing over her skin. "Should I be?" she whispered.

"Yes, you should be."

The trailing pleasure slipped lower, tightening parts of her body that had spent long months in slumber.

The MacLain's eyelids dropped. His gaze fell to her mouth, and Kenna realized she'd parted her lips to catch her breath. Nervous and too aware of his attention, she licked her lips, and his shoulders tightened.

His head lowered slowly, slowly, as if he were waiting to be stopped. She would have stopped him. *Should* have. But he was giving her a choice in this, offering her time to escape, and that made her want it.

That strange scent of snow clung to his skin. Kenna breathed it in as his lips brushed hers. And that was all it was. Before he'd even truly kissed her, MacLain raised his head and took a deep breath. Her mouth tingled.

"What are you doing here, lass?"

"I . . . I just wanted a moment alone."

"Nay, I mean what are you doing *here*, in this place?"

She shook her head. "I don't know what you mean."

"You don't belong here. That's why the men won't leave you be."

Kenna pressed her back harder to the wall, trying to put a little distance between them. "They won't leave me be because I have breasts and an arse."

His chuckle shook through her belly and trembled her bones. "True enough."

Her heart sped up in excitement, and Kenna blurted out the first thing that came to her mind. "Is it true you're cursed?" The words seemed to come from someone else's mouth.

His smile vanished. "Aye. I am."

"I shouldn't have—" she started, but if she thought she'd angered him, she was clearly wrong. MacLain kissed her again, and this time his lips pressed softly into hers and his tongue teased her lower lip. Startled, Kenna opened for him, and his warmth invaded her.

She would have sighed if she'd had the breath, but he'd stolen it all away. He *eased* into her, a slow assault that devastated her nerves. She could feel nothing of herself but her mouth where it touched his. And then his tongue as it rubbed against hers. His hands where they cupped her face.

Their bodies were separated by no more than two inches, but he didn't push himself into her. He didn't press her to the wall and grind against her.

And when Angus shouted her name loudly enough to rattle the walls, Kenna was struck with grief that the kiss was over.

"Kenna," MacLain whispered against her cheek. His mouth trailed down to her jaw and whispered over her neck.

For a moment, she refused to open her eyes. She clung to the belt of his plaid and squeezed her eyes shut and imagined they were in a hallway in her father's home. Later they would dance and flirt and Laird MacLain would lead her to her father and ask for permission to court her.

And that kind of dreaming was exactly the kind of idiocy that had led her to this inn in Larmuir.

Kenna let him go and slid to the side to escape the shadow of his body. "I'd best return," she murmured and spun to hurry back to the taproom. She heard the door open and glanced back to see him vanish into the yard.

Wiping the last tears from her face, Kenna went back to her work.

Finlay MacLain's fangs burned like slivers of metal pushed into his jaw. He paced the stable yard and let them descend with a groan of relief. They still throbbed, of course, aching with the need to sink into her body, but that he could bear. He'd learned self-control over the past fifty years, though he'd never faced a challenge like Kenna Graham before.

The woman was a temptation of scents. When she approached his table, she seemed to bring her own air with her, spiced with roses and green grass. It wasn't soap or perfume, he knew that. Over the years, he'd gleaned hints from conversations with other vampires. Scent had much to do with attraction, and as a vampire, his sense of smell was sending him a blatant signal. *Have this woman. Take her. She's yours.*

Kenna Graham was a mate. A woman perfectly suited to his body and his needs.

A mate.

Just the thought of the word terrified him. He'd been alone for so long. The choice had been his at first, but now it seemed a decree handed down by a higher power. God, perhaps, if he still existed. Or the Devil, as everyone else seemed to think. Either way, there was no room for a woman. His longing for her was already taking up too much space inside his skull and causing him to do foolish things. Like watching her. Following her. Kissing her.

At least he'd so far resisted the need to snap the necks of every man who touched her. It was a near thing each night, and getting harder, but he'd resisted. He hadn't even stood and shouted a demand that they cease their pawing. Being associated with the MacLain would not help Kenna Graham's station in life, and it was clear to him that she'd already fallen far.

Her way of speaking suggested an education in a far larger town than Larmuir. He'd even seen her scratch out a few numbers on a table top during a long discussion with the innkeeper.

Kenna did not belong here . . . but neither did she belong at Castle MacLain. He shouldn't have kissed her, and he wouldn't again. She might think her current life low, but Finlay would bring her lower still.

No one should have to live the way he lived.

"One more," he muttered as he paced the length of the yard and back again. The rain soaked through his shirt, but Finlay didn't feel the cold. His body simply adjusted to it, dropping down to a lower temperature.

One more murderer and he would be done. His fifty-year hunt would be finished. The monsters who'd killed his family would all be dead. But this last one . . . This last one would assuage some of his own guilt, too. Surely.

Finlay glanced up at the moon and watched it with a measured eye. Another hour and he'd need to leave, and still no sign of his quarry.

The last week of September. That had been the deal. But Jean was nothing if not smart. As wily as a serpent. And he could likely smell a trap from hundreds of miles away.


"Move, girl!" Angus shouted, giving her a push between the shoulder blades. She would have turned to snarl at him, but she was too tired and still in shock.

The MacLain had *kissed* her. Quite nicely. If he was cursed by the Devil, the evil hadn't affected his lips.

Nor his hands, which had touched her with such gentleness. How long had it been since anyone had touched her with care?

Frowning, Kenna made her way to a table to set new tankards down. A hand cupped her bottom. She brushed it away. That kiss had thrilled her, jostled her nerves into excitement. But now that her pulse had slowed to its normal pace, she only felt wearier, more exhausted than she'd been in weeks.

"Just let me have a peek of that sweet little kitten," a thin old man mumbled, his hand closing over her knee. Any other day Kenna would have knocked her elbow into his head, but this time she just gathered up the empty tankards nearest him and tried not to yawn. She was too tired to care, and the idea frightened her. A month from now, or a year, what would she allow? A hand down her bodice? A playful quest under her skirts? And then what?

She didn't want to think of it. This one night was enough to get through. And then the next night. And the one after.

When the door opened, sweeping in wet air, Kenna glanced up only to see if it was MacLain. When a thin black-haired man walked in, she rushed to the back to ladle up more stew for the tables not yet served. Mary, the other serving girl, flounced down from the dark stairway followed closely by the blacksmith, still rearranging the folds of his plaid.

Kenna averted her eyes. Mary seemed to feel no shame in it, but Kenna did not like the glimpse into her own likely future.

It wasn't until she'd begun to serve the stew that Kenna realized a strange quiet had fallen over the inn. Her heart leapt in anticipation. *MacLain.*

But when she looked for him, he wasn't there. In-stead, the black-haired man sat at the MacLain's cor-

ner table. It shouldn't have angered her, but it did.
That was *his* seat. This stranger didn't belong there.

The man crossed his legs, his mouth angling up
into a smirk as Kenna watched. When his eyes met
hers, her whole body flinched. He smiled.

Heart flailing like a frightened bird's, she spun
away and pretended to swipe at spilled ale.

"Wench." The man's voice crawled over her skin
like spiders.

She froze, staring at the scarred table.

"*Wench.* Approach."

She'd never had any compunction about ignoring
patrons before, but despite her fear, Kenna turned
and walked toward him.

"I have need of sustenance," he purred, the vow-
els of his words thick with a French accent.

Still two feet away, she stopped and bobbed a curtsy.
"Yes, milord. I'll get the stew." There. That hadn't been
so bad. So why were her knees shaking as his gaze slid
over her? He only wanted stew.

But it seemed her instincts were right. Before she
could escape, his hand whipped out and latched on
to her wrist. The fine leather of his glove held the
chill of the night.

"What is that scent?" he asked, while Kenna tugged
at her arm.

"I don't know what you mean, sir."

"That smell. It's familiar." He tugged her closer,
and though she strained to resist, he moved her as if
she were a small child.

Smiling up at her, he pulled her between his knees
and slowly inched his face toward the skin above the
neckline of her gown.

"Stop," she whispered, her whole body shaking now.

His nose touched her breastbone, and the stranger
closed his eyes and inhaled deeply. "Ah, yes," he sighed.

He pressed the side of his cold face to her skin and slid higher. "It's the boy."

"What? Stop!"

His nose nudged her chin up just before he slid high enough that his mouth touched hers. "What lovely memories."

Terror soaked into her bones. A tear leaked from her eye and rolled down her cheek. The stranger dragged his cool tongue along her skin and caught it.

"He never did mind sharing," he breathed. Even the air flowing from his mouth was cold. Panic bloomed where it touched her, then spread down her body like ripples in a pool.

She reared back, but his arms didn't even strain as he held her. His smile swept into a grin, then the grin turned into something truly terrifying.

His mouth *changed* as she watched. Sharp teeth descended. Teeth like the fangs of a wolf, only sharper, narrower.

"Oh, sweet God," Kenna whispered.

"No," he drawled, his voice light with amusement. "Not God."

She drew air into her lungs, unable to stop until they strained at her ribs. And then she screamed.

The beast laughed as she twisted, straining away from him, screaming. He laughed and let her struggle.

"Help me!" Kenna cried out, eyes rolling to find someone willing to rush to her aid. Every eye was cast toward the floor. *"Please."*

One man rose, and then another. "Please," she prayed thankfully. But the men scurried away from her, toward the door, and left it swinging open as they ran away. Three more men followed. The others all seemed frozen to their seats.

The beast's hand curved around her neck, and Kenna expected to hear the snap of her own spine, but instead he only bent her down, drawing her closer to those glistening fangs.

"No," she sobbed, but his eyes sparked with delight at her terror. The fear snapped into desperation and Kenna began to fight like an animal, twisting and bucking and scratching at his arms. Despite his leanness, his body seemed sculpted from pure strength, and soon enough, the wet of his mouth touched her throat.

The sure knowledge of her own death rose over her like a wave. She could see it, looming and dark, brutal in its blankness. The end of her.

She screamed. She screamed until she thought something must rupture in her throat. Then she made one last, desperate attempt at survival and let her body drop as a dead weight.

It worked. She slid low, feeling one sharp edge of a fang cut her chin as she dragged by it.

"You stubborn bitch," the beast growled, curling his fingers into her hair. Pain exploded across her scalp as he yanked her up. The laughter in his eyes was gone. Now he looked angry.

She'd thought herself terrified before, but now she knew true fear. "Oh, God," she breathed.

"On your knees," he ordered, and Kenna felt her legs do as he demanded as if she had no say over them.

"Offer your throat."

"No!" she cried, terrified because her chin was tilting up.

"When I am done feeding, you will retire upstairs and await my pleasure."

"No. *Please.*"

His laugh held not a touch of warmth. "Save your begging for later, my sweet."

Behind her, the door slammed hard enough that it sounded of a tree branch cracking. Another patron escaping. A man who wouldn't stop her attack, but not willing to sit and enjoy the spectacle, at least. Small comfort.

"Unhand her!" The voice exploded through the room. *MacLain.*

The beast glanced up, but instead of alarm or annoyance, welcome flashed over his face in a quick smile. The fangs gleamed. "Ah, Laird MacLain. Never fear. They'll remember none of this."

"Get your hands off her," MacLain growled. Despite that her body shook with relief, the hair on the back of her neck rose at the sound of that rough voice.

No alarm showed in the beast's eyes, but he shoved her aside all the same. "You would threaten me over a woman? She's a tavern whore, you fool."

Kenna scooted as far away as she could, dragging herself until the wall stopped her retreat. "He's a demon," she whispered in warning just before her eyes focused on MacLain. His snarl matched the growl she'd heard, but that wasn't what squeezed her throat tight. *He's a demon*, she'd warned, but she needn't have bothered.

MacLain had fangs, too.

"Sweet God above," Kenna breathed, hastily crossing herself before she pulled her knees to her chest and made her body as small as she could. She barely saw the claymore rise, MacLain moved it so quickly.

"What's the meaning of this?" the stranger barked too late. The heavy blade descended in a blurred arc. The stranger became a blur too, sliding away from sure death. An awful sound jumped through the air . . . flesh and bone rendered from its body.

"Please," she breathed as the stranger roared. He drew his own sword—a miracle considering that his left hand tumbled across the floor toward her.

Whimpering, she pulled her feet in closer as the horrible remnant rolled to a stop six inches from her toes. But she didn't have time to dwell on that macabre sight. MacLain's claymore clanged hard against the other beast's sword. Though MacLain pushed forward, trying hard to cleave the stranger in two, the man managed to dart to the side and slide past MacLain's reach. He moved impossibly fast. More like a darting rat than a man.

His blood sprayed across the room. And then he was gone through the open door, leaving not even a shadow in the doorway.

Kenna watched, wide-eyed, as the MacLain turned, shoulders tight, claymore raised to fight. He seemed frozen like that, his body leaning slightly forward as if it needed to give chase and was held back by an unseen force. His back expanded with a deep breath. And then he turned back toward her.

She'd thought herself a relatively brave woman, but Kenna had no hesitance in playing the coward now. She buried her face in her knees and squeezed her eyes shut, as if she were a child frightened by shadows at the foot of her bed.

The thump of his booted step drew close.

"Lass? Are you hurt?" His hand touched her hair, and she flinched.

"Please," she begged.

"Your throat . . . let me tend to it."

She shook her head and pressed her nose harder to her knee.

"Kenna. Please."

He said please, but there was no plea in that word.

It was an order. But she couldn't raise her face to him, despite that he'd just saved her life. Perhaps he'd only saved it so that he could take it for his own pleasure. "Please don't hurt me."

"I won't. I swear it."

"You're not a man."

He did not answer. Instead, his fingers drew a gentle line down the side of her throat. "You're bleeding," he whispered, a low rumble that shook against her skin.

He hadn't denied the truth, at least. He wasn't a man. He was a devil or a demon or a goblin. But he also wasn't that beast who'd tried to eat her. Kenna opened her eyes and raised her face, but she didn't meet his gaze. As he tilted her chin slightly, she kept her eyes on his shoulder.

"It's only a scratch. He didn't bite you?" He sounded confused.

"I jerked away."

"You've a strong will."

She slid her jaw from his grasp and looked down.

The MacLain sighed, his breath ruffling the hair that had come loose during her struggle. "Come, lass. We must go."

That finally snapped her eyes up to meet his. He looked sad and weary and not at all evil. "Go where?"

"Away. Jean will return. It's not safe here."

Kenna pressed her fingers into the floor. "But I've nowhere to go."

"You'll come with me. To MacLain Castle. There's no other way."

"No!" she shouted, but she might as well have saved her breath. The MacLain leaned down, wrapped his hands around her waist, and tossed her over his shoulder. Despite her screaming, his step was sure and steady as he stole her away from her last chance

at a home. And not one person met her eyes as she
was carried away.

She was well. Unharmed. Terrified and facing a
life he wouldn't have wished for her, but unharmed
all the same. Finlay sent up a quick prayer of thanks
to a nameless god.

He'd been several roads away when he'd heard that
terrified scream. He'd known it was her but tried to
convince himself it wasn't as he'd raced toward the
inn.

Now new doubts swirled in his mind. He should
have left her. Should have gone after Jean when he'd
fled. But he hadn't known what that bastard had done
to Kenna. Hit her or bitten her or violated her in a
worse way. She'd been so pale and small, huddled on
the floor, terror and the scent of blood glowing off
her.

A few seconds of hesitation and he'd known Jean
was gone. The injured vampire would have left a trail
of blood for only a few feet before the wound closed.
Finlay would've been chasing shadows.

He sighed at the lost opportunity, then flinched
when both of Kenna's fists landed on his back with a
strength that hadn't waned in the two minutes since
he'd stolen her from the inn.

"All right, lass," he murmured over her curses as
he leaned down to set her on her feet.

She scrambled away so quickly that she tripped
and landed on her rump.

"Don't run," he warned as she lurched back up to
her feet. He saw the determination in her eyes and
shook his head. "You may run straight into Jean if
you do."

That pushed the gleam of flight from her eyes.

She looked nervously behind her and edged a bit closer to Finlay.

The new moon left it dark as pitch. Finlay knew Jean was nowhere near, but he felt no guilt in keeping Kenna on edge.

She shook her head. "But he must be dead. You cleaved off his arm!"

"He will heal. Quickly. He is in pain, but he is not mortally injured."

Her eyes narrowed as if his words angered her. "This makes no sense. None of it," she snapped. "What is it you want? Do you mean to eat me?" Despite the defiant tilt of her chin, her mouth trembled.

"Eat you? Nay. Jean didn't mean to eat you either. He was . . ."

*"Tell me."*

"He meant to drink your blood."

"Oh, merciful Lord. You're a powrie!" Her hand curved protectively over her throat.

"No. I'm no' a faery." *Nor am I small and wrinkled and ugly,* he wanted to add, in the hopes that she would agree.

"You're a servant of the Devil in some way." She shook her head. "I canna believe I let you kiss me!"

"Kenna, we've no time for this now. I'm not evil. I promise you. Now let's hurry. We must find a horse."

"Are you mad? I shan't stroll off to MacLain Castle with a monster! Just kill me here if you mean to do it."

"Oh, for God's sake, woman. Would you prefer to ride on my shoulder the rest of the way? I can handle the walk, but I wager your belly would get sore."

"What do you want with me?" she cried.

Finlay flinched when he saw the tears shimmering in her eyes. Her bravery had let him believe that she wasn't still overcome with terror, but now he could see that she was too scared to do anything but fight him. Kenna *was* brave. And she was terrified.

Having experienced more than his fair share of fear in his life, Finlay felt his heart twist. "If I leave you here, he'll return for you."

*"Why?"*

"To get to me. He'll kill you for revenge or keep you as bait." He sighed at the desperate confusion in her eyes. "I'm sorry," he added softly.

"I'll stay somewhere else, then. Angus has a daughter who lives on the other end of the lane and—"

"Jean would have no problem tracking you within Larmuir or even outside it."

"But . . ." She shook her head, helpless.

Though he wanted to reach out and gather her into his arms, Finlay knew she wouldn't welcome it. More likely, she'd scream. "Let me keep you safe, Kenna. Please."

"You're like him," she whispered.

"I'm not," he insisted. "I am cursed. But I won't hurt you. I swear on my father's soul that I won't."

Her hands rose slightly before falling to her sides. "I don't know what to do. *What do I do?*"

She wasn't talking to him in truth, but he answered. "If you want to live, Kenna Graham, you'll come with me."

Her hands found each other and her fingers laced together. She stared at them and seemed to find some calm within herself. A dog howled in the distance, and though she flinched, she didn't look up. "All right then. You havena hurt me yet. And he has. I suppose that makes the difference."

Anger washed over him, trying to mask the prickle of hurt beneath his skin, but there was no ignoring it. She thought him a monster.

And she was right.

# Chapter Two

The horse shied again, dancing toward the edge of the trail. Kenna noticed that MacLain let it step sideways and calm itself before urging it on. His arms were curved around hers, pressing tight, just as the rest of his body was pressed to her side.

For the first few minutes she'd tried to keep her ankles crossed together so her thigh would not fit so snugly to his, but her muscles had threatened to cramp at the awkward angle. Soon she would have to give up on propriety altogether and hike up her skirts to ride astride. A twinge twisted up her spine every time the horse put a hoof down too hard.

"Are you warm?" he asked softly. The horse faltered, then caught itself.

"I am. Thank you." His body glowed with heat where it touched hers, though she imagined his calves must be half frozen beyond the edge of his plaid. His legs would be covered if he hadn't loosened the length of it to wrap around her. "This horse does not like you, Laird MacLain."

"I paid enough for it to buy its undying affection, but apparently the beast does not adhere to his master's bargain."

"How is it that you don't own a mount?"

"Horses do not like me, as you said."

"Because of your . . ." She glanced over her shoulder, but jerked her eyes back toward the shadowed path when his breath touched her cheek.

"Yes," he answered carefully. "Because of that."

Well. Even an animal could sense his true nature. What a disappointment to know she hadn't the good sense God gave a horse. "How do you travel, then?"

"I run."

"But . . ." She glanced back again. His skin brushed her jaw, making her jump. Had that been his mouth or his chin? Gooseflesh bloomed on her skin. "But . . . but you said MacLain Castle is ten miles on."

"Yes."

How could a man run twenty miles in one night? How powerful must he be to travel such a distance?

The sounds of the night swelled around her, tightening the muscles of her shoulders into knots. Owls and crickets and little beasties rustling in the dry grass. Not one light sparkled in the distance. Not even the faintest hint of wood smoke tainted the air. She was alone here, the only daytime creature in this night world. And they were riding deeper and deeper into the darkness.

"Shh," MacLain whispered. She thought he was trying to soothe the horse again until his thumb rubbed against her knuckles. "It's all right."

"I don't think it is," she whispered back, her voice hitching on the last word. A few hours ago, she'd thought she had nothing, yet something had been lost since then. She could feel a space, empty and hollow, inside her chest.

"Dinna cry," he murmured. She felt his lips move against her hair. "I'm sorry."

The space filled up with tears, and though she tried

to hold them back, they spilled over and dripped down her cheeks. When MacLain urged her head toward his chest, she gave in and leaned against him.

"Sleep, lass. You've had a long day. Sleep now."

"I can't." But she didn't raise her head. The slow beat of his heart was as soothing as a lullaby. And regardless of what she'd seen tonight, the man still smelled of heaven. Of icy clouds and crisp air. "What are you, MacLain?"

He sighed, and the sound of it rushed against her ear. "I'm not sure I can explain it."

"Have you not done so before?"

"Nay. Never. And it's a difficult thing. Have you ever heard stories of a creature called a revenant?"

"I don't think so."

He shifted and tucked his plaid more tightly around her. Heat crept higher over her back. "There are tales of cursed creatures . . . Dead men who rise from their graves to exact revenge against those who've wronged them. They wander the land, living on the blood of their victims."

"Is that . . . Are you one of those revenants?" She couldn't keep the doubt from her voice. He hardly felt like a corpse. His heart still thundered against her cheek.

"I never truly died," he said. "But I have spent fifty years hunting for my enemies. And I do drink blood."

She felt him holding his breath after those words. She could hear the silence, because she held her breath, too. He'd been alive for more than fifty years? He drank *blood*? "Whose blood?" she rasped.

"I, uh, try to confine myself to cattle. I keep several cows."

"Why?"

"Well, it's easier that way, as—"

She pushed up. "I mean, why would you drink blood?"

"I must. To stay alive. I am a vampire."

*Vampire.* The word raised no alarm inside her head. It meant nothing to her. "Do you like it?"

"What?"

She felt his gaze touch her face as she looked up at him. "The blood."

"Oh. I see." He leaned back a bit, rolling his shoulders away from her. "Cow's blood is only passable."

Well, that answered nothing, but she could hear the embarrassment in his voice, and somehow his discomfort eased her own nervousness. However old he might be and whatever he might drink to keep himself alive, he seemed nothing more than a man in that moment. And what could she do, anyway? Question him until he agreed to release her? And then where would she be? Homeless and helpless against the attack of that French beast.

Sighing, she eased back to the hard comfort of his chest. "You won't bite me, then?"

"No," he rumbled in response.

She hadn't realized his hand had hovered over her shoulder until he eased it down to rest against her arm. His fingers curled to hold her. The heavy muscles of his arm were a weight against her back, and Kenna became suddenly aware of how much she'd missed that. A man's arm finding rest on her shoulders.

This man wasn't a man at all. And yet when he'd kissed her, she'd felt like a woman for the first time in years. Kenna was frowning in confusion when the night floated her up into dreams of bloody demons with angels' wings.

*  *  *

The sky was lightening to a midnight blue in the east. Occasional birdsong broke the silence of the predawn.

Morning usually filled Finlay's soul with exhaustion, at the least. Not physical exhaustion, but a bone-deep weariness that sometimes spiraled into despair. But as this dawn approached he felt something entirely different. Anticipation. Such delicious anticipation that he wished they were more than a half mile from the castle.

The cold had soaked into him in the past two hours, turning his flesh cool. But where his body touched Kenna's, he retained his warmth and absorbed hers as well.

Finlay drew in a deep breath, pretending to scent the night for danger, but his real goal was to draw the taste of Kenna Graham deep into his lungs. His whole body tightened as if his skin were drawing close.

He hadn't thought much of holding her when they'd first mounted. He'd been busy worrying over Jean and berating himself for letting the man escape. And then there had been the added distraction of the skittish horse. Still, he'd quickly made room in his thoughts for the roundness of her hips between his thighs and the feather softness of her hair when it brushed his face.

His regrets were vanished now. Strange. Very strange. He'd lived for nothing but revenge, nothing but absolution . . . nothing more than that for fifty years. Perhaps the talk of mates and what that might mean to a vampire, perhaps the tales had been accurate.

Finlay closed his eyes and pretended that Kenna Graham wasn't asleep. If she wasn't asleep, that would mean she leaned into him because she wanted to. It would mean her body curved so effortlessly into his because she desired his touch.

A brief wave of dizziness overtook Finlay for a moment. Feeling foolish, he forced his eyes open. It didn't help. Instead of picturing her in his mind, he found himself staring down at her mouth, faintly parted. Tiny wisps of white fogged in the cold when she exhaled. His cock tightened at the thought of leaning down and breathing her in.

He hadn't exactly been celibate since becoming a vampire. In fact, at the start of his new life he'd lowered himself to shameful depths of immorality. That shame had worked itself into his bones, but not deep enough to stop his body's needs.

So, yes, he'd had women, but he'd tried his best to keep his lust contained. He'd pressed it down until it was a flat, hard thing. Something bitter instead of sweet.

But now there was this.

Kenna sighed and rubbed the side of her face against his chest. His heart squeezed in response. He barely even glanced at the thick bailey walls as they passed. He'd made this journey countless times, but he'd never had Kenna Graham in his arms before.

A lithe, silent figure approached as Finlay led the horse past the inner walls. The mount was too tired to protest anymore. Its ears barely even flickered at the approach of a stranger.

"Gray," Finlay murmured to his manservant. "I've purchased a horse. I hope you remember how to care for one."

"Not so different from a cow, my laird," Gray whispered.

"All right," he responded, though he wasn't so sure of that. "I've also brought home a visitor."

Gray said nothing. Luckily, the care of Kenna would fall under Mrs. McDermott. Gray did not like people.

When the servant took hold of the bridle, Finlay swung his leg over and tried to slide off the horse in one smooth motion. Lines creased into Kenna's forehead just before she opened her eyes, arms flying out as if to catch herself.

"Dinna fear. We're at my home."

Despite his soft tone, her eyes rolled wildly from side to side. The hint of dawn was too faint for her, he realized. She could see nothing.

"Mistress Kenna, we've arrived at MacLain Castle. You've a chance to sleep in a bed now." Her jaw tightened, so Finlay added, "And nothing more."

He was anxious to get her inside, but Gray's voice stopped him. "Laird, we have a visitor. Another one, I mean."

That froze him in his tracks. He inhaled sharply, testing the air for the smell of Jean. No. That wasn't the scent he found. "Who?" he barked.

"A servant of the king."

A courtier. Damn it. They were after him again, and he'd put them off too long. This would be trouble and he had no time for it.

Kenna twisted a bit, making clear that she wanted to be set down. Finlay reluctantly eased her to her feet. "What's wrong?" she demanded.

"Nothing. It's nothing. Politics."

"Who is it?"

"Just a courtier. Nothing more."

Kenna frowned. "They know about you?"

"No." The king didn't know about him, but he and his people suspected something. Something that might benefit the crown. "It's nothing," he said again. "Let's get you to bed."

Kenna shot him a sharp glance, but Finlay pretended he hadn't meant what he'd meant, and led her quickly across the courtyard. Not his bed, then. Not tonight.

"Laird MacLain." The lanky young man bowed just low enough to convey the appropriate amount of respect and no more. "I am Guthrie, here as a servant to our king."

Finlay inclined his head. "And here I thought you'd come to break bread with me." The man's tight smile offered the exact opposite of amusement. Finlay's gut turned with dislike. He hated court and everything about it, and here was a man who clearly thrived on politics.

"The king requested that I come personally to remind you of your promise to present yourself at Stirling before month's end. In case it has escaped your notice, the month draws quickly to a close."

"I haven't time for this right now," Finlay snapped.

The man smirked. "You should be careful not to displease him. Again."

God's blood. He'd ignored James as long as he'd been able, but his refusal to show himself at court had only sharpened the royal curiosity. Finlay was aware of the rumors floating beneath the surface of polite society. No one suspected he was a vampire, of course. No one at court knew what a vampire was.

No, they thought he was a sorcerer, able to bend people to his will through magic. The king wished to find out if this was true, and if it was . . . Well, then Finlay would prove a permanent asset at court.

Ironically, if they knew the true extent of his powers, he wouldn't be allowed anywhere near the king. Finlay tried one last excuse.

"I have no special skills to offer the king, and I am needed here."

The courtier's scornful glance about the hall made clear what he thought of Finlay's words. "Regardless of your duties here, the king's patience is at an end. Either you arrive at Stirling Castle before the end of the month, or you'll be tried for witchcraft."

"Witchcraft! That's an outrageous insult."

"Come now, Laird MacLain. All of Scotland knows you sold your soul to the Devil. But only the king knows what you received in return."

"God above, that's ridiculous."

"I'm sure our liege will be pleased to discuss it with you. Or see you burned at the stake, of course."

*If I punch him, I will kill him,* Finlay told himself. His fist clenched, but he managed to keep it by his side and didn't even consider reaching for his sword. This preening bastard had no idea how lucky he was. Years ago, Finlay hadn't known the meaning of self-control. Destroying everyone around him had finally taught him that lesson. He wished it hadn't been so damned hard to learn.

"I've had a long journey, Guthrie. If you'll excuse me, I mean to take my rest. We can speak over supper tonight, if you like."

"Ah, I'm afraid I'll have to extend my sincere regret, Laird MacLain. I left my men in Doune and must rejoin them for the journey back. I arrived last night, you know. In fact, I can't imagine how I missed you on the road as you left. Passing strange, don't you agree?"

"Not particularly. I wish you well on your journey, then. Godspeed."

"And on yours as well, Laird MacLain. May it be soon." The courtier touched a finger to his brilliant blue bonnet, put his other hand on his sword hilt, offered a tiny bow, and left.

Christ, he hoped the man had the good sense to remove the peacock feathers during his ride or he'd likely be killed by hunters. Or set upon by brigands. Finlay tried, and failed, not to smile at the thought.

Light eked past the tight seams of the shutters, so it was past time for him to find his bed. He wondered if Kenna had managed to fall asleep yet. She'd been as skittish as that horse when he'd led her inside. The sight of Mrs. McDermott had seemed to offer only the barest comfort. Then again, the woman was fantastically old. Perhaps Kenna thought the housekeeper was a walking corpse as well.

He waited for Gray to confirm that the king's man was well and truly gone, and then Finlay took the stairs. The twisted hallway led to ten rooms, then up to the parapets above. But aside from his room, there were only three kept ready. Two of the doors stood open; the third was closed. This was Kenna's room.

Before he even reached her door, he knew he would end up standing before it. He'd stand there and wonder. He'd imagine her inside. Finlay knew all this even as his feet came to a stop.

Worried that she might be cold, he drew in a deep breath and caught the scent of woodsmoke and hot iron. Yes, Mrs. McDermott's grandson had laid out a good pyre of wood. The smell of fresh bread crept into the hallway as well, satisfying his next worry.

She was warm and fed and safe, and the sound of her breathing made clear she'd found sleep as well. Finlay could move on now, but he didn't. Instead, he stared at the latch and told himself not to touch it.

It didn't matter that she'd let him kiss her earlier. It didn't matter that her bonny body had heated at his touch and grown wet as he kissed her. It didn't matter because she'd thought him a man then, and now if she woke to find him watching her sleep, her heart might stop with sheer terror.

Ah, well. When she woke later, perhaps sleep would have stolen some of her fear. As for his own . . . Well, he didn't have much hope that his fear would fade before he woke.

Kenna Graham was his mate, and he had no idea what to do with her.

# Chapter Three

At first, the darkness was like a cocoon, warm and safe and familiar. But slowly, as Kenna tried to ease free of the muffling bonds of sleep, she realized something was not right. Her tiny room beneath the attic eaves of the inn might be dark and relatively safe, but it was decidedly not warm. And her regular pallet wasn't thick and springy beneath her back.

Eyes wide open, Kenna lay still and tried to see something, anything. Finally, an ember caught her eye, then another spark of deep orange. The glowing coals looked like the gaze of a beast for a brief, frightening moment, and that was when she remembered.

The MacLain.

A tiny squeak escaped her throat before she could stop it, but then Kenna swallowed her breath, forced it back, and held it tight within her lungs. Was he here with her? Was he in the bed? She listened for breathing, but heard nothing and sensed no one. If only it weren't so *dark*.

Before ten heartbeats had passed, Kenna had already grown impatient with her terror. She'd never been impulsive, and she couldn't stand to lie there wondering what might be happening, so she sighted her eyes on those glowing embers and eased her feet over the side of the bed. She could picture the room now, a simple square furnished with nothing more than a bed and chest. The door was to her left, and it hadn't been locked behind her when she'd been left here.

Forcing herself to stand, she moved three feet forward and reached her hand to the left. After a few tense moments of groping, she finally touched the wood of the door. The latch opened when she pushed it, and the door swung silently in.

Finally, a bit of light. Not much, but enough to see that her small chamber was empty. A candle sat on a table. Kenna wrenched it from the holder and pushed it into the embers. The wick caught, and she could see. Yes, she was alone, aside from the ghosts who lived here, and there had to be plenty. But after facing the hell-beast who'd tried to eat her earlier, Kenna couldn't summon up fear for mere wisps of spirit.

And what of the hell-beast who'd kissed her?

Kenna slumped back down to the feather bed. She was in MacLain Castle. With the MacLain. And he was some sort of faery or demon or *vampire*, whatever that might mean.

She couldn't imagine that she'd managed to sleep, but the bread and mead had filled her belly and muddled her mind, and sleep had been the only clear answer as to what to do.

But what to do now? Was it day? Night? She glanced at the shutters of the window and the three thick iron bars that kept them closed. Then she glanced at the open door. Well then. The easiest path seemed the best answer. Kenna pulled on her shoes.

Though she began with weak knees and a rattling heart, as the minutes passed and Kenna found nothing and no one in the passageway, she grew weary of her cowering and simply explored. She found the stairway easily enough, but when she reached the great hall, nothing moved there but two flickering rush lights.

Had she been left here alone then? The last traces of her fear hardened into irritation. For a great laird with the power of the Devil on his side, MacLain led a decidedly severe life. There were no servants rushing about, no pot bubbling over the fire, no fire at all, for heaven's sake.

Shivering from the cold and scowling over her empty stomach, Kenna ventured toward the small door set next to the hearth. Pray God there was a kitchen there, complete with fire and food. She could not face life with monsters without something warm in her belly.

Her perseverance was rewarded. In the kitchen, Kenna discovered a pot of parritch steaming in the hearth. No servants still. Perhaps the laird had called them all to his chambers to bathe and perfume him.

Laughing at the very idea of MacLain wearing perfume, Kenna retrieved a wooden bowl and spoon from a shelf and ladled out a generous helping of parritch to fill her belly.

She sat at a small wood table, but after the first bite found herself nervously glancing between the doorway that led to the hall and the smaller door that likely led to a garden. How vulnerable it felt, sitting here, waiting for a stranger to stumble upon her.

Kenna grabbed up her bowl and carried it with her to wander the hall. There was not much to see in the huge square room. One large table sat before the cold hearth. Four benches were pulled 'round it. An old claymore hung above the mantel, and two tapestries flanked it. The bright colors of the pictures told her nothing, though, aside from the fact that some long-ago ancestor had greatly enjoyed hunting stag. And perhaps that the wife had resented the time he spent hunting.

There was the arched opening that led to the stairway and on the opposite side of the hall, another opening to a room that looked to be a chapel. Kenna was hardly surprised to see it empty. She swallowed another large bite of parritch and headed toward the last point of interest: the heavy, iron-studded door at the front of the hall.

The bolt hadn't been thrown, so when she tugged the door open, she expected to see bright daylight, but she found the orange glow of a setting sun instead. It bounced off the birch trees that had been allowed to crowd into the flat yard. The lack of servants had extended to groundskeeping, it seemed. Only a few stones remained exposed in the bailey floor. The rest was grass and tamped dirt.

If she hadn't seen people here already, she'd assume the place deserted.

Had she dreamed it all? Everything? That seemed more likely than not, considering the memories.

But someone had made this parritch. And someone had brought her here. Someone with fangs and a bonny smile. Surely those two things shouldn't go together.

Kenna propped herself against the edge of the doorway and watched the light turn from orange to red to dusky violet. She was just scraping the last of the oats from the bowl when she spied a hooded figure come around the corner of the keep. It moved close to the edge of the castle wall, like an animal comforted by the nearness of shelter.

She felt a bit like a wild animal herself, frozen to the spot and hoping not to be spotted. But it was futile. The thing was headed right toward her.

Suddenly, its head lifted and dark eyes locked onto hers.

A girl. Kenna blinked, and for a moment, she wasn't sure why she thought the person was female. But there was something ineffably feminine in the small mouth and delicate bones of the face. Beyond that, she could have been a boy. Her black hair was shorn close and her sickly pale skin offered no hint at vanity.

"Good even'," Kenna said, because she could think of nothing else.

The girl watched her for a long moment, scowling, and the scowl identified her as the servant who'd held the horse that morning. Kenna had thought her a boy at the time. Without a word, the girl walked on, right past Kenna, as if she hadn't intended to enter the door. She looked angry, as if she wanted Kenna gone. Because Kenna added to her work, or was there another reason?

"If you're thinking of escape, I'd wait till morning," a deep voice rumbled from behind her shoulder.

Kenna dropped the bowl and whirled around with hands held high. They bounced harmlessly off MacLain's chest. Her little slap neither hurt nor offended him, it seemed. He merely inclined his head.

"You slept well, I hope, Mistress Kenna?"

"Aye," she croaked. "And you?"

"I admit to a bit of restlessness, worrying over you." He smiled and knelt to retrieve her bowl and spoon. "I see you've broken your fast."

"Yes, I-I apologize. There was no one about and I . . ."

"Will you sit with me while I break mine?"

What could she say? *No, I prefer to stay here and watch the moon rise?* But it seemed wrong to dine with a monster.

He decided the question by offering his arm and another of those smiles. Kenna gingerly put her hand on his, surprised when he flinched slightly at her touch.

"Are you hurt, Laird MacLain?"

"Nay, nothing like that."

And what could that mean? She glanced toward him to find his jaw tense, but he said nothing more. She'd never been much for subtlety. "What is it, then?"

He looked down, frowning, and seemed to study her for a moment. Then he shrugged and stared straight ahead. "I was watching you, standing there, and I was thinking of our kiss, and of how I admire you."

Oh. "Well, I . . ."

"And then you turned and I saw the look in your eyes."

"What look?"

A corner of his mouth turned up. "The look that sees me for what I am, Mistress Kenna. The truth is not always easy to bear."

She didn't know what to say. He'd been thinking of their kiss? Kenna ducked her head. It had been a lovely kiss, soft and hot, and she'd been thinking of it herself before. Before.

He was a beast, and yet he'd been the first man in years to treat her as a woman, as a person.

When they reached the kitchen, Laird MacLain waved her toward the table and served himself. Her husband would never have done that. He'd expected to be cared for by all and sundry. But the laird himself retrieved his own bowl and scooped up parritch as if it were a natural occurrence.

He took the next seat at the square table, his left knee jutting out toward her. As he ate, Kenna found herself sneaking glances at his leg. Crisp bronze hairs dusted the length of his lower leg, more sparsely on his calf than on his shin. Muscles bulged, as sharp as cut rock beneath his skin. She could just see the bottom of his knee beneath the dark edge of his plaid and was suddenly overwhelmed with an urge to touch it. To lay her hand on his bare skin and feel his flesh jump at her touch.

Her husband had often teased her about her physical appetite. Stronger than any man's, he'd said. And he'd been right. She'd loved that part of married life, and she'd missed it after his death. Until she'd grown too tired to miss it.

But now her fingers itched to smooth over those crisp hairs and listen for the shock of his indrawn breath.

Kenna fisted her hands tightly in her lap. "How can you possibly be fifty years old?"

"I'm not," he answered. "I'm past seventy."

"Good God! But you look so . . ."

He flashed a smile. "Bonny?"

"Bonny? No, I wouldn't say bonny. Not at all."

"Oh." He looked a bit crestfallen at that, and Kenna couldn't help but smile.

"I was going to say braw, Laird MacLain. You're a bit too big for bonny."

"Really?"

The smile was back, and Kenna had to remind herself that sometimes his mouth held fangs.

"Big and braw, did you say?" He looked exceptionally pleased with himself, just as any man would.

"Aye. Big and braw . . . and terribly old."

MacLain slapped a hand over his heart with a grimace. "Och, lassie. Such cruelty in a wee babe." His plaid rode up a bit, exposing an inch of his thigh as it flexed with the movement. A bonny sight despite her previous words.

And what the devil was she doing thinking such things?

The world sat heavily and suddenly on her shoulders. Her life had been tossed high in the air and she was flailing aimlessly. Flailing, indeed. Tumbling toward the ground and thinking of this man's *legs*?

"Laird MacLain, when can I go home?"

His eyes dropped to the empty bowl and he set his spoon carefully inside. "After I've hunted down Jean Montrose."

"You said you'd been after him for fifty years."

"Aye." He looked up to her, regret clear in her eyes, and Kenna knew this was worse than she'd allowed herself to imagine.

She shoved up to her feet. "What of me, then? What of my life?"

"I'm sorry."

"I canna stay here forever in this godforsaken place!"

"I ken that. I'll do my best to find him quickly. He's a foul-tempered rat. He'll try for revenge before going to ground."

"A fortnight," she muttered. "I shall give you a fortnight to find him. He'll have forgotten me by then, surely."

"A man who lives for hundreds of years does not forget things so easily, Kenna. It isn't safe."

"And this is?" She threw a hand out, trying to encompass his whole world into her scorn, but suddenly found that she was pointing toward a dour-looking Mrs. McDermott. Kenna quickly dropped her hand. "Good even', Mrs. McDermott."

The woman sniffed and shuffled to the hearth.

"Pack two days' worth of food," MacLain said. "We're off before the moon rises."

Kenna snapped her chin up to meet his eyes. "We? Me?"

"Aye."

She shook her head in confusion. "Am I to help you find Jean, then?" She'd do what she could, but truly her belly trembled at the thought.

The MacLain rubbed a hand over his face as if he'd already spent two full days on a horse. "Nay. We're going to meet the king."

"That makes no sense! Why would the king wish to see *me*?"

"He doesn't. He wishes to see me and I canna leave you here, not with Jean free. So we go together."

"But . . ." She wanted to sputter out a protest, but what could she say? *Leave me here in your cave of a castle?*

"If you've anything needs doing, do it," he muttered. Had she thought him charming before? "I can only travel by night, so there's no time for gnashing your teeth."

"Gnashing!" she snapped, but she spoke to his back. By the time she'd drawn enough air to yell, Mrs. McDermott was her only companion.

"Humph," the old woman sniffed. Kenna had no idea if her displeasure was directed at Kenna, MacLain, or both, but she'd learned from her grandmother that one couldn't win an argument with a woman that close to death, so she gathered up her pride, set her chin, and pretended she had things to pack.


"My apologies," Finlay muttered as he approached Kenna. "I had to bid farewell to the cattle." She stood with arms crossed, a plaid pulled low over her brow. The same plaid he wore, and it moved him to see it so dark against her pale skin.

One of her pretty eyebrows rose. "You really say good-bye to your cows?"

"No. Not really."

"Oh!" Shocked realization widened her eyes. "I . . . see."

He'd meant to lead the horse and leave Kenna be. He really had. But each time he moved into the horse's vision, it shied away in panic, eyes rolling. "Damned idiot beast," he cursed. Now that it had rested, it remembered its terror of his kind. Likely it could smell the cow's blood on him as well, though he'd rinsed his mouth with whisky afterward.

"Can I give you a hand up, lass?" He cupped his hands, standing well back of the horse's line of sight to boost her up. She accepted his help gracefully, though he could see by the tight set of her mouth that she was angry or disgusted or both. Likely both.

But as he tossed his leg over and settled in behind her, his body didn't worry over her state of mind. It thrilled at her warm curves, sending sparks of approval chasing up his spine. *She is warm and soft and lovely*, it crooned. And she was.

The blood he'd drunk had been meant to hold some of his lust at bay, but he might as well have filled his belly with goat's milk. His fangs began to ache the moment her round bottom pressed between his thighs. Finlay clenched his eyes shut and took a deep breath. It didn't help. As a matter of fact, it hurt quite a lot.

"If it wouldn't offend you, laird, I'd prefer to ride astride. My spine still aches from that last ride."

"Aye!" he answered too fast. "'Tis a grand idea."

If her hip weren't pressed quite so snugly to his cock, perhaps he could think of something other than tossing up her skirts. She shifted immediately, swinging her leg around and wiggling her skirts into place. When she finally sighed and settled back, Finlay's eyes nearly popped out. Now it felt as if he were riding her instead of the horse. Her thighs pressed all along the length of his now, from hip to knee. The cheeks of her bottom cushioned his pelvis. And if his cock got any harder, surely she would feel it pressing along the cleft of her arse.

Ah, Jesus.

He cleared his throat hard enough that she jumped against him. "Right, then," he croaked. "Are your feet covered? I'll have Mrs. McDermott bring another cloak if you need."

"Nay. I'm warm."

God, yes, she was warm. He sneaked his arms around her waist and urged the mount forward, his hips tilting forward with the movement. Pleasure heated his skin as they rocked together with each step of the horse.

For a half mile or so, he was so absorbed in his own torment that he almost felt alone. Foolish, considering the source of his pain. But as they passed the burned stumps of wood that had once been a village, Finlay scolded himself for his distraction and took a deep breath to clear his mind.

Instead of clarity, he found a brightness that struck him like lightning. "Oh," he breathed.

"What is it?" Kenna asked, her voice a bit rough around the edges. Rough, because she was aroused. As aroused as he was. He could smell the slippery desire of her sex as clear as if he were nestled between her legs.

If he let his hand fall an inch to her thigh, would she shiver and sigh? Would she lean her head against his shoulder and let her thighs relax? By God, he could slip his hand beneath her skirts so easily. Make her moan. Bring her to her peak right here.

He lay the edge of his hand carefully on her thigh . . . and his fangs descended.

Good God, they'd never done that unless he'd willed them to. He glanced at her neck where the plaid had dipped down, and he knew he'd bite her, full belly or not. He'd run his tongue along the line of her neck, and then he'd open his mouth against her skin and scrape his fangs over that pulsing vein.

A shudder stretched his spine. She smelled so good that her taste must be a banquet meant for gods. He couldn't imagine it. Couldn't imagine the hot flow of her essence flooding his mouth.

"MacLain?" she whispered.

"Aye, lass?" Her neck was so close now. Only an inch away. And her arse was a snug furrow rubbing against his cock.

"Um . . . Why does . . . Why does the king wish to see you? Are you in trouble?"

The king? She wished to speak of politics? He stared at her sweet white neck. So close. She'd feel pleasure if he bit her, especially if he aroused her first. More than she was already aroused, that is.

Finlay laid his hand flat on her thigh and closed his eyes at the tiny hitch in her breath.

"Laird MacLain," she said on a rush.

"Aye, lass," he murmured, stroking his thumb across the rough wool of her skirt. All he had to do was dip his chin and his lips brushed the hot skin of her neck.

"You!" she yelped, jerking forward so that her back no longer curved into his chest. "You didna answer my question!"

She tugged the plaid forward so that he could no longer see her neck, but her hips were pushed back even more firmly against him. *She jerked away,* his brain tried to explain as his hips urged him to rock against her. *She does not want you.*

But there was no question that she did want him. Her body made that clear. His mind eked out a bit of clarity from the cloud of need. *She does not* want *to want you.* And that was the last word. For now.

"What—?" His voice was a growl when he tried to speak, so Finlay had to pause to clear the lust from his throat. He tried again after exhaling very carefully. "What question was that, Mistress Kenna?"

"W-why does the king wish to see you if he does not know of your . . . truth?" Her breathlessness was small comfort, but it soothed his pride, at least. My God, she was responsive, as needful as he was, if not more cautious. As cautious as she should be. Canny lass.

Still, Finlay wasn't so burdened with caution, and he needed a distraction. Talking about Stirling and the king just might be the thing.

"There are rumors about me at court. They say I can bend any man to my will."

"Can you?"

"Not truly."

She twisted suddenly toward him, looking over her shoulder. "Why do you sound . . . Oh. I see. Your, uh, teeth are . . . down."

"They are," he said, relieved that she could not see the flush creeping up his face. "Sorry." Finlay closed his eyes and pulled them in with a grimace.

"Does that hurt?"

"Only—" Realizing what he was about to say, Finlay changed course. "Only sometimes."

"You're not . . ."

*Painfully aroused?*

". . . thirsty?"

"Och, no. I shan't bite you unless you want me to."

"*Want* you to? Who would want that?"

"Er . . . Women."

"Why?" she scoffed.

Should he tell her the truth? That his bite could bring her to her peak faster than another man's tongue? "It is considered extremely pleasurable."

"To be *bitten?* You must be mad. I wager *you've* never been bitten."

"On the contrary." She twisted toward him again and he flashed her a smile.

"Not by another man?"

"Oh, no. Not by a man."

Lips parted, she gaped at him. "There are women like you?"

"Aye."

"And they are your, um, lovers?"

Finlay's enjoyment in teasing her fell away for a dark, cold moment. He pushed back at the memory, slamming it shut like a door. "They have been in the past, yes."

"I see." Her body slowly twisted back to face front. "Is that girl your lover?"

Finlay shook his head. "What girl?"

"The girl who works in your stables."

"Gray?" he asked, half laughing. "She's my man-servant."

"She's a woman!"

He cocked his head, thinking. Perhaps Gray had been a woman once, but not anymore. Not if she had any say about it. "She is a girl, I suppose. I found her in Germany, living in a cellar. She does not like to be touched, Kenna."

"Oh," she responded quietly.

"She is like me, but she was turned too young and . . . used. By a whole family of vampires, you see."

"Och, that's awful. How old is she?"

"I'm not sure. Nearly a century old, I think. I found her about twenty years ago."

A shiver racked her body, and Finlay realized that her shaking didn't affect him now. The talk of Gray had successfully tamped down his arousal. Even now he was haunted by the memories of that cellar, and of Gray, chained and silent and as dead as a living thing could be. He still didn't like to think how close he'd come to missing her in the corner, though perhaps she'd have been relieved to starve to death there in the dark.

The horse sidestepped suddenly, as if it had been startled. Finlay held up a hand and swung down, handing the reins to Kenna. He silently stepped back, moving away from the horse so that it wouldn't bolt, then he drew a deep breath. He smelled not blood and cool flesh as he'd feared, but dank fur and urine. A wolf perhaps, marking its territory. Listening closely, he heard the faint rustle of brush far away and then farther still. There was no danger, unless the beast led a pack back toward them.

Trying to hum a soothing noise deep in his throat, Finlay moved back toward the horse, willing it not to startle. Though it shifted nervously, it stayed still as he remounted behind Kenna.

"What is it?" she whispered.

"Not Jean," he answered simply, and she nodded, needing to hear no more than that.

It had been a very long time since she'd been so aroused, and Kenna had forgotten how singularly distracting it could be. And she couldn't escape it, not with Laird MacLain's body wrapped so thoroughly around hers. Even past her skirt and his plaid, she'd felt the ridge of his arousal against her. It felt exactly like a normal man's, as did his hard thighs and hot arms and wide, solid chest behind her.

Normal, yes, but all of him very, very large.

But he wasn't just another man, and she had to remind herself of it every ten seconds or so. Yes, he had a lovely mouth. And yes, his long fingers made her think of lovely things, but he had *fangs*. Fangs he wanted to bite her with, apparently.

She wasn't as scared of that as she should be. And the longer she stayed in his arms, the less frightening he seemed. "How long before we reach Stirling?"

"Hopefully we'll be there by daybreak. We'd best be."

"Why?"

"I canna travel by day. We are night creatures. The light blinds us. You should remember that if we become separated. Jean cannot see in the daylight, and the sun will easily burn his skin."

"Oh." Well, she had the opportunity to ask the question that had been haunting her for miles. "If I were, um, bitten, would I become like you?" she blurted out. She could have sworn that she felt his gaze fall to her neck again.

"Nay. It can be done, as it was done to me, but it takes purpose. Nothing so simple as a single bite."

"I see." The silence seemed too fraught with meaning as she wondered if he knew why she'd ask. Not because of Jean, but because of the vampire whose hand rested even now on her thigh. "Thank you for answering my questions, Laird MacLain," she blurted out.

He only grunted in answer, but did his fingers spread wider over her thigh? He had to rest his hand somewhere, of course, and her waist would be no better, for she'd spend her time tracking any movement of his thumb, wondering if he meant to brush a touch against the underside of her breast.

Kenna's nipples tightened at the thought.

His quiet voice startled her. "Will you call me Finlay?"

"Finlay? Why?"

"'Tis my name."

"Well, I gathered that." Finlay. It fit him, somehow.

"'Tis my name and no one's called me it in fifty years." His words were so careful that she knew he was saying something important.

"Why?" she whispered.

"Because," he answered simply, pausing as if that were all he would say. "Because they're all dead."

The night seemed too dark of a sudden. Perhaps a cloud had passed over the bare light of the new moon, or perhaps it was the emptiness of his words.

"But the legends say that your father and your grandfather and—"

"Nay, 'tis only me. 'Tis always me, Kenna."

"But . . ." But that was horrible. He'd lived in that empty place for fifty years? "Laird MacLain—" she started, and felt him flinch behind her.

"Finlay," she corrected, "what happened to the rest of your family, your clan? There must have been others before."

"Aye. We were a small enough clan, but we were fierce and proud. As to what happened . . ." She felt him roll his shoulders behind her, his spine giving in with a faint pop. "I bear the blood of sixty-two souls on my hands, my father's blood included."

"But you could not have killed them!" Her strange conviction made no sense, but she felt so sure of him.

"I may as well have. But it doesna matter now. After I kill Jean Montrose I'll be done."

"Done?" she whispered. His hand had left her leg and now her thigh was cold. "Done with what?"

She held her breath, waiting. His answer was important, though she couldn't say why. So she held her breath and listened carefully for an answer that didn't come. In the end, he only shrugged, and a cold chill swept down her body.

That place he lived in might be called Castle MacLain, but it was no home. It was a place where he slept. She thought of his time at the inn where he sat and waited. He spoke to no one, never tapped a foot when the piper struck up playing. He had only ever waited, his eyes on the door. Waiting for it to be done.

"Will you live forever?" she asked.

"Nay. A few hundred years, I gather."

"And can you be killed?"

"Are you planning to rid yourself of me, lassie? Well, it won't be easy, but it's hardly impossible. I've got to bleed out quickly, ye ken? A knife to the heart or across the throat will do it. But I'd prefer you use your knowledge against Jean and not me."

"Aye," she whispered. "Of course."

"Enough of that, now, or you'll have bad dreams. Tell me about your marriage. You must have still been in your cradle when you married."

She was so surprised by the sudden charm in his voice that she laughed. "Are you trying to flatter me into changing the subject?"

"Perhaps. Now tell me of your husband."

"My husband," she murmured, settling back against his chest. "I met him when I was seventeen and we were married within the month. My family did not approve and so we depended on his. He was very handsome and funny, and lazy as the day was long. We were happy for a while, and then we were not, and then he was dead."

"I'm sorry."

She felt his chin settle on her shoulder and sighed with contentment. "I was young and foolish, a common enough condition. Did you never marry?"

"Nay. I was young and foolish as well, but more interested in falling in love with as many women as I could, preferably several at once."

"Ah, yes. An even more common ailment among young men."

"I was quite afflicted."

She smiled, turning her head toward his chin. "I can't really imagine."

"Ha. Neither can I. Not anymore. Now I cannot even charm an old widow trapped between my thighs for miles at a time."

"Oh, goodness." She laughed, clapping a hand over her mouth as the sound echoed through the trees.

"It's all right," he said. "There's no one about."

And so Kenna laughed, loud and long, and wondered when she'd last done so.

# Chapter Four

"Try your best not to speak with anyone," Finlay murmured as the gates of the castle came into view. Dawn glimmered on the horizon. "Once we are shown to our rooms, you must remain there until I come for you. You cannot trust anyone."

"Come now. It can't be so bad as all that. My mother dreamed of being invited to court."

"Kenna, they are threatening to charge me with witchcraft. They would rather I be burned than walk free of their web."

"*Witchcraft?* What is it you can *do?*"

"I am quite good at persuading people to my point of view."

She shook her head. "You implied that already. How do you do it?"

A sleepy-eyed soldier watched them as they rode up the hill. "Later, Kenna." He tucked her cloak more carefully over her legs, mindful of the number of soldiers they'd be passing. She'd rearranged herself to sit aside before they'd entered the town, but she'd grimaced in pain as she'd done so. He'd see her tucked into bed before he presented himself to the king.

"You willna . . . ?" he started, then paused to wonder if he should ask. She'd seemed to accept him, but then she'd not had much choice alone in his castle. "You willna tell them the truth?"

"Why would I do that?"

"You've made clear you think me a beast, Kenna. A monster cursed by the Devil himself."

She didn't answer for a long while, and Finlay held his breath, waiting for her response.

"I believe that you're cursed," she finally said, her voice low as the breeze. "But 'tis clear to me now that you're not so different from other men."

Finlay pulled his chin back. What did that mean? He opened his mouth to press her further, but then they were passing through the outer gates under the careful watch of eight armed soldiers.

"Laird Finlay MacLain," he announced to the two soldiers who stepped in front of the mount. "Here at the request of the king."

The soldier on the left glanced to his side and must have received a signal, because he waved them on toward the inner gate. They were stopped once more, and then they were through.

He felt Kenna shift in the saddle as a boy rushed forward to grab hold of the bridle.

"Finlay," she whispered. "I'm not sure I can."

"It's all right. I've got you." He jumped down and eased her slowly to the ground, aware that her weight rested heavy on his hands.

"Are you not the least bit stiff?" she muttered.

"Nay." He glanced toward the east. "But my eyes are beginning to burn, if that soothes your pride."

"Oh!" She stood a little straighter, though he clearly felt the way her muscles stiffened and twitched. "We must get you inside."

The worry in her voice made him smile. "I'll survive. Would you like me to carry you?"

"Of course not!" Her outrage gave Kenna the last bit of strength she needed to stand on her own, but she moved slowly as they followed a servant inside and were shown upstairs to a small room. With one small bed.

"I canna pass you off as my wife, I'm afraid."

She shrugged. "I understand. It's not such a hardship to be known as your leman. An elevation from serving wench, I'd say."

"I'll take that as a compliment, lass."

"You would."

He left her to her privacy for a moment and hunted down some hot food. Not easy at this early hour, but there was fresh bread and warm mead, at least. The closed shutters of their chambers provided all the protection he needed from the sun, as they faced north and couldn't have coaxed much light if they tried. After the hurried meal, Kenna slumped with weariness.

"The king won't receive me for hours, at least. We should sleep."

With only a mildly concerned glance at the bed, Kenna nodded. He tried his best not to anticipate anything other than sleep. That alone seemed a fine enough pleasure at the moment.

He laid his claymore on the floor within reach and Kenna took the other side. But there wasn't much of a "side" to the narrow frame. When he stretched out on the straw ticking, his front pressed against her back in several interesting places.

"I'm sorry," he said, but Kenna raised a hand to wave his apology aside.

"We've been closer than this for hours."

Yes, but they hadn't been in a *bed*. Did she not know the difference?

He'd grown used to the smell of her hair on their

journey, but now he was aware of it again, the scent tempting him to bury his face in the nape of her neck and breathe. The same scent as her skin, only warmer.

Closing his eyes, he tried not to think of her fragrance. Or her plump bottom pressed against his groin. Or the way his knees fit so close behind hers.

"Kenna," he whispered, smoothing back a lock of hair from her face. His fingers memorized the feel of her cheek beneath them.

"Mm?"

"If I'm not here when you wake, don't venture out. Wait for me."

"Mm-hm."

He watched his fingers stray down to the soft skin behind her ear. She was nearly asleep. If he kissed her there, would she even notice? It would gain him nothing but aching, but Finlay couldn't resist. Her scent tugged at him, swelling more than just his cock. Despite everything she'd been through in the past twenty-four hours, she was still so strong and steady. A mate he could be proud of, if only his life were fit for her. It wasn't.

He stretched forward, letting his breath touch her ear. Kenna didn't move. She didn't protest. But he knew she wasn't asleep after all, for her breath hitched. He waited two heartbeats, then three. Finally he shifted the smallest amount and his mouth touched that spot, the bare skin just behind the shell of her ear.

He pressed his lips there and drew in her scent, holding it in his lungs as long as he could. Her heart sped, pounding until he could hear the individual thumps of the blood rushing in and out, in and out. The life of her, pulsing below his mouth.

His fangs stretched, but he ignored them with only a small bit of difficulty. She was tired. Exhausted.

But it seemed she did know the difference between a horse and a bed. Her body needed no more than that small kiss to rouse itself and call to him. Finlay lay back and let her be, but the scent of her quick arousal followed him deep into sleep.

Kenna woke to the slamming of a door. "Oh!" she gasped, disoriented by the pale blur that surrounded her.

"I'm sorry," MacLain's voice said. "I didna mean to startle you." Part of the blur shifted, and Kenna realized he'd pulled the bedcurtains around her before he'd left.

"Have I slept too long?"

"Nay. The king willna see me. He's making a point, I believe." The anger in his voice raised the hairs on her arms.

"What will we do?"

"We'll wait till the morning. If his man refuses me again, I'll have no choice."

She shook her head, still muddled by too much sleep in the middle of the day. "What do you mean?"

"I must find Jean. I canna lose him again." He gave her a hot look. "I canna."

"You'll defy the king?"

"On the contrary. I will see him. And I'll show him the skill he's so eager to witness."

Kenna started to nod and then found herself shaking her head. "I don't understand any of this, Finlay."

His eyebrows twitched up at the sound of his name. Then he nodded and sat hard on the mattress. "I ken how strange this must be to you. You're verra brave."

"I'm verra confused!" And she was. She did not know whether she should run from him or pull him down upon her. Each time he touched her, she burned with want and pleasure. That couldn't be right. It couldn't. "Why must you kill Jean?"

"Because he's a monster."

"But why *you*?"

His head bowed and he sat quietly, not even breathing as far as she could tell. She watched him, noticing the fine white leine he wore and the silver pin that held his plaid in place. His hair was neatly combed and his jaw freshly shaven. He even wore stitched stockings that hugged his calves.

"I met him here," he said softly. "Him and his band of Frenchmen. I was nae more interested in politics then than I am now. But I liked the women here, you understand. I was twenty-two and I cared for little but women and whisky."

"Aye. As most young men do."

"And the women with Jean, they were beautiful and verra . . . wicked."

Kenna felt her face flush as she nodded. A mixture of embarrassment and jealousy warmed her skin.

"And when he suggested we all retire to MacLain Castle for a spell, it seemed a grand idea. My father remained at court, so he had no idea what was happening."

"What was happening?" she whispered.

MacLain shrugged and she watched his face grow pale. "Jean liked it there. It was secluded. The people were . . . unsophisticated. And I was . . . I don't know. I entertained him, I suppose. So they turned me. I'm not even sure when."

"What do you mean?"

"They took turns draining me of blood and feeding me their own."

"That's how it's done?"

"Aye. It takes a few days, but I'm not even sure when I stopped being human and became a vampire. They'd turned the castle into a . . . *den*. It was endless blood and sex and whisky and opium. The women simply lay about naked, eager to take on any man who wanted them. I lived like an animal for weeks, Kenna, blind with the pleasures they lay before me."

She felt horror and disgust and fear. What kind of a man could turn his ancestral home into a *harem*?

"And then my father returned." He said the words as if that were the final line of the story. As if it had ended there.

"But what happened? What happened when your father returned?"

Taking a deep breath, he lifted his bowed head and stared straight ahead. "I heard him shouting, but the woman I was with pulled me back down to her and I let myself forget him. When I woke in the evening, everyone was gone."

"Who? The vampires?"

"Everyone. I was alone. I wandered the castle and found no one."

Kenna clutched the bed linens closer to her chest. "Where were they?"

"Dead," he said softly. "My clan was dead. As the weeks had passed, they'd fed on them or killed them outright. Left the bodies in a pile behind the bailey wall so as not to be bothered by the stink. My father's fresh corpse was at the top of the heap."

Sickness rolled through her belly. She pressed a fist to her mouth to hold back a groan.

"I was feasting and rutting and filling my gut with blood while my people were being slaughtered. Day by day. My family. Everyone. I didn't even notice."

"Finlay," she started, but he cut her off.

"So that is why Jean must die, and why I must be the one to do it. He's the last one left. I've killed them all. Even the women."

She saw his jaw clench at that, and wondered what that would do to a man like him. To kill women. Women who'd been in his bed. What would it do to any man, to know he'd allowed the murder of his entire family?

When he pushed suddenly to his feet, Kenna jumped.

"We must dress for dinner," he said, reaching toward the bedside table for a package she hadn't seen. "I've a dress for you. I'll leave you to your privacy."

Though she held out her hands, he set the twine-wrapped material on the edge of the bed, avoiding her touch. Before she could ask him anything more, he slipped out the door and closed it quietly behind him.

He was a demon and a murderer . . . and he was her only protection in this place. Kenna's mind spun with helpless confusion.

# Chapter Five

"Stay by my side," he said as Kenna laid her hand gingerly on his arm. Her mind still shook with dismay at the story he'd told her an hour before. As they descended toward the roar of the great hall of Stirling Castle, she wanted to pull him aside and pelt him with more questions about the horror he'd lived through. But more than that, she wanted to know nothing more about it, ever.

And when she stole glances at MacLain, she wished she'd never asked. His face had changed. It was stiff now, as if something in him would break if he smiled. Fifty years had fallen away with the telling of the story, and now he seemed to be back in that place of death and guilt.

"I'm sorry," she murmured. He glanced down at her impassively, as if he knew what she spoke of and had no interest.

Then they were in the hall, and Kenna's eyes were too busy taking in the crowd to watch MacLain.

She'd never seen so many people. Hundreds of people, all of them dressed in bright layers of clothing and furs and jewels.

When she'd unfolded the length of blue velvet he'd left her, she'd been thankful. Now she was doubly so. Only the servants wore brown or gray, and the serving girls here looked even more harried than she had been at the inn.

As she watched, a fat gentleman with gold-puffed sleeves reached for a young girl passing. Her mouth became an *O* of shock as he pulled her into his lap and pressed his face into the crook of her neck.

"Do not let yourself drift away," MacLain said, bending low to warn her, and Kenna nodded. The man let the girl go after a taste of her flesh, but the night was early yet. She did not want to see what would happen to the serving women after the ale had been flowing for hours.

The atmosphere grew calmer as they moved closer to the central dais. Here, the people were watchful and more reserved, their eyes shifting over the crowd with sharp interest. These people meant to be near the king, and they had purpose.

Kenna saw eyes slide toward MacLain and widen. He was recognized, but no one approached to offer a friendly welcome.

He stopped and let his gaze skip over the tables. "There," he said, and led her toward the far side of the hall.

They approached a table crowded with young men. Not one woman sat among them. Either they had no wives or they did not bring them to court.

"Guthrie," MacLain said. One man glanced carelessly up, his fingers idly stroking the wide arch of rubies that nestled in his puffed collar. When he saw who stood above him, he smirked.

"Laird MacLain, you've finally arrived."

"Aye. I am here as an eager servant to the king, yet now he refuses to see me."

The man cocked his head. "The king will entertain you at his leisure, I'm sure."

"Of course," Finlay ground out. "But I'm afraid I am needed on urgent—"

"Why, Laird MacLain! Who is your lovely companion?"

She felt his body stiffen next to her, and her fingers curled into his skin in nervousness. "I present," he growled, "my lady, Kenna Graham."

She dipped a quick curtsy as Guthrie's gaze swept down her. "Graham, eh? She's enchanting."

"Yes," he snapped.

Guthrie smiled. "Perhaps Kenna Graham may be better at gaining access to the king than you are, Laird MacLain. She looks as if she could be much more charming."

The man's companions roared with laughter as Kenna flushed.

MacLain snarled. "I don't find your statement amusing, Guthrie."

"Oh." The man chuckled. "That's because I wasn't trying for amusement. Send her to my room tonight. You'll be in to see the king tomorrow before he breaks his fast. Will that suffice?"

A brief, hard shock of alarm jumped through her. MacLain was desperate to be on his way, after all. And she was a serving wench he'd met two days before. She clutched his arm harder. *I won't do this,* she prayed. *Please, I canna do this. Not this.*

But who would stop it here? Who would help her? No one.

His hand curved over hers and peeled her fingers from his arm. Good Lord, would he hand her over right this moment? His fingers laced into hers.

"Guthrie?"

"Yes, Laird MacLain?" The mocking laughter faded slowly from Guthrie's expression as he stared into MacLain's face. A shiver jumped through his body, and he raised a hand to the back of his neck to rub hard.

MacLain leaned a little closer. "I *will* see the king tomorrow. Before noon. This is an urgent matter, after all."

Frowning, Guthrie nodded. The deal was done. Kenna's throat burned with humiliation. She would be sent to this pup's room and forced to take him between her legs. She'd fought so hard to avoid this, and all her struggles had been for naught.

When MacLain stood straight, Guthrie shook his head and dropped his eyes immediately. But MacLain seemed to change his mind before turning away, and he stepped forward to grab the man's chin.

"And you will not set your eyes on Kenna Graham again. Ever. Understood?"

"Aye," the man breathed, all the color melting from his face.

Her legs were shaking as he swung her around and led her back toward the far tables.

"You won't give me to him?" she whispered.

He could not have heard her over the din, but he shook his head all the same.

"Why?"

"You're not mine to give, Kenna."

"Oh. Of course." Her relief felt strangely like hurt. "Thank you."

"And I'd kill him before I'd let him touch you."

She couldn't understand the tears that sprang to her eyes, but they would not stop despite her blinking.

"We'll have a real meal tonight at least," he grumbled, leading her to an empty table at the very corner of the room.

"Aye," she said as the tears slipped free and slid down her face.

"Will you—? Kenna, why are you weeping?"

"I'm not." She sat down on the bench and ducked her head, trying to wave him toward his seat.

"Lass, what's upset you?"

"Nothing. I only . . . You wanted to be on your way so badly. And I . . ." What had she come to in life, that she could weep with gratitude at not being treated as a worthless whore? "I expected . . ."

His hand touched the crown of her head, and that small touch made her breath catch and the tears fall faster. "Kenna," he whispered, his fingers sliding down her temple and beneath her chin. "I would not have given you to him."

She nodded, pressing her lips tight together.

"Did you think that I would?"

"I don't know. I don't *know*. I think I have . . . I fear I've lost all sense of myself. I cannot even recognize kindness anymore."

"Christ, lass," he murmured, sinking down to his haunches to meet her eyes. His fingers whispered over her cheek. "I am not kind."

"You've been kind to me from the moment we met, Finlay MacLain. And I am so hard and weary that I don't know what to do with it."

"No," he whispered. "I am not kind."

"What you told me tonight . . . You made a mistake, all those years ago. A terrible, awful mistake. And you've tried to make it right. You're not a monster."

His fingers spread out to cup her cheek in his warmth. "You've no idea what I am."

"I serve ale to dozens of men a night. Rich and poor. Young and old. I know what you are, Finlay. You're a man, and a good one."

"Ah, Christ, Kenna." His words were so soft that she barely heard them. But she felt better now.

Stronger. Less like a woman who expected to be used as barter.

"Sit," she ordered him, straightening her shoulders and grieving the loss of his heat when his hand fell away. "I'm famished."

They ate pheasant and goose and salmon, and drank fine ale, and Finlay's face lost some of the stiffness that had broken her heart earlier. But as the stiffness left, it revealed sadness, and a lost look in his eyes when he watched the revelers that surrounded them.

Excitement had bloomed through the hall with the arrival of King James, and Kenna had hardly believed herself in his presence as the trumpets sounded. But her excitement had sloughed off as the night had worn on. It was just as she had expected, no different from the inn, except that there were more serving girls and the men expected easy submission from the women they harassed.

When the king took his leave, MacLain pulled her to her feet and escorted her back to their chambers.

"I'm sorry, I must leave you here. I must discover what the king wants of me, and I dinna wish to expose you to that . . . vulgarity."

"I've seen it all before," she said, but slumped with relief when he shook his head in refusal.

He loosened the laces of her dress with brusque hands, fed the small hearth until the fire roared, and then he left her alone. Despite that she'd slept half the day, Kenna was exhausted, and climbed quickly beneath the linens to warm herself.

When she realized she missed MacLain's presence behind her, she wasn't even surprised by her loneliness. She just hoped he'd return soon.

\* \* \*

The sound of water woke her, trickling into her dreams. Then the crackle of new wood catching flame. And the strong smell of ale.

Kenna opened her eyes and found the flames casting stretching, shifting shadows on the wall.

The soft splash of water caught her attention, and then she saw him. Finlay MacLain stood before the fire, his back bare from the waist up. He'd loosened his plaid and removed his leine. As she watched he scrubbed a square of linen over one arm and shoulder. His muscles jumped and bulged.

Butterflies skipped over the skin of her stomach. My God. She'd admired many a bonny man in her day, but the sight of his naked back stole her breath away.

He washed his neck and beneath his arms. When he swept the linen rag over his chest, she willed him to turn and let her watch, but he cruelly faced the hearth.

"Some clod spilled ale on me," he said into the silence.

Kenna held her breath and closed her eyes.

"Kenna, I know you're awake."

"Oh?" she whispered. "How?"

He took a deep breath, his back expanding. "I can hear you. And . . ."

"And what?" She lay in complete contentment, watching him.

"Nothing." He laid the rag in the bowl of water and turned to reach for his leine.

Kenna gasped. By God, he was a powerful man. His chest curved with muscle. His arms bulged with it. What would it feel like to be beneath him, to feel the weight of him above her, to feel protected and surrounded by all that power?

"Kenna!" he snapped. "You canna do that."

"Do what?" His belly was long and lean, marred only by a white scar that curved around his ribs. Her fingers twitched with the need to trace it.

"Kenna, I can . . . I mean to show you respect, do you ken?"

"Aye," she answered as her eyes traced the faint path of hair that disappeared beneath the dark edge of his plaid. She'd felt his cock press against her, felt its hardness and width. Her sex tightened and pulled at her nerves.

"Damn it!" he snapped. "I can see and hear and smell far better than any man."

"So?" He'd taken off the stockings he'd donned for his visit to the king, and even the sight of his naked feet aroused her.

"So I can . . ." He kicked the wooden bowl, spilling everything across the floor. "I can smell you! When your body grows slick I can taste you on my tongue, and I'm trying to ignore it and I can't!"

He could *taste* her? Every time? Blood rushed so hard to her face that her skin prickled.

"And it wasn't *kindness* that made me threaten Guthrie. It was selfishness. I want you for myself, and if I canna have you, at least I can keep that bastard's eyes off you."

She pressed a hand to her thundering heart. He wanted her. Badly. "Why . . ." Her mouth was so dry that she could hardly swallow. "Why can you not have me?" It was too dangerous, probably. With the fangs and his dark soul and beastly nature. It was foolish of her to even want it.

Finlay walked to the hearth and pressed both hands to the narrow stone mantel. "I want you, lass, but I canna offer more. Marriage or love. Not even bairns, as they'd be like me. So I canna have you, and it is one thing to lie in a bed beside you, burning. But it is another thing entirely to smell your body grow warm and wet for me, and tell myself I should not touch you."

Oh. Well, that didn't sound dangerous at all. He had been aware of her arousal every time, and still he hadn't taken her? She'd never known a man to turn down even the most grudging offer of pleasure. "But you kissed me. At the inn."

" 'Twas just a kiss. And it nearly got you killed. Imagine what a mistake it would be to lie with me."

His hands clutched the stone, throwing his muscles hard against his skin. The plaid had slipped a bit lower, exposing the hollow of his spine just above his buttocks. Running her tongue down his backbone seemed a grand idea at the moment. "You would hurt me?"

"Nay! Of course not! But it would not honor you, either, would it?"

"Honor," she muttered. Honor. She had honored her husband and what had it gotten her? Nothing in the end, but loneliness and shame. She had honored her family her whole life, and they had tossed her out like rubbish after her marriage. This man had shown her more honor than any other. He'd asked for nothing in return.

"I am a widow."

He started to shake his head, but she cut him off.

"I know what it is to lie with a man. And I know what it is to miss that. I do miss that, Finlay. I want to feel a man inside me again. I want to feel *you*."

His whole body flinched as if she'd struck him, and he pushed back from the wall to pace. "Kenna, don't. Please. I am . . . *especially* drawn to you. I willna be able to resist if you offer. And I mean to *take* from you, Kenna, do you not understand?"

She touched her fingertips to her neck, and his

gaze flew there. When his lips parted, she saw his fangs. Sharp and long. Fear and sharp desire pulsed through her. Finlay groaned, and the sound of his need shivered against her.

"Would it . . . Would it cause harm? To my body or my soul?"

His face twisted, torture writ clear on his features. "Nay, but—"

"I am a woman," she insisted, rising up and letting the bed linens fall away. "And I *need*, Finlay, just as much as you do."

"Stop," he ordered as she reached for the hem of her shift. He took a step toward her, eyes fierce, hand reaching to halt her movement. But Kenna cared nothing for caution and honor and good sense tonight. Tonight she wanted a warm body against hers and a need that matched her own. She wanted to be a woman again, and feel her body rise with pleasure.

Before he could reach the bed, she gripped the shift in her hands and pulled it over her head.

"Ah, Christ above," he gasped, stuttering to a stop just a foot from her. He closed his eyes, but too late. She saw in the tightening of his face that her nakedness could not be shut out so easily. She slipped from the bed and took one of his large hands in her own.

"Will you lie with me tonight, Finlay? With only the honor of my invitation between us?" Though she asked the question, she forced the issue by pressing his hand to one of her breasts.

He didn't resist, but she felt the shaking in his fingers. Kenna held her breath and waited.

He wanted. He wanted so much.

For a brief moment, Finlay thought he might be able to walk away. Somehow, he fooled himself into thinking that even the soft give of her breast beneath his fingers could not convince him. But only for one heartbeat. Then the nerves of his fingertips woke, and her skin was hot and fine and yielding. She pressed his hand closer and her breast filled the curve of his palm and pushed up against his fingers.

When he shifted his thumb, Kenna sighed, her breath puffing against his chest. And then she touched him.

She flattened her palm to his chest, spreading her fingers wide. A simple touch. And nothing close to enough.

Finlay opened his eyes and he was lost. Her body was perfect and lush. Her breasts full and firm and so pale under his roughened hands. Her hips curved out from a small waist, forming the perfect angle for his hold.

"Kenna," he breathed as he wrapped his arms around her and pulled her to him. The bedcovers had kept her heat close, and now it soaked into him, warming more than just his skin. Something inside him thawed as he drew the fragrance of her warm body deep into his lungs. The thawing revealed pain, and Finlay felt his breath hitch.

Kenna's hands swept over his back and down to his waist. After a deep breath, she slipped from his arms and pulled him to the bed.

He went to his knees before her. "You are a fine and lovely thing, Kenna."

"As are you," she whispered as she slid her hands into his hair and pulled him to her for a kiss. The taste of her swept him into another world. Nothing existed but their bodies. No past, no future, no horrors of his own making. It was just Kenna's tongue rubbing shyly over his. Her taste, like the sun and summer, flooding through him.

They kissed until her hands began to move restlessly over his shoulders, and he couldn't resist tasting more. First her neck, then her shoulder, then the soft rise of her breast.

She inhaled hard. He felt the thundering of her heart beneath his mouth, but he would not rush this. Not this. It would last forever if he could will it so.

He kissed down to the full roundness at the underside of her breast and felt her fingers dig into his shoulders in frustration. When he began to chuckle, Kenna growled. "You mean to tease me, then?"

"Aye," he breathed, just before he licked a slow circle around her rose pink nipple.

Her breath hissed between her teeth.

"Aye, I mean to tease you." He touched his tongue to the pebbled peak, wetting it just enough to draw it tighter. He circled it again.

"Oh," she moaned. "Finlay, please." She didn't wait for his generosity, though. Kenna simply wound her fingers into his hair and pulled him to her.

He obliged, sucking hard at the peak until her groan turned from frustration to joy.

He'd thought her arousal enticing before. But now he was so close to her, and her sex so wet, that he soon found himself too distracted to tease any longer. Setting his hands to her thighs, he eased her legs open and dragged his mouth down her belly.

"Ah, God," she moaned, arching back. Her thighs shook.

Had it been years for her as it had for him? It must have been. When his mouth touched her sex, she jumped as if a spark had landed on her skin.

This he could not take his time with. It seemed his mouth had watered for her taste forever, so Finlay sank his tongue deep, thrilling at the sound of her cry.

He lapped at her, swallowing her taste, then he traced the lines of her sex before settling in at that hard nub that made her sob. Her restless legs rubbed his shoulders until he curved his arms beneath her thighs to spread her wider.

"Finlay," she breathed. "Finlay."

What power, to feel her body shake and strain at his kiss. To hear her call his name in pleasure. Her heels dug into his back as if she could pull closer.

"I . . . canna . . ." she panted. Her thighs tightened and her moans turned to whimpers. *"Please."*

And then she was screaming and shaking, her sex hot and wet against his mouth. When she quieted, he pressed kisses to her thighs and drank her in with his eyes. If this was the only time, he wanted to remember the sight of her sex, swollen with lust for him.

She had barely gotten her panting under control when she said, "More now."

Finlay found himself grinning with delight as he rose to his feet. "More?"

"Oh, aye. More."

"All right then, lass." He reached for his thick belt.

Eyes gleaming, Kenna rose to her elbows and watched him, a smile starting small on her mouth before spreading wider.

"A moment," he murmured. "It'd be a sad thing if I didn't memorize the picture you present."

Kenna glanced down at her naked body, her thighs still spread and open to him. "You canna embarrass me, Finlay MacLain. I'm too well pleased to care."

"And that's a beautiful thing." His clumsy fingers finally freed the belt. It clunked to the ground and his plaid fell free.

"My God," Kenna sighed. "So is that."

She shocked him into a laugh, but her hot look soon chased his amusement away.

He'd thought his cock as hard as it could get, but her gaze proved him wrong. He throbbed as she rose to her knees and backed farther onto the bed.

"Come now, man," she said. "I mean to ride you."

"Lord," he huffed, shocked despite the lust that exploded through him.

She simply cocked an eyebrow and waited. What could he do but lay himself down? He half expected her to laugh and cover her face in embarrassment, but true to her word, Kenna climbed atop him.

Her sex pressed into his throbbing cock, and when she leaned close to kiss him, her breasts brushed over his chest. Finlay curved his hand behind her neck and held her to him, her hot body hardly any weight at all atop him. She was so wet that she slipped over his shaft as she moved, setting white light flashing behind his eyes.

This was more than he'd hoped for. He'd thought he'd be able to seduce her if he put his mind to it, but he'd never imagined that she would climb atop him and take what she wanted. Though she seemed content to take naught but kisses at this moment. His hands strayed to her hips and eased her up.

"Mm," she purred and rubbed her sex slow against him.

"You weren't lying, lass," he groaned. "You've definitely got the skills of a widow."

Her laughter made her shake quite delightfully against him. "Wait 'til I lose my shyness, Laird MacLain."

Her hair flew back as she pushed herself up, resting her hands against his chest. When her neck arched, Finlay became suddenly aware of his fangs, and they throbbed in response at being remembered.

Laughter forgotten, he let his gaze wander from the dark curls of her sex to her belly and breasts and pale, delicate neck. Her smile faded, and she let his hands lift her hips.

When he felt his cock notch into her sex, Finlay pushed his hips up and eased hers down. Tightness. Heat. Kenna's body took him in. Finally. *Finally.*

Her nails dug into his chest. "Wait," she breathed. "Wait."

*Wait,* he told his hands. They shook with the need to defy him.

She eased up, then down again, slipping a little lower. "You're so big," she breathed. "Go slow."

And how was he to control himself now? His fangs descended. He eased her up and down, up and down, until finally he slid as deep as he could go and Kenna's panting turned to a moan.

"Yes," she urged. "Oh, yes." Her sex squeezed him as she raised up and then took him hard and deep.

"Jesus, lass." He ground his teeth hard together.

"It's been so long," she panted. "You've no idea." She rolled her hips as she moved, so that the up and down became one long movement that never ended. The constant assault of pleasure glowed through him, as if the sun shone on his body for the first time in fifty years.

It was all he could feel. The heat of her, the slide. His heartbeat filled his ears.

No, not his heartbeat. *Hers.* Thumping like a war drum calling up his bloodlust.

"Ah, God," he growled.

She rode him faster, her pulse speeding to meet her excitement as he slid his hands from her hips to her breasts. He could *see* her pulse now, beating just beneath her jaw. Pressure built at the base of his cock. His fangs pushed out to their full length as he gently pinched her nipples.

Kenna tossed her head back, gasping. Her neck was stretched so long . . .

Desperate with need, Finlay wrapped his arms around her and flipped her to her back without drawing even an inch out of her body.

"Oh!" she cried, though her shock didn't prevent her from wrapping her legs around his hips.

"If you need a man," he muttered, "then you shall have one." He drove deep and fast, sinking himself in her tightness.

"Aye," she moaned, as he took her hard. "Aye."

But the harder he had her, the more he wanted. Her heels dug into his arse, as if she wished for more, too. Her face turned away, exposing that beating place.

"Kenna," he growled, and opened his mouth over her neck.

She tensed beneath him, as if she'd suddenly remembered that he wasn't just a man, but he'd heard the faint scrape of his fangs against her skin, and Finlay was lost.

He sank his fangs deep, and her blood filled his mouth.

"Ah!" she screamed, her spine arching as the sound twisted from pain to ecstasy. The taste of her was pure and thick in her blood, and it washed over him, through him, *into* him as he swallowed. Power filled him, tightening his bollocks.

Her moaning started soft, each breath getting louder as he slowed his thrusts, drawing them out as he sucked gently at her neck. He shifted above her, so that his shaft rubbed rough against her with every draw of his mouth.

"Ah, Finlay," she moaned. Her sex squeezed him. "Finlay." Just as her body began to stiffen, he sank his fangs deeper, and her voice rose to a scream as her hips jerked against his. *Aye*. Aye, she was *his*.

Finlay let go of his control and followed her down into that bright oblivion, his own shout muffled by her throat. There was nothing besides Kenna. Nothing in the world but his body inside hers and her blood in his mouth.

*Kenna.*

As soon as the waves of pleasure abated, he gently freed her neck and let his forehead collapse to the bed beside her. It seemed to take all his strength to support his weight above her.

His body was heavier than it had been . . . as if something hollow had been filled up.

# Chapter Six

She was the same woman she'd been the day before. She must be.

And yet she felt utterly different.

Kenna touched a hand to the sore spot on her neck, the place where Finlay had taken her blood. She should feel weak. She'd been injured. Her sex felt as tender as her neck, and she was almost certain Finlay had left bruises on her hips with his desperate hold.

But despite the loss of blood and the tender places that made themselves known when she stretched, Kenna *glowed*. Her body hummed. And her soul felt years younger. Nearly as young as she actually was.

She stretched again, and felt Finlay's hand close over hers.

"Are you ill, lass?"

"Nay," she answered with a smile, snuggling deeper into the bedcovers. She pulled his hand over her hip and felt him turn to press into her back. Ice seemed to cover her skin.

"Och!" she yelped, scooting away from him. Frightened, she swung around and pressed her hand to his chest. "Finlay, you're frozen!"

"My apologies. I did not mean to frighten you." His face stiffened.

"What's the matter?" she cried.

"Nothing. We are just . . . I must have kicked the linens off and our flesh cools easily in the air."

"But . . ." She watched as he slipped out the other side of the bed. His buttocks flexed with fascinating rhythm as he rounded the bed and approached the dead hearth. "Does that not hurt you?"

"Nay."

He crouched to the task, and soon had a cheerful fire crackling. "I'll warm soon enough," he muttered. "But I must leave you regardless. The king awaits."

"Right now?" she asked, not bothering to hide her disappointment. It seemed to cheer him, though, for his scowl turned immediately to a smile.

"I'm afraid so. But it shan't take long."

"No?"

He pulled on his leine, hiding his bonny nakedness. "No. I'll make sure of it."

"Good." She was sore, but she meant to have more of him while she could.

He began to fold his plaid around him. "I'll send a girl with bread and ale to break your fast."

She watched him dress, satisfaction swelling her heart. It felt good to watch a man ready himself for the day. And it felt wondrous to lounge about and sigh over the sight of him. It hadn't been marriage itself she'd enjoyed so much, after all. The marriage had been a burden. It had been the physical pleasure that came with it that she'd loved, the feel and touch and taste of a man.

Finlay had said he could not offer her marriage, but perhaps she wanted no more than a good, long while in his bed.

"I'll return soon," he said, crossing the room to

kiss her forehead. She considered pulling him down for more, but his eyes were already distant, thinking ahead to his audience with the king.

"Have a care," she warned, but as he unbolted the door, his arm flexed, distracting her into a sigh. And Kenna realized she had best take care herself.

"Sire." Finlay bowed low, leg outstretched, eyes pointed toward the ground. He could smell the fear coming off the other members of the king's audience. They all wanted something and feared the king's judgment. Finlay was the only one with nothing to lose.

"Laird MacLain," the king muttered with an irritated glance toward the archway. Guthrie stood there, arms crossed and eyes glaring at Finlay. "You have not pleased me. I have had need of you these many months now, and you have declined my invitations."

"My apologies, Sire. As you know, my clan has suffered great hardship, and I hesitated to separate myself from my home."

"Even for your king?"

"I am here, Sire."

"Yes." His eyes slanted toward Guthrie. "Though I am not sure why you are suddenly filled with eagerness. I mean to enjoy your company here at court for quite a while."

Finlay managed to bite back a curse.

"I have need of your special . . . strengths."

"I have no particular strengths, Sire."

He cocked his head, eyes narrowing. "On the contrary, Laird MacLain, I am quite convinced you do. I am told you live alone. How is it that a solitary man can hold his land with no mischief from his neighbors?"

"I am not alone."

"No? Who are your clansmen, then?"

He had no answer to that. He'd had no clansmen for fifty years. No men or women or bairns. Most had been killed. The others had fled and burned their homes down behind them in an attempt to break the curse that had fallen over them.

"You've a pact with the Devil," the king said.

"Nay."

"And," he went on as if Finlay hadn't spoken, "you've a way to make men come 'round to your opinion. Guthrie, for example."

At the edge of his vision, Finlay saw the way Guthrie's fists twitched.

"He was adamant that I let you cool your heels. 'He is arrogant,' he said. 'He has disobeyed you.' And then this morning, he comes to attend me, insisting that I must see you immediately. He was quite urgent."

"I spoke to him last even'."

"Aye, you did. Quite convincingly. Yet Guthrie only responds well to obsequiousness, and you do not strike me as the type to bow your head to the likes of him."

Guthrie's heartbeat sped and the scent of his anger reached Finlay's nose. Perhaps the king was a vampire, too, because he bellowed, "Leave us!" and the crowd of petitioners and courtiers snapped to attention. A moment passed, and then they all filed out. Only a guard remained, his eyes sharp and impassive all at once.

"Even if your skill was granted by Satan himself, your duty is to Scotland, Laird MacLain."

He felt a twinge of guilt at the words. He did have a duty to his country, regardless of whether he was man or vampire.

"I canna fight England's greed on my own. I need the support of all Scots."

"Aye. Of course." His guilt formed a stone in his gut. If the king asked, could he help keep the English in check? Would this be a way to help make amends for the many wrongs he'd done? Perhaps . . . Perhaps after he killed Jean, this would give him another purpose. A reason to keep going despite his weariness.

"The MacKenzie clan is being needlessly stubborn," the king muttered. "I have need of more land on the coast, and they refuse to give it, even for the sake of their king."

"The MacKenzies." Finlay's heart, which had begun to rouse itself with pride for his country, sank like a stone.

"Aye, and Fergus Stewart is not much better. His youngest daughter has caught the eye of my uncle. Stewart says his daughter is already promised to a cousin and he will not break the betrothal. Can you imagine? Defying his king over a fifteen-year-old girl's supposed love? It's damn near traitorous, I tell you."

Finlay closed his eyes and drew a deep breath. "You'd like me to convince Stewart to give his lass to your uncle."

"Aye. But the MacKenzies first. They are here at court, so it should take little effort. I want that land, MacLain. For the sake of Scotland, of course."

Right. Land. Alliances. Intrigue and power. Stirling Castle never changed. He could have stood here fifty years ago and had the same conversation with that king.

"And Alistair Bruce," the king muttered. "Does he think me blind? It's clear he's had dealings with the Irish behind my back."

Finlay could find no more purpose here than he'd found in the crumbling remains of his home. The king did not want him to use his powers against the English queen; James was too busy expanding his influence in Scotland.

"Sire," Finlay said. "I'm afraid you are mistaken. I have nothing to offer you."

The king's eyes narrowed. "You'd best reconsider, Laird MacLain. Your land may not be valuable, but it is subject to my power all the same. And it is well known that you are"—he swallowed and rubbed a hand across the back of his neck—"associated with . . ." His sharp eyes clouded and he looked up at Finlay in confusion. "What were you saying?"

He had not wanted to do this. He'd avoided Stirling for months just so he would not feel a traitor. Still, he narrowed his eyes and pushed his thoughts straight out. "I'm afraid you were mistaken, Sire. I have no special hold over men's minds. My presence offers no benefit for you or the crown. And while my clan is small and ragged, we have no trouble raising taxes or holding the land. You are better served to send me back to MacLain Castle."

"I see," he murmured. His face softened with concern. "You are right, of course. You had best return. There is never any trouble from the MacLains, which is more than I can say for half the families in Scotland."

"Thank you, Sire," Finlay said with a bow. It brought a man low to use his liege so. To know that a king was just a man, after all.

"Guthrie!" the king shouted. The door opened before his voice had ceased to echo. "You were wise to argue Laird MacLain's case this morning. He has served us well at Castle MacLain, and must return as soon as he is able."

Guthrie's eyes widened with alarm. "Your Majesty, did he injure you?"

"Of course not, you fool. Escort him out. We are done here."

Guthrie's worry was so evident that Finlay could not doubt the man's genuine affection for his king, but unfortunately that affection turned to glittering rage when he gestured Finlay toward the door.

"What did you do to him?" he hissed.

"I canna know what you mean."

"You snuck inside his head!"

Rumors and legends could only make his life more difficult. He did not need an enemy at court. He did not need to be noticed at all. Unfortunately, he'd already twisted Guthrie's mind once and there was a good chance it wouldn't work again.

Finlay stopped and faced the fuming man. "If I could really control men's minds, do you not think I would have installed myself at the king's side? What kind of man would pass up that kind of power, Guthrie? If I could rule the king, I could rule Scotland."

Thoughts turned behind the man's eyes.

"You've seen my home, man," Finlay insisted. "Do you really think me powerful?"

Here was a man who coveted power. Who'd dedicated his life to his king just for the chance to gather up as many scraps of influence as he could. He could understand Finlay's desire for solitude no more than he could understand the turnings of the stars.

The surety of his expression faded, but the hostility remained.

"I do not trust you, MacLain. Neither do I like you. In fact, I rather hope that Frenchman catches up with you."

Cold flashed over Finlay's skin like sliding ice. "What Frenchman?" he asked, knowing full well who it was.

Guthrie's smile was the grin of a wolf. "Have you no' heard? He's got only one hand, and I'd wager you had something to do with the loss of the other. He was prowling between Stirling and Larmuir two nights ago, and I gather he headed out for MacLain Castle about the time you left it. Do you think he might make it back to Stirling today?"

Gray. And Mrs. McDermott and young Rabbie. Had they obeyed the orders he'd given before leaving?

Ignoring Guthrie's triumphant laugh, Finlay spun and hurried toward the hall, narrowing his eyes against the sunlight that trickled weakly through the small windows. If the tale was true, Jean was either at MacLain Castle or on his way to Stirling. Finlay would've welcomed the knowledge of a coming confrontation if not for his worry over Kenna.

He could not leave her here alone, and he could not expose her to the dangers of the night.

"Damn it," he muttered as he bounded up the curved staircase. If they stayed here, they were simply waiting to be found. But if they left at sundown, they might find Jean standing at the gates of the castle, his sword in hand.

He pushed open the door of their chambers and found Kenna mid-pace.

"Finlay!" she cried, rushing toward him. Her outstretched arms briefly overrode his worries. Here was his woman, wrapping her arms around him. "What did the king say?"

"We're free to leave—"

"How?"

"But there is a more dangerous problem now. Jean has been to MacLain Castle. We must go."

The horror on her face did not stop her from drawing herself straight and offering a curt nod. "Of course. We must see to your home. Tonight—"

"Nay. We leave now."

"Now? But . . ."

"We've no choice. I won't be trapped here like a rat when the sun sets, not with your life at risk."

"But, Finlay, you said—"

"Come now. Let's gather our things. You will be my eyes, and we'll find shelter before sunset. God willing, Jean will be unawares. I'll circle back to Stirling if it's safe to leave you."

Kenna raised her hands, lips parting as if she would speak in earnest, but then her arms fell, and she stood quiet.

"All will be well," he whispered, touching his fingers to her precious cheek. "I will see you safe, Kenna Graham."

"I am not worried over me, you great lummox!"

"No?" Even his urgency to be gone could not keep him from smiling down at her. "Will you keep me safe then, lass?"

"Aye, unless I kill you first."

When he saw the tears in her eyes, Finlay pulled her into his arms and pressed his lips to the top of her head. She felt right there, her head resting just beneath his chin, her hands clutching his back. And her scent glowing 'round him like a sun. Only now she smelled of his body, too.

His lust was no longer a flat and bitter thing. This need for Kenna was pulsing and warm and growing so fast that it hurt his chest.

"Come now," he murmured. "Let us find this wretch and be done with it."

# Chapter Seven

He sat behind her on the horse again, just as he always did. But now it was different, feeling his body pressed against her after it had pressed so thoroughly into her the night before. The rocking of the horse was another reminder of what they'd done. Her sensitive sex pulsed with the movement.

But there was guilt, too. Finlay was hunched over her, his plaid pulled low over his eyes, his hands hidden beneath the wool to keep the sun from his skin. He was suffering and she could think of nothing but having him again.

Thank God the sky was thick with clouds. Even in the weak light, his eyes streamed tears. Two hours had passed, and he'd grown quiet. Kenna tried to think of some way to distract him . . . and herself.

"I canna understand why the king let you leave after he was so eager to get you to Stirling."

"He changed his mind."

"Why?"

He did not answer for a long while, as if he were thinking of what to say. As if he might lie. Kenna squared her shoulders and waited for the sound of falsehood. Her husband had lied to her often enough, so why did she feel shocked?

He shifted behind her, his thighs tensing. "What the king accused me of . . . It is true, to an extent. I can influence men with my mind. It's one of our powers."

He'd hinted as much, but she still felt a shock. "How do you do it?"

When he shrugged, his body rubbed against hers. "I think very hard what I'd like them to do. Like glaring at someone, I suppose, only with your mind."

"That's all?"

"Yes, that's all. But 'tis not as powerful as it seems. It only works on a person once or twice and then . . . nothing."

"Have you done it to *me*?" She gestured frantically and heard a hiss of pain behind her. She turned to find Finlay tugging his plaid more thoroughly around him. "I'm sorry."

"You've a right to be shocked. And no, I havena done it to you, but only because you're very strong willed. When I came to the inn, I tried to be sure that no one noticed me, that they *wanted* never to notice me, but it did not take with you, Kenna. You kept *looking* at me."

"Well, I thought you verra fine to look at."

His laughter rumbled into her. "I can't deny I was rather pleased with my failure. And even if I'd meant to make you obey, I didna want to push hard enough to hurt you."

She glanced over her shoulder. "Strong willed or not . . . I think Jean did that to me. I felt . . . I felt that I could not resist him."

His arm tightened around her. "He didna care if he hurt you, but I'd not hurt you for the world."

Ah, God. Her heart clenched so hard that pain sparked through her chest. He'd said he had nothing to offer her, but his consideration was enough for now. His consideration, and affection, and, yes, his kindness. Kenna sneaked her hand beneath the plaid to lay it on his. His fingers laced into hers and she leaned comfortably back against him. They'd ceased to pass any other riders for a few long minutes.

"Are you sure Jean willna find us in the day?"

"He's arrogant. He thinks he has us run to ground. Jean is canny but too confident, perhaps. I should have challenged him outright instead of trying to trap him."

His head was hanging lower as he spoke, and Kenna began to worry at his weariness. Until she felt his teeth graze her neck.

"Oh!" she yelped, shocked by a lightning rush of arousal.

"I canna stop thinking of you above me," he whispered.

*"Oh."* Her sex clenched hard as his thumb feathered over her wrist. She felt the slight pressure of his mouth sucking at her neck. Would he . . . Surely he wouldn't bite her right here, would he?

"Och, lass. You smell so perfect."

"Finlay," she gasped. "Are you not in pain?"

"Aye, but you're doing a fine job of distracting me from it."

Well, she could hardly object to that, could she? Kenna closed her eyes and let her head fall to the side while Finlay laughed against her skin. "You're supposed to be watching the road for strangers," he warned, not sounding the least upset.

She forced her heavy eyes open.

His mouth drew a line down to her shoulder. "Will you ride me again tonight, lass?"

Her face burned. "If . . . Did you like it, then? My husband used to scold me for my eagerness. Not at first, but . . . later."

"No offense to his everlasting soul, but your husband was a dolt. I am man enough to take you, lass, whatever you have to give."

She was grinning like a fool when they rode up on a shepherd and his flock. The shepherd watched them with a wary eye, and the sheep scurried away with panicked bleats. Finlay pulled back on the reins.

She stayed silent as he questioned the man, as he'd questioned others along the way. So far, no one had seen Jean or heard aught of a stranger traveling through under cover of night.

"Were you here last night?" Finlay pressed.

The shepherd shot him an irritated look. "Aye. We slept right off the road two miles on. I'd 'ave seen 'im."

Finlay tossed a coin in the man's direction and they were on their way. A few minutes later, they rounded a curve, and the lowering sun threw light into her face. Finlay gasped and recoiled.

"I canna see a damn thing. Can you tell where we are?"

Kenna cast a worried eye down the road. It seemed to head straight into the sun for a good long while. "There's a small stream ahead and a stone bridge. Just beyond that we ride through a notch in a ridge."

"Good. There's no point going farther. He'll have to pass this way. Can you guide the horse south along the river? Before we cross the bridge."

Kenna nodded and tightened her hands on the reins. The horse shied a bit at her heavy hand. She'd guided it along the road, but that was a far cry from taking it over hill and hollow.

"You're doing well," Finlay murmured, but she couldn't deny the strain in his voice. The sun hurt even her eyes at this point. He must be in agony.

"Not much farther. I can hear the falls. When you

see them, stop. There's a cave." She heard him draw a deep breath, scenting the air. "And Jean isna here."

She spied the falls soon after, and the dark, narrow mouth of the cave. Finlay dropped to the ground when she halted the horse, and Kenna followed him down, gratefully. They'd made it.

As she led him toward the darkness, Kenna caught a glimpse of his face. His skin was an angry red, his eyes nearly swollen shut, the whites dark with blood.

"Your eyes!"

He shook his head and she pulled him into the stone room. Suddenly, she could see nothing, and Finlay was sighing with relief.

"Is it . . . Are we far enough in?"

"Come, there's a ledge here." Now he was leading her, directing her to sit on what felt remarkably like a bench.

"Will your eyes heal?"

He answered, "Aye," but she heard the clear hesitation on his voice.

"What is it?" she asked into the dark. "Tell the truth."

"I will need your help. Your blood."

The fear was a small thing this time, swamped by the anticipation of pleasure.

"But let us rest a while."

She thought of the arousal she'd fought all day. "No. Now. Let's do it now."

"Kenna," he said, as if he meant to say no, but then he turned her to him and kissed her. She melted into his arms, as if she'd been weeks without him instead of hours. He pulled her up, and she climbed onto his lap and straddled him, kissing him as though she might devour his mouth.

A faint pain pierced the inside of her bottom lip. Before she could even gasp, Finlay was apologizing.

"I'm sorry. I'm sorry, love." But his tongue dragged along her lip and his breathing grew labored.

"Take what you need," she urged, already hot for him.

He groaned, his breath breaking as he fumbled with her skirts and dragged his plaid aside. His hand slid roughly over her sex.

"How can you be so ready for me?" he whispered, but the question needed no answer. He pulled her hips forward and lifted her, and the next thing she knew, his cock was driving deep.

She keened at the painful pleasure, her cry nearly drowning out his animal growl.

His hand wound into her hair to arch her neck. Kenna braced herself, and then he bit her.

There was the pain she'd been expecting. A sharp, small stab, no more than the sting of a bee, but then it turned to a strange warmth, like a hand held too close to a candle. That warmth spread and dimmed before gathering at the points of her pulse. Her wrists and neck and heart . . . and her sex.

She set her knees against the stone and began to ride his shaft.

Oh, God, yes. Each stroke of his cock was a spark against that warmth the bite had created. And her sex had been swollen all day, wanting and needing. His thighs were hard beneath her, strength against her softness. His arms like bands of steel around her ribs. He was everything she was not. Everything.

He drew at her throat and rose up to meet the fall of her hips, and Kenna screamed as her body tightened around him. She was peaking already, shaking against him and crying his name.

He swallowed for a long while before drawing his fangs free. Then he lifted her hips once, twice more, roaring with pleasure as he sank himself deep.

She collapsed against him, limp as a rag doll and just as brainless.

"Christ, woman," he panted, his hand smoothing against her hair. "You're a miracle."

"That's sacrilege, Finlay MacLain," she said, though her scold sounded more like a purr.

"I'll worship you privately, then, and keep my prayers to myself."

"Are you better now?"

"Aye. I'll be good as new in an hour or so, and the sun willna set for a while yet." He eased back. "And you, Kenna? How do you feel?"

"Full," she answered honestly, loving the sound of his laughter. "And drained all at once." He laughed harder, and she realized what she'd said and laughed with him. There was no reason to move, so they sat still for a long while, arms tangled and breath mingling. She thought she could stay like this for months and years.

But how long did she have, really? "After you kill Jean, will you be done with me then?"

His body turned to rock beneath hers. "What?"

She gulped at the coldness of the word.

"You wish to be on your way, I suppose," he muttered. "Free of this madness."

"No! 'Tis not that. You said that once you'd killed Jean you'd be done, but you never said with what. I worried you meant . . . I worried you meant you'd be done with your life."

"Oh. I did."

Her gut clenched as if he'd hit her. "What do you *mean*?"

"I mean my life has been worth nothing more than this revenge. I brought death upon my clan. Shame to my father's name. There is no one left who even depends upon me."

"What about . . ." She bit her tongue. "What about Gray? And Mrs. McDermott?"

"They've both been provided for."

Kenna didn't know what to say. Did he mean to take his own life? How would he even do it? She leaned into him and wrapped her arms around his waist.

Finlay drew in a deep breath. "I thought you were asking to leave."

Kenna shook her head and squeezed him as hard as she could. "Nay, Finlay. Not now."

There were things to be done. Plans to be made. But she was glad he was content to hold her and sit still for a long, long while.


"Do not leave the cave." He held both her arms and tried to meet her gaze, even knowing she could see nothing in the dim.

"I've said I won't."

"No matter what happens," he insisted. "Even if you think me dead, do not come out. The waterfall will hide the sound of your breathing, and your scent as well, so long as he does not draw close. Do not come out."

"All right." She was agreeing, but the stubborn set of her chin told a different story.

"Promise me."

She rolled her eyes. "I promise."

By God, she was so lovely and wild. He wanted another taste of her, but she must be sore. And there was no time. And he wanted her so badly.

"If he kills me, he'll have no need of you. Wait here until—"

"Finlay!"

He ignored the flash of panic in her eyes. "Wait

until day, then go to MacLain Castle. There is gold in the chest in my room."

"Stop! I willna listen to this!"

He glanced out the opening of the cave. The sky was nearly as dark as the cave now. "I must go."

"Finlay," she said, retrieving his attention. She rose on her toes to press a kiss to his mouth. "Be careful. Please. You are such a good man."

He could say nothing to that, so he kissed her back and then walked into the night, his movements silent as a creeping cat. The wind was at his back, so he crossed to the other side of the road and ducked down into the space beneath the bridge.

If Jean had been to MacLain Castle, he must take this road to reach Stirling. He must cross this bridge. And Finlay would have him.

The stars winked one by one to life. The moon rose. The wind died down around him, swelling the night with silence. Even the dying leaves ceased to tumble across rock. He was left alone with his thoughts.

He'd had no plans for what he would do after finally killing Jean. He'd only known his purpose in life would be done. His slow work of the past fifty years would be over.

For a while he'd despaired of ever finding Jean Montrose. The man hadn't been hiding, he'd simply disappeared into the strange world of the Orient, emerging for short periods to roam through Europe before returning to the East. He was some sort of restless demon, wandering the earth, leaving chaos in his wake. What he'd done to Finlay, he'd done to others, as if he took joy in using up the people around him. He used them until there was nothing left, and then moved on to another victim.

But Finlay would put an end to that, finally, if he

wasn't killed himself. And if he did emerge the victor, then what?

His mind filled with images of Kenna Graham. Her head thrown back as she took her pleasure, her mouth tightening with anger at his high-handedness, her bowed head as she wept in loneliness. She was a mate, so the lust was there, but in truth, he simply liked her.

If only his life were something—*anything*—to offer a woman. If only he'd made himself something more than a murderer.

A noise floated on the air.

Finlay tensed, cocking his head. "This is ridiculous," a male voice complained in French. "He's disappeared like a snake into the grass."

"He will be at Stirling," another voice responded. *Jean.*

"You said he would be at his castle."

There was a loud crack, followed closely by the panicked scream of a horse and a woman's laugh. "Stop it," the woman scolded, her voice husky with amusement. "You fight like small children. This trip was supposed to be entertaining, and I am growing bored."

"Hold your tongue, wench," Jean growled. He was getting closer. His words echoed off rock. They were riding through the notch.

Finlay raised his head above the bank of the stream. Two horses approached. Jean was on one, a man and woman on the other. The wind shifted for a bare moment, carrying the scent of old smoke with it. Not opium smoke, but the stench of burning houses. Finlay's heart sank.

"I need a new woman," the younger man said, causing the woman in his arms to hiss. Her fangs flashed in the moonlight. "Bah," her companion complained as he pulled too hard at the reins. "You are too eager. I like the scent of fear while I'm fucking."

She rained a flurry of words down on his head in a language Finlay had never heard, so he shut them out. The man's words, on the other hand, penetrated Finlay's brain like a knife. "After you kill the Scotsman"—he chuckled—"can I have the wench?"

If Finlay failed in this, Kenna would suffer at the hands of these creatures.

He tightened his hold on his claymore and counted to ten. They approached the bridge. Closer, closer. The first horse stepped onto the bridge. *Jean.*

Finlay waited.

When he heard the first horse's back hooves touch the stone, Finlay rose up with a banshee's cry and swung his claymore toward the male rider on the second horse. While the woman was still drawing a breath to scream, his blade sliced into flesh and the man's head tumbled toward the water.

The horse snorted and pawed the ground as if it would rear. Finlay slapped its hindquarters and sent it running, the woman's scream escaped to trail behind her into the night.

Jean wheeled his horse around with a shout of fury.

"Get down," Finlay ground out. "Get down and fight."

"You crazed bastard!" Jean's horse pranced sideways, eyes rolling. "You've been alive only seventy years. Don't tell me you've already gone mad."

"Get off the horse and *face me*!" He circled around, trying to trap Jean against the low stone wall of the bridge, but Jean pulled back on the reins, sawing into the horse's mouth and forcing it backward.

"You took my arm, you Scottish bastard. I can't imagine what the fuck you are so angry about."

Finlay heard the blade sing through the air just in time to jump back. "You killed my entire clan, Jean. And now I will kill you." He swung the claymore over his head, power pushing through him as he aimed for Jean's thigh.

The vampire slid off the other side, and Finlay pulled back just in time to avoid killing the horse. "Damn it."

"Your *clan*," Jean spat, backing off the bridge toward the far side of the road. "They were humans. Cattle. The only reason we spared you was because you were one of us."

"You *made* me into one of you!" he screamed as he moved toward him, matching Jean step for step.

"You begged for it," Jean sneered.

Rage exploded through him. Aye, he had begged for it. He'd wanted power and women and strength. Finlay raised his claymore with a scream and rushed toward the man he'd waited fifty years to kill. The swords clashed so hard that sparks flew into the night.

Jean's sword slid down and he spun away, stepping just out of the reach of Finlay's blade. "Where is the wench?" he sneered.

Finlay swung again, meeting Jean's blade with another jarring crash.

"I can smell her on you. Fresh. Very fresh. She's here. Hiding."

*Clang.*

Jean danced away again. "After I kill you, I'll find her, and I'll fuck her."

*No.* He swung with the full force of his body, spinning Jean to the left, forcing him onto the uneven surface of the grass.

Jean laughed. "And then," he panted, "I'll take her home with me. Perhaps I'll even turn her and keep her forever."

He'd counted on his words turning Finlay's world red, and it worked. Roaring, he dove toward Jean as the man's sword swung suddenly up. Finlay twisted just in time. The tip caught him, ripping open his shoulder, but it did not kill him, and it did not slow him down.

He used the force of his spin to turn him back around, and swung his claymore in a wide arc. "May you rot in hell!" he screamed as his blade sunk deep just at the juncture of Jean's neck. It sliced through his shoulder and rib cage, traveling all the way to his belly before it stuck. Jean's eyes widened, his body split, and he was dead as he fell to the ground.

Kenna was safe. She was safe. So Finlay hardly even minded the sword that stuck straight from his chest. Still, it was a surprise to look down and see it.

He'd told her not to leave the cave. He'd made her promise. But the shouting had started and there had been more than two voices, and fear for him had overwhelmed her. So she'd sneaked closer. Just to be sure. Just to know he was safe.

And now she could not move.

Finlay stood. He stood *alive* over the body of his dead enemy. Thank God.

But as she watched, frozen, Finlay looked down. Even in the moonlight she could see the confusion on his face. The stunned question. She followed his gaze . . . and she screamed.

Her wail chased the confusion from his face and replaced it with fury. "You . . ." he croaked as his legs buckled and he fell hard to his knees.

"Oh, my God. Finlay." She ran as fast as she could across the grass and over the road. "Oh, God, no."

"You weren't to leave the cave," he rasped. Blood bubbled from his lips, black in the moonlight.

"Don't die!" she cried as she went to her knees beside him. "Don't die."

"There's a woman on a horse. Do not trust her. She's a vampire." He swayed forward, terrifying her. If he fell on the blade, he would surely die. He would surely die anyway. She grabbed his shoulder to hold him up, as if she could support his weight.

"Did it hit your heart? You said it must hit your heart. Please tell me you won't die."

"I canna be sure." Blood trickled down his chin. "Close enough, perhaps. But you are safe, Kenna. He's dead and you're safe."

"Please."

His body swayed. "Don't forget the gold."

"Damn you," she hissed, terrified into anger. "You will not die. I won't allow it. You are the best man I've ever known, and I want you, Finlay. Do you understand? I mean to keep you. You *canna* die."

His smile was made grotesque by the blood. "You're a miracle, Kenna Graham."

"Stop speaking that way. Tell me what to do! Tell me."

He coughed, and blood sprayed across her arm.

"No, please. Please, Finlay. Don't deny me this. Stay with me."

He drew in a deep, bubbling breath.

"I love you. You're a good man. *My* good man." She shook her head and begged. "Tell me what to do. *Please.*"

His eyes met hers for a long, quiet moment. They were so dark in the night. So beautiful. "Leave . . ." he whispered. "Leave the blade in. If I fall, help me to my side. When the blood stops, if I still live . . . pull it out."

"Aye," she sobbed. "Aye."

His breath rattled. In and out. Kenna waited, her hands braced against his shoulder. Blood dripped from his mouth. He swayed.

"I do . . ." he started. "I do love you, Kenna. Lay me down now, lass."

"Oh, God," she prayed as she guided him down to his side. "Oh, God, please save him. He's a fine man. *Please.*"

The blood bubbled faster in this position, forming a black puddle beneath his cheek. Finlay's eyes drifted shut and stayed that way.

On her knees, she prayed. If he was a demon, God would not save him. But if he lived, Kenna would know that he wasna truly cursed. She would convince him to believe it, too.

The rattling stopped.

"Finlay," she cried, dropping to her hands to feel his breath. It was there. The bleeding from his chest had stopped. And he breathed. She waited longer, not sure if she should touch him. But the breathing continued.

Her knees went numb. Her voice faded away from praying.

Finally, she grasped the handle of the narrow sword. If it had been a claymore, she couldn't have budged it. But it was a French sword, and when she pulled, it slid free of his flesh with a sickening squish.

Finlay awoke with a roar, both hands flying to the wound she'd left behind.

"Finlay! Finlay, don't touch it!"

"Nay," he coughed. "Press it hard."

He tumbled to his back and Kenna pounced on him to press against the seeping wound. He grunted in pain, but she didn't even flinch. "You will live," she ordered.

He didn't smile this time. He was too busy grimacing in pain. Kenna took that as a good sign and pressed harder.

"Jesus Christ, woman!"

Kenna smiled. He was going to live.

He was going to *live*.

# Chapter Eight

Finlay stood expressionless, staring at the ruin of the last remains of his life.

Smoke still curled from the black, blank windows of the castle. Embers glowed in the faint glimmer of dawn. The gray stone of the castle had turned black at all the edges.

Kenna's hand squeezed his. "Do you think Gray and Mrs. McDermott were gone?"

He'd ordered them gone, but Gray was stubborn. He shook his head. "I canna be sure."

"Let's look around."

Nodding, he let Kenna pull him toward the stables, which still stood whole and undamaged. When they were ten yards from the door, Gray stepped out.

"Gray!" he shouted, and her solemn eyes rose to meet his.

"Laird MacLain."

"You left as I ordered?" He couldn't keep the doubt from his voice.

Gray shrugged. "I sent Mrs. McDermott and her boy on to the cottage. I hid in the stable loft while the others were here. They didn't notice."

"Well, it's a relief to see you."

Gray shrugged again and went about her business, taking the reins of the horse and leading it into the stables.

Finlay simply stood and stared, unsure what to do.

"I think you should build a new castle, Finlay."

He glanced down to the woman at his side. Dark shadows marred the skin beneath her cheeks. "Why?"

"This one was full of ghosts. You need a new home." Her jaw edged out. Finlay almost smiled.

"I don't think we should stay here, Kenna. Let us go somewhere else."

She bit her lip, uncertain for a moment. "We will do what you like. But you are the leader of the clan, and there are MacLains out there still. You can call them home and start again."

He shook his head. "I don't know." But the idea lodged beneath his breastbone and he knew it could find purchase there.

"Whatever you decide, Finlay," Kenna said. "But not today. Today we will sleep."

"Aye. But just to be clear, Kenna, you're about to bed down with me in a stable."

"Aye?"

"In a plaid stained with my blood."

"And?"

"And you still think me a good enough man for you?"

"Ha," she huffed, her mouth curving up into a grin. Her hands reached for him, brushing his chin before she found his jaw and pulled him down to her. "You're my man, Finlay MacLain, and you shan't get rid of me so easily. Hay and blood and burned out castles willna scare me off. I'm yours."

His heart swelled so large that it pushed against

his ribs. "Aye, Kenna, you're mine. My old life is done. And you're still mine."

"Take me to your stables, Laird MacLain." She laughed.

And so he did.

Dear Readers:

I hope you've enjoyed HIGHLAND BEAST. For my next single-title historical romance, I'm returning to visit the Murrays, the Highlands, and the heather. Sir Simon Innes—who appeared in both HIGHLAND WOLF and HIGHLAND SINNER—has been whining for his own story and his own special heroine. And who better for him than a Murray lass? A lass raised to be strong, quick of wit, adventurous, and destined to find trouble if it doesn't find her first.

Ilsabeth Murray Armstrong is the daughter of Elspeth Murray and Cormac Armstrong from HIGHLAND VOW. Following in the footsteps of her illustrious ancestresses, she stumbles her way into a lot of trouble. She overhears her betrothed speaking with another man of a plot against the king. Before she can get home to speak to her parents she is warned that a man has been murdered, her dagger found in his heart, and that the king's men were already searching for her.

Knowing that she cannot drag her family into the midst of such treachery and suspicion, she seeks out a man who has already saved two Murrays from the hangman—the dark, sober Sir Simon Innes. Ilsabeth finds him to be a man very much to her liking despite the distrust he reveals as she pleads for his help. She is not one to back down from a challenge and sets her heart and mind on proving her innocence. But can she prove to him that she is the perfect woman for a man who is too much alone, his spirit burdened by the evils he has seen?

Sir Simon Innes is a man dedicated to finding the truth and he is not all that sure that the beautiful Ilsabeth is being completely honest with him. She may have Murray blood but she is also an Armstrong and they do not have a particularly sterling reputation. He finds himself tempted by her big blue eyes and her lively spirit, however, and is drawn deep into the danger and betrayal surrounding her. Passion soon rules them both and he risks his position as a king's man to try and save her.

Oh, yes, Simon and Ilsabeth have a hard row to plow, enemies to fight, and doubts to conquer. Will she win? Or will treachery defeat all her plans? And what of Simon? Can he give his well-protected heart to a woman he is not sure he can trust?

After the tale of Simon and Ilsabeth I do plan to return to the Wherlockes. There are so many stories about their vast and gifted family that need to be told. I am thinking it is time the cocky, randy, but oh-so-charming Sir Argus Wherlocke gets his tale. He is certainly demanding one. Nudging at my mind even as I turn my attention back to the Murrays.

But what sort of woman would deal well with a man who has two illegitimate sons? A man who has bedded far too many women, starting at a very young age? A man who can make anyone tell him their deepest, darkest secrets?

She would have to be a very strong woman. She would also have to have some defense against that strange gift of his. After all, what woman wants a man who knows all her secrets? Where would be the mystery in that? Matching that arrogant rogue will not be easy but I know there is a woman out there ready to take him on. And I think Argus should have to work very hard to deserve her, don't you?

Here's hoping you will enjoy a return to the Murrays!

Happy Reading!
Hannah Howell

Secrecy and intrigue ignite dangerous passions in *New York Times* bestselling author Hannah Howell's seductive new novel. . . .

It is whispered throughout London that the members of the Wherlocke family are possessed of certain unexplainable *gifts*. But Lord Ashton Radmoor is skeptical—until he finds an innocent beauty lying drugged and helpless in the bedroom of a brothel.

The mystery woman is Penelope Wherlocke, and her special gift of sight is leading her deep into a dangerous world of treachery and betrayal. Ashton knows he should forget her, yet he's drawn deeper into the vortex of her life, determined to keep her safe. But Penelope is no ordinary woman, and she's never met the man strong enough to contend with her unusual abilities.

Until now . . .

**Please turn the page for
an exciting sneak peek of
Hannah Howell's
IF HE'S SINFUL,
now on sale!**

*London—fall, 1788*

There was something about having a knife held to one's throat that tended to bring a certain clarity to one's opinion of one's life, Penelope decided. She stood very still as the burly, somewhat odiferous, man holding her clumsily adjusted his grip. Suddenly, all of her anger and resentment over being treated as no more than a lowly maid by her stepsister seemed petty, the problem insignificant.

Of course, this could be some form of cosmic retribution for all those times she had wished ill upon her stepsister, she thought as the man hefted her up enough so that her feet were off the ground. One of his two companions bound her ankles in a manner quite similar to the way her wrists had been bound. Her captor began to carry her down a dark alley that smelled about as bad as he did. It had been only a few hours ago that she had watched Clarissa leave for a carriage ride with her soon-to-be fiancé, Lord Radmoor. Peering out of the cracked window in her tiny attic room she had, indisputably, cherished the spiteful wish that Clarissa would stumble and fall into the foul muck near the carriage wheels. Penelope did think that being dragged away by a knife-wielding ruffian and his two hulking companions was a rather harsh penalty for such a childish wish borne of jealousy, however. She had, after all, never wished that Clarissa would die, which Penelope very much feared was going to be her fate.

Penelope sighed, ruefully admitting that she was partially at fault for her current predicament. She had stayed too long with her boys. Even little Paul had urged her not to walk home in the dark. It was embarrassing to think that a little boy of five had more common sense than she did.

A soft cry of pain escaped her, muted by the filthy gag in her mouth, when her captor stumbled and the cold, sharp edge of his knife scored her skin. For a brief moment, the fear she had been fighting to control swelled up inside her so strongly she feared she would be ill. The warmth of her own blood seeping into the neckline of her bodice only added to the fear. It took several moments before she could grasp any shred of calm or courage. The realization that her blood was flowing too slowly for her throat to have been cut helped her push aside her burgeoning panic.

"Ye sure we ain't allowed to have us a taste of this, Jud?" asked the largest and most hirsute of her captor's assistants.

"Orders is orders," replied Jud as he steadied his knife against her skin. "A toss with this one will cost ye more'n she be worth."

"None of us'd be telling and the wench ain't going to be able to tell, neither."

"I ain't letting ye risk it. Wench like this'd be fighting ye and that leaves bruises. They'll tell the tale and that bitch Mrs. Cratchitt will tell. She would think it a right fine thing if we lost our pay for this night's work."

"Aye, that old bawd would be thinking she could gain something from it right enough. Still, it be a sad shame I can't be having me a taste afore it be sold off to anyone with a coin or two."

"Get your coin first and then go buy a little if'n ye want it so bad."

"Won't be so clean and new, will it?"

"This one won't be neither if'n that old besom uses her as she uses them others, not by the time ye could afford a toss with her."

She was being taken to a brothel, Penelope realized. Yet again she had to struggle fiercely against becoming blinded by her own fears. She was still alive, she told herself repeatedly, and it looked as if she would stay that way for a while. Penelope fought to find her strength in that knowledge. It did no good to think too much on the horrors she might be forced to endure before she could escape or be found. She needed to concentrate on one thing and one thing only—getting free.

It was not easy, but Penelope forced herself to keep a close eye on the route they traveled. Darkness and all the twists and turns her captors took made it nearly impossible to make note of any and every possible sign to mark the way out of this dangerous warren she was being taken into. She had to force herself to hold fast to the hope that she could even truly escape, and the need to get back to her boys who had no one else to care for them.

She was carried into the kitchen of a house. Two women and a man were there, but they spared her only the briefest of glances before returning all of their attention to their work. It was not encouraging that they seemed so accustomed to such a sight, so unmoved and uninterested.

As her captor carried her up a dark, narrow stairway, Penelope became aware of the voices and music coming from below, from the front of the building, which appeared to be as great a warren as the alleys leading to it. When they reached the hallway and started to walk down it, she could hear the murmur of voices coming from behind all the closed doors. Other sounds drifted out from behind those doors but she tried very hard not to think about what might be causing them.

"There it be, room twenty-two," muttered Jud. "Open the door, Tom."

The large, hirsute man opened the door and Jud carried Penelope into the room. She had just enough time to notice how small the room was before Jud tossed her down onto the bed in the middle of the room. It was a surprisingly clean and comfortable bed. Penelope suspected that, despite its seedy location, she had probably been brought to one of the better bordellos, one that catered to gentlemen of refinement and wealth. She knew, however, that that did not mean she could count on any help.

"Get that old bawd in here, Tom," said Jud. "I wants to be done with this night's work." The moment Tom left, Jud scowled down at Penelope. "Don't suspect you'd be aknowing why that high-and-mighty lady be wanting ye outta the way, would ye?"

Penelope slowly shook her head as a cold suspicion settled in her stomach.

"Don't make no sense to me. Can't be jealousy or the like. Can't be that she thinks you be taking her man or the like, can it. Ye ain't got her fine looks, ain't dressed so fine, neither, and ye ain't got her fine curves.

Scrawny, brown mite like ye should be no threat at all to such a fulsome wench. So, why does she want ye gone so bad, eh?"

*Scrawny, brown mite?* Penelope thought, deeply insulted even as she shrugged in reply.

"Why you frettin' o'er it, Jud?" asked the tall, extremely muscular man by his side.

Jud shrugged. "Curious, Mac. Just curious, is all. This don't make no sense to me."

"Don't need to. Money be good. All that matters."

"Aye, mayhap. As I said, just curious. Don't like puzzles."

"Didn't know that."

"Well, it be true. Don't want to be part of something I don't understand. Could mean trouble."

If she was not gagged, Penelope suspected she would be gaping at her captor. He had kidnapped the daughter of a marquis, brought her bound and gagged to a brothel, and was going to leave her to the untender care of a madam, a woman he plainly did not trust or like. Exactly what did the idiot think *trouble* was? If he was caught, he would be tried, convicted, and hanged in a heartbeat. And that would be merciful compared to what her relatives would do to the fool if they found out. How much more *trouble* could he be in?

A hoarse gasp escaped her when he removed her gag. "Water," she whispered, desperate to wash away the foul taste of the rag.

What the man gave her was a tankard of weak ale, but Penelope decided it was probably for the best. If there was any water in this place it was undoubtedly dangerous to drink. She tried not to breathe too deeply as he held her upright and helped her to take a drink. Penelope drank the ale as quickly as she could, however, for she wanted the man to move away from her. Anyone as foul smelling as he was surely had a vast horde of creatures sharing his filth that she would just as soon not come to visit her.

When the tankard was empty he let her fall back down onto the bed and said, "Now, don't ye go thinking of making no noise, screaming for help or the like. No one here will be heeding it."

Penelope opened her mouth to give him a tart reply and then frowned. The bed might be clean and comfortable, but it was not new. A familiar chill swept over her. Even as she thought it a very poor time for her *gift* to display itself, her mind was briefly filled with violent memories that were not her own.

"Someone died in this bed," she said, her voice a little unsteady from the effect of those chilling glimpses into the past.

"What the bleeding hell are ye babbling about?" snapped Jud.

"Someone died in this bed, and she did not do so peacefully." Penelope got some small satisfaction from how uneasy her words made her burly captors.

"You be talking nonsense, woman."

"No. I have a gift, you see."

"You can see spirits?" asked Mac, glancing nervously around the room.

"Sometimes. When they wish to reveal themselves to me. This time it was just the memories of what happened here," she lied.

Both men were staring at her with a mixture of fear, curiosity, and suspicion. They thought she was trying to trick them in some way so that they would set her free. Penelope suspected that a part of them probably wondered if she would conjure up a few spirits to help her. Even if she could, she doubted they would be much help or that these men would even

see them. They certainly had not noticed the rather
gruesome one standing near the bed. It would have
sent them fleeing from the room. Despite all she had
seen and experienced over the years, the sight of the
lovely young woman, her white gown soaked in blood,
sent a chill down her spine. Penelope wondered why
the more gruesome apparitions were almost always
the clearest.

The door opened and, before Penelope turned to
look, she saw an expression upon the ghost's face
that nearly made *her* want to flee the room. Fury and
utter loathing twisted the spirit's lovely face until it
looked almost demonic. Penelope looked at the ones
now entering the room. Tom had returned with a
middle-aged woman and two young, scantily clad females. Penelope looked right at the ghost and noticed that all that rage and hate was aimed straight at
the middle-aged woman.

*Beware.*

Penelope almost cursed as the word echoed in her
mind. Why did the spirits always whisper such ominous words to her without adding any pertinent in-
formation, such as what she should *beware* of, or whom?
It was also a very poor time for this sort of distraction. She was a prisoner trapped in a house of ill repute
and was facing either death or what many euphemisti-
cally called a fate worse than death. She had no time
to deal with blood-soaked specters whispering dire
but unspecified warnings. If nothing else, she needed
all her wits and strength to keep the hysteria writhing
deep inside her tightly caged.

"This is going to cause you a great deal of trouble,"
Penelope told the older woman, not really surprised
when everyone ignored her.

"There she be," said Jud. "Now, give us our money."

"The lady has your money," said the older woman.

"It ain't wise to try and cheat me, Cratchitt. The lady told us you would have it. Now, if the lady ain't paid you that be your problem, not mine. I did as I was ordered and did it quick and right. Get the wench, bring her here, and then collect my pay from you. Done and done. So, hand it over."

Cratchitt did so with an ill grace. Penelope watched Jud carefully count his money. The man had obviously taught himself enough to make sure that he was not cheated. After one long, puzzled look at her, he pocketed his money and then frowned at the woman he called Cratchitt.

"She be all yours now," Jud said, "though I ain't sure what ye be wanting her for. T'ain't much to her."

Penelope was growing very weary of being disparaged by this lice-ridden ruffian. "So speaks the great beau of the walk," she muttered and met his glare with a faint smile.

"She is clean and fresh," said Cratchitt, ignoring that byplay and fixing her cold stare on Penelope. "I have many a gent willing to pay a goodly fee for that alone. There be one man waiting especially for this one, but he will not arrive until the morrow. I have other plans for her tonight. Some very rich gentlemen have arrived and are looking for something special. Unique, they said. They have a friend about to step into the parson's mousetrap and wish to give him a final bachelor treat. She will do nicely for that."

"But don't that other feller want her untouched?"

"As far as he will ever know, she will be. Now, get out. Me and the girls need to wrap this little gift."

The moment Jud and his men were gone, Penelope said, "Do you have any idea of who I am?" She was very proud of the haughty tone she had achieved but it did not impress Mrs. Cratchitt at all.

"Someone who made a rich lady very angry," replied Cratchitt.

"I am Lady Penelope—"

She never finished, for Mrs. Cratchitt grasped her by the jaw in a painfully tight hold, forced her mouth open, and started to pour something from a remarkably fine silver flask down her throat. The two younger women held her head steady so that Penelope could not turn away or thrash her head. She knew she did not want this drink inside her but was unable to do anything but helplessly swallow as it was forced into her.

While she was still coughing and gagging from that abuse, the women untied her. Penelope struggled as best as she could, but the women were strong and alarmingly skilled at undressing someone who did not wish to be undressed. As if she did not have trouble enough to deal with, the ghost was drowning her in feelings of fear, despair, and helpless fury. Penelope knew she was swiftly becoming hysterical but could not grasp one single, thin thread of control. That only added to her terror.

Then, slowly, that suffocating panic began to ease. Despite the fact that the women continued their work, stripping her naked, giving her a quick wash with scented water, and dressing her in a lacy, diaphanous gown that should have shocked her right down to her toes, Penelope felt calmer with every breath she took. The potion they had forced her to drink had been some sort of drug. That was the only rational explanation for why she was now lying there actually smiling as these three harpies prepared her for the sacrifice of her virginity.

"There, all sweets and honey now, ain't you, dearie," muttered Cratchitt as she began to let down Penelope's hair.

"You are such an evil bitch," Penelope said pleasantly and smiled. One of the younger women giggled and Cratchitt slapped her hard. "Bully. When my family discovers what you have done to me, you will pay more dearly than even your tiny, nasty mind could ever comprehend."

"Hah! It was your own family what sold you to me, you stupid girl."

"Not that family, you cow. My true parents' family. In fact, I would not be at all surprised if they are already suspicious, sensing my troubles upon the wind."

"You are talking utter nonsense."

Why does everyone say that? Penelope wondered. Enough wit and sense of self-preservation remained in her clouded mind to make her realize that it might not be wise to start talking about all the blood there was on the woman's hands. Even if the woman did not believe Penelope could know anything for a fact, she suspected Mrs. Cratchitt would permanently silence her simply to be on the safe side of the matter. With the drug holding her captive as well as any chain could, Penelope knew she was in no condition to even try to save herself.

When Cratchitt and her minions were finished, she stood back and looked Penelope over very carefully. "Well, well, well. I begin to understand."

"Understand what, you bride of Beelzebub?" asked Penelope and could tell by the way the woman clenched and unclenched her hands that Mrs. Cratchitt desperately wanted to beat her.

"Why the fine lady wants you gone. And you will pay dearly for your insults, my girl. Very soon." Mrs. Cratchitt collected four bright silk scarves from the large carpetbag she had brought in with her and handed them to the younger women. "Tie her to the bed," she ordered them.

"Your customer may find that a little suspicious," said Penelope as she fruitlessly tried to stop the women from binding her limbs to the four posts of the bed.

"You *are* an innocent, aren't you." Mrs. Cratchitt shook her head and laughed. "No, my customer will only see this as a very special delight indeed. Come along, girls. You have work to do, and we best get that man up here to enjoy his gift before that potion begins to wear off."

Penelope stared at the closed door for several moments after everyone had left. Everyone except the ghost, she mused, and finally turned her attention back to the specter now shimmering at the foot of the bed. The young woman looked so sad, so utterly defeated, that Penelope decided the poor ghost had probably just realized the full limitations of being a spirit. Although the memories locked into the bed had told Penelope how the woman had died, it did not tell her when. However, she began to suspect it had been not all that long ago.

"I would like to help you," she said, "but I cannot, not right now. You must see that. If I can get free, I swear I will work hard to give you some peace. Who are you?" she asked, although she knew it was often impossible to get proper, sensible answers from a spirit. "I know how you died. The bed still holds those dark memories and I saw it."

*I am Faith and my life was stolen.*

The voice was clear and sweet, but weighted with an intense grief, and Penelope was not completely certain if she was hearing it in her head or if the ghost was actually speaking to her. "What is your full name, Faith?"

*My name is Faith and I was taken, as you have been.*

*My life was stolen. My love is lost. I was torn from heaven
and plunged into hell. Now I lie below.*

"Below? Below what? Where?"

*Below. I am covered in sin. But I am not alone.*

Penelope cursed when Faith disappeared. She could
not help the spirit now, but dealing with Faith's spirit
had provided her with a much-needed diversion. It had
helped her concentrate and fight the power of the
drug she had been given. Now she was alone with her
thoughts and they were becoming increasingly strange.
Worse, all of her protections were slowly crumbling
away. If she did not find something to fix her mind
on soon, she would be wide open to every thought,
every feeling, and every spirit lurking within the house.
Considering what went on in this house, that could
easily prove a torture beyond bearing.

She did not know whether to laugh or to cry. She
was strapped to a bed awaiting some stranger who
would use her helpless body to satisfy his manly needs.
The potion Mrs. Cratchitt had forced down her throat
was rapidly depleting her strength and all her ability
to shut out the cacophony of the world, the world of
the living as well as that of the dead. Even now she
could feel the growing weight of unwelcome emotions, the increasing whispers so few others could hear.
The spirits in the house were stirring, sensing the
presence of one who could help them touch the world
of the living. It was probably not worth worrying about,
she decided. Penelope did not know if anything
could be worse than what she was already suffering
and what was yet to come.

Suddenly, the door opened and one of Mrs.
Cratchitt's earlier companions led a man into the
room. He was blindfolded and dressed as an ancient
Roman. Penelope stared at him in shock as he was led

up to her bedside, and then she inwardly groaned. She had no trouble recognizing the man despite the blindfold and the costume. Penelope was not at all pleased to discover that things could quite definitely get worse—a great deal worse.